# BFF: BEST FRIEND'S FATHER CLAIMED

DEVON MCCORMACK

Editing: Keren Reed

Proofing: Lyrical Lines and Judy's Proofing

Cover Photography: Paul Reitz Photography

Cover Model: Stuart Reardon

Cover Design: Jay Aheer

*Special thanks to Nikki for helping me help Eric.



Warning: While BFF CLAIMED is a steamy romance novel, a main character's backstory includes sexual assault.

## ALSO BY DEVON MCCORMACK

**Romance**

Still Your Guy

Between These Sheets

FU: Fixer Uppers

Filthy Little Secret

Tight End

**Romance Co-Authored with Riley Hart**

**The Metropolis Series**

Faking It (Metropolis Series, #1)

Working It (Metropolis Series, #2)

Owning It (Metropolis Series, #3)

Finding It (Metropolis Series, #3.5)

Trying It (Metropolis Series, #4)

~

Weight of the World

Up for the Challenge

**The Clipped Saga (Erotic Fantasy Adventure)**

Clipped (The Clipped Saga, #1)

Bound (The Clipped Saga, #2)

Gagged (The Clipped Saga, #3)

**Bastards Series (Erotic Thriller Novellas)**

Cheating Bastard (Bastards #1)

Lying Bastard (Bastards #2)

**Young Adult Titles**

The Pining

When Ryan Came Back

The Night Screams

# 1

# JESSE

I still have my arms around Eric.

In all the times we've held each other, I've felt some distance between us, a sort of coldness from Eric. Now I understand why—the scope of the betrayal in his life...the bastard who's the reason he carries this pain with him every day.

As he trembles, still caught up in a fit of tears, my total adoration and appreciation of Eric intensifies. But with that comes hatred, anger, rage. Not toward Eric, but toward the motherfucker who hurt him.

I wish I could hunt down this uncle who violated his trust...and his body...and beat the shit out of him. I want to tear him apart with my bare hands and make him plead for his life.

The sorts of thoughts I have about vengeance are horrible. They make me judge myself, yet I don't see why anyone should have any consideration for him when he didn't have any for my Eric.

I kiss Eric's hair, pulling his body closer against mine.

He needs me, yet I wonder if he can understand how

much I need him, how much I've come to care about him in such a short time, and how much I appreciate that he was willing to share this with me despite how painful it must have been.

I don't try to pressure him or make him get up off his knees any faster than he needs to. We shift our position on the floor, so soon I'm sitting on my butt with him curled up, nestling his face into my chest, taking deep breaths as a calm settles between us.

"I didn't think it would be like that," Eric says.

"We're going to get Ty back," I remind him.

"No, Jesse. His reaction was pretty much what I expected, if not better. But telling you about what happened to me… I've been carrying that around for so long. I didn't think I would ever be able to tell anyone about it. It was a fight to push the words past my lips."

He sits up and turns to me, his sun-kissed face redder than usual, especially under his eyes, where he's been wiping his tears. As much of an emotional wreck as he looks like, he's as beautiful as ever, with that jet-black hair that matches the trim, even scruff decorating his sharp jawline. Those thick pink lips are as kissable as ever, even more so now that he looks like he needs me to kiss away all his agony. Captivated as I am by his face, it's those striking blue eyes that always have the power to take my breath away.

Those eyes look different than they ever have before. I can't tell if it's because of what he shared with me about his past or what we shared together through our experience of revealing our betrayal to Ty…or if it's just in my head, a sort of imagined connection because of all that's happened.

"How did it feel to tell me?" I ask him.

His face quivers. I'm not used to seeing Eric like this. He's not one to show his vulnerabilities—he's a front of confidence and strength. There's always been a wall, and in one moment, with our confession to Ty and his confession of what his uncle did to him, the wall came crashing down. Now I see a man who's totally exposed, someone who makes so much more sense—how he acts, his guardedness, his pushiness...and also his extreme consideration for me, his constant care and protectiveness when we were first messing around. In some ways, I think he was trying to show me the care and thoughtfulness that he was never offered when he was abused.

"It was hard," Eric says, "but once the words came out, this pressure that had been weighing on my chest for so long lifted. I was ashamed, still angry and hurt. It was similar to the time I came out to Ty's mother. There's something about disarming secrets that feels so good on your conscience."

"I agree, and we got some big ones out tonight."

I should give him space. That seems like the right thing to do, but I can't help myself. I set my hand on his face and run my thumb through his scruff. I'm wondering how he'll react, but he leans into it, closing his eyes and inhaling, as though he's never really had a refreshing breath of air since what happened to him when he was sixteen.

Those rage-filled sensations return to me.

I shake them off because right now I need to be focusing on loving Eric, on giving him what he needs, which is for me to be here for him.

I can do that. I can just sit here and appreciate what we shared.

*"I'm falling in love with you too."*

What it did to me to hear those words pushing past his lips...what it does to me knowing he's been falling the way I have been.

And falling for Eric has been like falling from the hundredth story of a skyscraper—fast and terrifying.

"Eric, you don't know how much it means to me that you shared that with me."

"I've never told anyone that," he says.

In some ways, I'm shocked.

No one? At all?

Although, considering how he's reacting, I shouldn't be surprised. "What have you been telling your therapist all these years?"

"Anxiety," he replies. "This and that. There have been a lot of times where I didn't even want to admit that was the reason for my issues. That my stress and those things that stay with me were part of who I was. I mean, there were things that set me off. That's life, right? I hear some people can repress trauma. I wish I was one of them, because for me, I think the more I've tried to push it away, the more I've tried to forget, the more it's always been there fighting for attention, trying to make me vividly aware of every detail, creeping up on me in my nightmares."

I see his pain, his hurt. I see Eric, the real Eric—the one I want to know better.

"Part of me still feels as though I shouldn't have told you how fucked up I am," he says.

"We're all fucked up, Eric, and you didn't do anything wrong. He took advantage of you. He hurt you. If I could fucking hunt this guy down..."

I calm myself once again because I know my anger can't be helping him. "There was nothing you could have done differently back then. That man was clearly fucked up, for what he did to you, for the way he did it to you. You deserved so much more."

"Thank you, Jesse. You've been so incredible about all

this, and if you had pushed any harder than you had, I would have done what I always do with people. I would have found a way to push you out of my life."

I honestly didn't think it was a good idea to push even when I did. He was weak and hurt, but I could feel he wanted to tell me something...wanted to share, and three simple words—quid pro quo—were clearly enough to help him free his mind.

"But I don't want you out of my life, Jesse. I don't think you understand how much I want you *in* my life."

He leans into me, offering a kiss, soft at first, but then he grips the back of my head and pulls me close.

He pushes me down to the floor.

This chemistry, this spark we've always shared, helps diffuse some of the fury pulsing through my veins, fury about what was done to him. His pain helps me remember what's important, and that's this incredible connection we share. And if that can give him some relief in this moment, then he deserves that.

He lies stretched out on top of me, feeling so fucking good with his weight pressed against me. He pulls away and glances down at my lips in a way that leaves me curious as to what he's looking at.

"You scare me, Jesse."

I worry he's talking about bottoming for me, which set him off so dramatically. He mentioned he couldn't give me that, but Jesus Christ, that's the last thing I'm worried about. "We don't have to do anything you're not comfortable with," I assure him. "That shit about bottoming—"

"That's not what I mean. Yes, bottoming scares me. But you don't scare me in the bedroom. You scare me because even when I've been with guys, I've never wanted to put my heart on the line. I've never wanted to be the kind of man I want to be with you. I can't explain it entirely, but you make me want to get better, to change, because I want to be the kind of man you deserve."

"Eric, you don't have to change for me. I just want you to get help."

His gaze sinks, and I can tell that he sincerely fears that. He must know that the road to recovery isn't a simple confession. It might have been cathartic, but considering how long he's carried this, how much pain he's held within him, it's not something he can wish away. It's something he'll have to work on.

"Hey," I tell him, reaching out and resting my hand on the back of his head. "You're not on your own in this. Not anymore."

He chuckles, a nervous chuckle, it seems. His face trembles slightly once again. "How about we make some cookies? I have a feeling neither of us is going to be getting sleep anytime soon."

"We'll just be getting fat," I tease.

He smiles, doesn't laugh at it the way he normally would, but I can tell he's coming back into his own after everything that's occurred this evening.

*One step at a time*, I tell myself. I know what I've signed up for isn't easy, but I don't need it to be. My life hasn't been easy. I've never met anyone like Eric before, never shared this sort of connection with another person, and I know deep down that this is worth it.

That *he's* worth it.

# 2

# ERIC

I fetch ingredients for Jesse, which he collects into an aluminum bowl. Every once in a while, he'll glance over and offer a warm expression, as though he wants me to know he's here for me.

*Quid pro quo.*

Three such simple words. They almost make me laugh, thinking about how a silly movie quote turned into a game of learning about one another...and then to so much more. Those words allowed me to reach deep within, pull out something so painful, and share it with Jesse.

Before I spoke the words, shared my experience of what happened to me that evening with my uncle, I was expecting some sort of judgment from Jesse—not because he's ever given me any indication he would judge me or anyone else over something so serious, but because there's this fear that's always lingered in my mind about how others would respond to my secret.

I feared people would see me as incapable of taking care of myself, which is bullshit because I've always taken care of myself. When it was me and Dad, who didn't give a fuck about raising his son, it was still me on my own.

I fought and I fought long after I ran away from home. I kept going, pushed through, and persevered despite any obstacle that stood in my way. Still, it doesn't change that there's this part of me that feels weak...helpless even.

However, despite my fear of this judgment, when I look into Jesse's eyes—those beautiful chestnut-colored irises—and I see the soft expression on that clean-shaven, twenty-three-year-old face, the only thing I can read on it is simply: *I'm here for you.*

Regardless of how much I want to prove my own strength, there's something nice about not doing it on my own. Reminds me of those words he fed back to me: *"A really smart guy once told me no one ever gets to where they want to be without a little help."*

It's true too. I've believed it in all things, except about this.

When I finish getting Jesse all the ingredients for chocolate chip cookies, he mixes them into the bowl.

I rest my hands on the marble countertop behind me and lean back, appreciating how adorable he looks mixing the batter.

He purses his lips, the slight cleft in his chin shifting ever so slightly as he seems to be contemplating the gravity of all that went down this evening. A strand of his dark-brown bangs falls across his face, pulling from the rest swaying in a pleasant wave over his forehead.

It was a lot to put on a kid. Although, Jesse's so much more than that. Despite his youthful appearance, he's not some immature fuck-up. He's a man who's built a life for himself. A man I'm proud to have in my life.

"Had a lot of ideas about how tonight would go down," Jesse says. "And they didn't involve me baking chocolate chip cookies."

He's trying to crack a joke to lighten the mood—a familiar talent of his—but I'm having a hard time appreciating it the way I normally would. Not because it wasn't funny or because it wasn't nice seeing him try to cheer me up, but it's been such a rough night.

He gets this adorably awkward look on his face as his thick brows pull together. "Sorry, I'm just..."

"I know what you're trying to do." I reach out and rest my hand on his shoulder, holding it gently. His muscles are impressive, stressing the amount of time he spends at the gym, but it pales in comparison to the strength I know he's harnessed on the inside.

With my hand on him, I notice something has changed after sharing about that night with my uncle. There's a relief in touching him in this moment. It feels different than it did before, as though some barrier I hadn't even realized stood between us has come down.

It's how I feel Jesse deserves to be touched. What I feel he has earned from me.

He should be with someone who wants their hands all over him all the time. While I do most of the time, there are those moments when I want to keep my distance.

I don't want to keep any distance right now, though, but I know what we have to do. I know what the right thing to do is. And it's definitely time to do the right thing.

"I have to talk to Ty again," I say. "And I think it'll be best if we don't see each other again until after I do."

Jesse's gaze sinks to the bowl. "I agree. I was already considering that. You're going to do it in person, right?"

"Definitely. Now isn't the time for texts and phone calls. I'll go over to his place. I think this is the way to handle it, but fuck if I know what the best thing to do with something like this is."

"I'll give you your turn," Jesse says. "Then I'll reach out too. This is shitty as fuck, but I have to believe he'll talk to me. That he knows I care about him. I know it was selfish to get so caught up in what happened. We kept lying to ourselves, saying that it wouldn't affect him until it got to the point where we both knew it would. But I keep looking back at what we could have done differently, and I know that the only way would have been if I could have kept my greedy fucking hands off you, and the thought of doing that...hurts so fucking bad. Then I feel so guilty about how bad I wanted it."

I nod. "There's a part of me that feels like a bastard for letting it happen, but then there's this other part of me where I can't bring myself to regret it when it led to what we have now."

"I only hope Ty knows I really do value his friendship," Jesse adds. "I have to believe he won't walk away from that. He has every right to be mad...pissed. But...we were so close. We were there for each other. Whenever he was sweating about finals, I would grab a pizza and stay up all night, helping him cram to maybe get a B. I tried to be there for him whenever I could, and he was there for me. Even recently, when I broke up with Whitney, I was kind of down. Not because I thought Whitney was the love of my life, but she was who I did so much stuff with. Ty made sure to get me out there, kept encouraging me. Took me out to hang at the bars and made sure I got more involved in activities—flag football, basketball, volleyball."

Jesse smiles, and I can see how much their relationship matters to him.

Ty deserves a good friend and, of course, I had to be the thing to stand in the way of him and such a meaningful relationship in his life.

"He'll come around," Jesse repeats again, but as though he's not quite sure himself.

It doesn't instill much confidence in me, but I have to believe we'll find a way.

I care about Ty, and Jesse finally gave me hope that I can build a bridge and have a meaningful relationship with my son after all these years. It's something I'm determined to do. It won't be easy, but when has anything in my life ever been easy?

Jesse spoons some of the batter onto a cookie sheet before placing it in the oven. As soon as he does, he turns to me, and I can tell he has something else on his mind. Although, who knows what the fuck it's about, considering all the shit we've discussed tonight.

His face twists up. "Can I ask you something about... quid pro quo?"

I nod, even though I'm not sure I'm going to want to answer whatever question he asks.

"You said you were with your aunt and uncle," Jesse says, and already I don't like where this is going. "And you said your aunt didn't know what your uncle had done to you. I'm wondering, did you ever hear from her after that? I would assume she would want to know what happened to you."

I fold my arms and nod. "She looked me up some years later, when I wasn't difficult to find. She'd been searching for me for some time, but after what happened, I didn't contact anyone in my family. Not that she had anything to do with anything that fucker did, but I was so ashamed, and at the time, I wanted to pretend it hadn't happened. And... really, there was a part of me that felt as though she would blame me...that she would see it as her husband cheating on her with me. I know that sounds fucked up..."

"But I can see why you would have believed that," Jesse says quickly. "You were a kid. Hell, you didn't even understand why he would have done something like that. And you couldn't have known how she would have reacted to finding out about it."

"It got in my head and left me questioning so many things about myself and other people...about the whole fucking world. When she tracked me down, we had dinner. She wanted to know why I'd run off, and I said I was confused about Dad and didn't want to burden her or Uncle Andy."

"Was she still with him?" Jesse asks.

"He'd passed away...heart attack a few years earlier." Disappointment rushes through me as I reflect on the moment she told me.

"How did that make you feel?" Jesse presses.

"You don't think we've had enough quid pro quo, Dr. Lecter?" I tease, and I know it's because I'm uncomfortable with how much I'm sharing with him.

"You don't have to share anything you don't want to."

Jesse's words put me at ease, keep me talking. "In a way, I was relieved, but in another way, it was painful because I had to pretend to give a damn. To be sympathetic toward my aunt's loss. It felt like I had to pretend to be sad so that I wouldn't give away my real reason for leaving."

Jesse approaches me. "I'm so sorry."

He starts to reach for me but stops himself, as though he

doesn't want to push or make me uncomfortable in this moment. There's something about his hesitation, his appreciation of my boundaries that has a way of disarming me. I take his hand.

"Jesse, you don't have anything to be sorry for. Weren't you the one telling me I said sorry too much?"

He smirks subtly, appreciating my humor while discussing something so painful.

"I know I don't have anything to be sorry about," he says, hooking his free arm around me.

He moves slowly, cautiously, studying my expression like he's waiting for me to push him away...something I won't do right now. Even if my whole body didn't want him near me, barring some violent episode, I would fight it with all my being because I need to be close to him.

"I wish someone had been there for you when you needed them," Jesse says. "I wish, when you had searched for a friend to help you, you hadn't run to a monster."

"Sometimes life is shit."

"And sometimes it's not," he reminds me, looking directly into my eyes, and I don't have to read minds to know he's talking about what we have right now. It's true, because nothing from tonight—Ty shouting at us, or reliving the nightmare I experienced as a kid—could take away the pleasure I get in being with Jesse.

"Yeah, sometimes, I guess, I get pretty fucking lucky," I say before forcing a kiss on him. He receives it eagerly, and it helps diffuse some of the tension that's left in my body. The stress that has been bound up in knots in my chest has been cutting free ever since I confessed my dark secret. And gradually, the more we've talked and touched, the more I've been freed.

When we finally pull away from one another, Jesse says, "Please tell me you're going to get some sort of help for this. I want to be here for you as much as I can, Eric, but what you're going through, from what I have looked up—"

He must have detected how I've tensed up, because he stops talking for a moment. "Looked up?" I ask.

He bites his lip and takes a breath before saying, "I did some research after we went camping. Based on how you reacted, I knew something had to be related to some sort of assault in your past, so I Googled, and I'm so sorry—I wasn't meaning to intrude. I wanted to find a way to help you."

I knew he had caught on even before that, but I hadn't realized he would have bothered to figure out what was wrong with me. Such a simple thing as a Google search makes me feel tense because he was probing into something so private before I'd given him permission to. Yet at the same time, it makes me feel so cared for. He just wants to help.

"There you go apologizing again," I say, grabbing his chin, my thumb in the dip. I force him to look up at me. "You don't have anything to be sorry about, Jesse. It was incredibly thoughtful of you. And I know by the way I was acting about being a total top and having that episode camping, it was all easy to read on me. I know I pushed not to talk about it, and there's a part of me that is screaming, wishing we'd kept on like we were doing, but after tonight, after what I've been able to share, I know that was never the right thing to do, but it was so hard..." My jaw tenses up, and movement shifts about in my tear ducts.

This isn't me. I don't get like this.

"Eric, you've spent too long fighting this on your own. You don't have to do this by yourself anymore. I'm here. And we can get help together."

As cathartic as the experience of sharing with Jesse was,

there's something about the idea of telling someone other than Jesse that tenses me up again.

"I'm not going to push you into doing anything you don't want to do," Jesse says, "but you know that's the right thing."

I take a deep breath before Jesse goes on, "We can talk to your therapist in San Diego together...or find someone else...or I can go with you and I'll sit in the waiting room. I don't care, just let me help."

God, I love this kid. The fact that he's sitting here talking about not only going to a therapy appointment with me, but being willing to sit around in the waiting room if I don't want him in there. He is one of the most considerate human beings I have ever met in my life.

I keep wondering how he can be real...how someone so amazing, so understanding, so compassionate can be standing in my kitchen with me, making chocolate chip cookies.

It reminds me of what he said about how we are pretty damned lucky tonight despite all the bullshit.

"I would really like it if you helped me, Jesse."

I don't want to do this on my own, and maybe I do need to take some of my advice, reach out and get some help for this.

Jesse moves toward me quickly again, this time stealing his own kiss.

I feel safe as he wraps his arms around me.

I feel appreciated.

For the first time in so long, I'm not totally alone. I have an ally.

Funny to think that this kid, who most people would think I'm here to protect and keep safe, is doing all that for me. In many ways, he's stronger than I am, and maybe that has something to do with his own past, when he was that lost boy being kicked out of one foster home after another until he found the Morgans.

Whatever the reason he's so amazing, I'm glad he's here with me tonight.

I'm glad he's here with me through this horribly fucked-up situation.

# 3

# JESSE

I head into the office and slump down in the swivel chair at my desk.

Eric and I didn't get much sleep last night. We were too stressed about everything that happened...everything that was revealed. We ended up watching a movie together...and then another. I didn't go to bed with him, though. Instead, we stayed on the couch until it was time for me to go to work. Then it was time for me to go...and remain gone until he talked to Ty again.

That was our agreement, but the thought of being deprived of him—and his body—for any reason is fucking maddening. Makes me realize I'm fucking addicted to Eric Westright.

It's an addiction I don't have a problem with, even as I rub my eyes, thinking about how fucking rough it's going to be trying to make it through this day.

What's worse is that normally, when I'm stressed about something, I can turn to my buddy Ty to talk about it. That's not an option right now since we were such selfish bastards and because I couldn't keep my fucking hands off his father.

But it wasn't just about that steamy-hot chemistry between us. It had to be more, considering I've never felt that way about anyone else in my entire fucking life. And how is he so perfect? How is he everything I need in my life right now?

Whatever the reason we are where we are doesn't change that I'm a total asshole.

"Hey there, Jesse," I hear as Sam walks into my office. He starts around my desk and leans his ass against the desktop.

"Is this about me needing to review those reports you emailed me yesterday?" I ask.

"Aren't you going to ask me how my day's been first?"

I can tell he's flirting.

A friendly, lean blond, he wears a pink button-up and black bow tie. He's always dressed in the most adorable little suits and has never been subtle about his attraction toward me since I started my job. I've never done anything to suggest I'm interested in him, but I've noticed that my particular lack of interest in him, due to a certain Eric-addiction, has intensified Sam's interest. Not too surprising, considering Sam looks like he never has trouble getting some action.

If he knew how totally wrapped up I was in another guy, he wouldn't be going to all this trouble to try and capture my attention. Not when someone else has already captured my heart.

"How was your day?" I ask him, willing to entertain his little game.

"Well, it just started, so not too bad. Better now that you're here. But if you want the scoop, Teddy said something about Mindy to Roger, Roger told Mindy because he's been trying to get in her pants since our last Christmas party, and someone told Jeffers, so now we all have to have a big HR meeting about it."

"What time is the meeting at?"

"Thirty minutes. It's in an email I sent you earlier with some attached files you need to review by this afternoon, along with those I sent you yesterday."

"You guys are keeping me busy."

"You seem pretty good at handling whatever I give you."

And now he's getting dangerously close to crossing a line I won't mind shutting down. He hasn't crossed it yet. Keeps skirting around it, enough that I haven't needed to remind him about professionalism...or tell him about my boyfriend, Eric.

"Everything okay, man?" he asks. "You look like you were up late last night."

"Do I? Doesn't surprise me. I stayed up all night."

"And what could you have been up all night doing?" he asks in a very suggestive tone.

"Nothing terribly exciting," I assure him.

I would say I wish Eric and I had done something like that, but even with all that happened, I enjoyed my evening with Eric. We got to talk, to have a real conversation about important aspects of Eric's life, things I appreciated sharing with him.

"Well, that's too bad," Sam says. "Sounds like a waste of a night." He makes direct eye contact, but I guess he knows I'm not playing his little game because he quickly changes the subject. "Okay, I'm going to head out. I have to get over to my office and check out my task list for the day. Got some doozies."

He pats me on the shoulder before heading for the door, seeming to take a little extra time to show off the way he can shift his hips in a way that seems crafted. And that might work on me if I were on the market, but as of late, the only guy I'm totally consumed with is Eric Westright.

I push past my weariness as I pull up my work email. I'm going to have to force my way through this day.

I pull out my phone and look at Ty's number once again. I keep looking at it, not planning on talking to him until after Eric gets a chance. As his dad, he deserves that, but it's so fucking weird not being able to text Ty and tell him I'm frustrated as hell, to ask him to hang for a game of one-on-one at the gym and then pizza after.

I look at the image of him on my phone. He's flicking me off, which seems startlingly appropriate after what's gone down.

*Oh, Jesse. Why do you got to be such a goddamn bastard?* I think to myself before I get on my laptop and check my messages for fires.

That's the only way I'm going to get anything done, by sitting here and hammering it out. I'm not going to be shitty at this job. I've worked too hard to get where I am. I've paid my dues, and I have a lot to prove, since I'm still the new guy. I've always had a lot to prove, and I can do just that.

I take on my day the best way I can until I finish up and head out to meet with my parents.

I'm upset I won't be seeing Eric tonight. We've texted a little throughout the day to check in with each other, but this isn't enough. He gave me a taste of so much more, and now I want it all. Just like I did with his cock.

Now that we've talked about his past, that it's out in the open, we need to make a plan about how to handle everything we discussed...about that darkness he's carried with him since he had that horrible experience with his uncle... since he was *raped*. It's a word I have to almost force myself to so much as think. There's a part of me that wants to avoid it—to not face it—so I can only imagine how Eric feels about it.

STAN SETS a pan of lasagna on the table before taking off his oven mitts and tossing them on the counter.

I sit beside Charlotte at the round kitchen table, where we've shared so many dinners. Stan sits on the other side of Charlotte.

I feel guilty as fuck because my eyes are barely able to stay open and I can't stop thinking about Eric and Ty and whether they're having a talk right now. Eric said he was going to go over to Ty's condo after he got off work.

It might be too soon and Ty might snap, but God, if Ty only knew his father...really knew him the way I've come to know him...if he understood how badly Eric wanted to have a relationship with him, that would change everything.

"You've been so quiet, Jesse," Charlotte says. "Tell me about the new job. Tell me about this new special someone you're seeing."

"What?" I ask.

I haven't said anything to them about seeing anyone...at all. Not that I mind, but hell, I definitely wasn't going to say anything to them before Ty.

She looks confused for a second before tilting her head. "That was a joke. But clearly, there's something there, so are you seeing someone?"

God, if I wasn't so fucking tired right now, I'm sure I would have recognized that Charlotte was joking around, but now it's out there, and I can tell by the looks on both of their faces that I can't bluff my way out of this one. Not with them.

"I am seeing someone," I admit.

Charlotte smiles, and Stan immediately says, "Really? That's great. I guess you met her at work?"

"No." As soon as I say the words, I'm reminded of how complicated this situation is. How the hell am I supposed to fucking tell my parents, *Oh, you know my buddy Ty? Yeah, his father and I hit it off in Puerto Vallarta and kept seeing each other and couldn't stop, so now we're totally boyfriends. You mind if I bring him around for drinks and Christmas festivities?*

"It's probably gonna kind of surprise you. This person..."

"Person?" Charlotte asks. "What? It's not a guy, is it?"

Almost without realizing it, she picked up on the truth, and she must catch my surprised expression because she gasps. "It is? Wait, it's a guy?"

She puts her hand over her mouth as though she shouldn't have said even that much.

"Oh my God, did I just out you? Am I not supposed to say that? I'm so sorry."

She's totally thrown and bright red from obvious embarrassment.

Stan's quiet, and I can't help but chuckle because damn, this is awkward. "Yeah, it's a guy, Charlotte, and that reaction was actually flawless, so I think you win in terms of mothers handling their children coming out."

She fans her face as though she's trying to cool down. She takes short breaths.

"Charlotte," Stan says, "it's okay. He said he's seeing a guy, not that he's joining a cult."

She laughs, and I'm still laughing, and Stan's feeling clever as fuck for his timing on that one.

"So wait, have you always been this way?" Charlotte asks. "No, I'm sorry. That was a terrible way of putting that. I mean, obviously you've always been that way."

"I'm bi, Charlotte."

"Oh good," she says. "Wait. No. Not that it would have been bad if you were gay. I was worried you were unhappy with Whitney all those years...or that you didn't say anything because you thought we might be upset."

"I never thought either of you would be upset about me being bi." Maybe about the part that I'm screwing around with Ty's dad, who is a little closer to their age than mine, but not for being bi.

"Tell us about this guy, then," Stan says. "Guy or girl, we're expecting someone incredible if they're going to be seeing you."

"He is incredible," I say, my tone even more serious than I'd intended.

Their expressions shift from the playfulness we were just sharing to something more intense.

"Judging by the way you said that," Stan says, "this is clearly a lot more serious than we thought."

I smile.

It definitely is...so fucking serious, in an incredible way.

"Yeah, he's kind of amazing," I add.

Charlotte tears up beside me and wipes under her eyes.

Stan directs his attention toward her. "Charlotte, everything's fine. He's dating a man, not a goat."

"Stop!" she says, though the smile on her face assures me she's teasing him as much as he's teasing her. "I'm so happy you know that Stan and I support you in whoever you want to see, and that you didn't feel uncomfortable about being with whoever you wanted to be with."

"Unless they happen to be a Duke fan," Stan says, "in which case, I don't want them in my house."

We laugh together once again, and laughter feels so nice right now, considering how tense everything was last night and how my head has been totally absorbed in it all day at work.

Charlotte gets up, and Stan eyes her curiously. "Get up, Stan. Just do this for me."

"Okay." He rises from his chair. "Come on, son."

I obey as they force me into a group hug. Although, it's hardly forced. I need this, more than either of them could possibly realize.

"I'm so very proud of you, Jesse," Charlotte says.

"We're both very proud of you," Stan interjects. "We want you to be happy, and we love you for who you are." And once again, like when they took me in that first time, when I felt as if I was going to get in so much trouble for demolishing Stan's laptop, I realize that I have stumbled upon two of the most incredible people in this world.

Despite how cool they are about my being bi, I'm left wondering how they're going to feel about the guy being Ty's dad.

## 4

# ERIC

I knock again.

"Ty, please open up," I say as I stand outside his condo, knocking on his door.

He can't be that much better than he was last night when he stormed off. But I'm hoping that having a night to think on it might have given him a chance to reflect and calm down.

This might be a failed attempt at trying to talk to him, but I've got to give it a shot. He needs to know I'm here and care. And that I'm so fucking sorry. Not sorry that I love Jesse, but that it happened the way it did...and sorry for what that will do to his and Jesse's relationship.

"Ty, please..."

I've knocked so many fucking times that I'm surprised no one's come out to ask me to stop.

I struggle to breathe, this knot in my chest twisting as my anxiety intensifies.

I need him to hear me out. None of us were really listening last night. It was all about emotions and hurt and pain. I need an actual conversation with my son. He deserves that.

As I realize how futile my knocks are, I lean against his door. Tears well in my eyes as I reflect on what a fucking bastard life is.

I knew it wasn't going to end well when we told him, that there was the possibility I might lose him, but it seems so unfair because really, we never found a way to make it work.

He hates me. He's always hated me.

"Ty..." My voice strains and I cough, trying to keep it together. I can't lose it right now. So I pour out my heart... because I'm desperate here. "We got off to a great start, didn't we? Both of us filled with hope and believing we could find a way to figure out this fucked-up situation. I never wanted a kid, but I promise you, the moment your mom told me about you, I cried like a fucking baby because...I guess there was some part of me that really did want that and thought maybe I could be good at it.

"I'm sure you aren't thinking that could be true now, and I get that. But when I met you, I thought I could come in and be awesome at this dad thing, but it was tough. I started staying in Atlanta to spend more time with you, and going to your football games at school, thinking...naively...that I could slide on in and make it happen. But every time we were around each other, I guess I felt like a fraud...and I could feel this wall between us. I don't know if it was in my head or real...a little bit of both, probably. Before I knew it, you went off to college, and as much as I tried to do stuff with you, I didn't. I guess you got busy...and I got busy. It felt as though my chance was all over. I fucking hated it, but I have tried, Ty. I might have fucked up so big with this, but I do love you. And I'm so fucking sorry for making this shit situation even shittier."

Silence.

Painful, cruel silence.

It's what I fucking deserve, I know it.

I'm crying like I did when he walked out...when I revealed my secret to Jesse. Crying like a fucking baby. I never cry, but these days, I can't seem to stop myself.

I take a moment to catch a breath.

*Get it together. He doesn't need to hear you do this.*

I struggle to pull myself together once again. It takes me a good minute before I step away from the door, looking at it, having lost hope.

Maybe I'll have to come back.

"Ty, if you don't answer today, I'll be here tomorrow... and the next day, and the next, until you listen to me."

I bang on the door some more. "Ty, I know you're in there. I saw your car in the parking lot."

"I...uh..."

I turn quickly and see Ty rounding the corner at the end of the hall, his eyes wide with surprise as he comes to an abrupt stop. With two plastic bags of groceries and a gallon of milk in his hands, he glances around uneasily.

"Oh...your car," I say. "I assumed..."

"I Ubered."

I...am...such...an idiot.

I back away from the door and face him. "Got it..."

Even though we're both quiet, all I can do is appreciate how nice it is to see him again, especially since in that moment when he walked out, I was filled with such despair and pain. Such hopelessness.

He doesn't look mad so much as shocked. Unlike after Jesse and I confronted him about what we've been doing. Then he was mad *and* shocked.

He approaches slowly, cautiously. In a white tank and a

pair of sweatpants, his dirty-blond hair pushes out from under the beanie he wears. While that hair might be from Tricia's genes, those blue eyes and his jawline are unmistakably from mine. Even his facial hair grows about as fast as mine, as indicated by the clear five-o'clock shadow he's got despite appearing pretty clean-shaven last night.

"Do you mind if I talk to you?" I ask.

He tenses, looking less surprised, more annoyed. He doesn't reply as he approaches and opens his door.

Funny how such a simple thing can take so long. He forces it open and pushes inside, shoving the door back the way I'm sure he wants to shove me away from him.

He leaves the door ajar, as though he's allowing me to choose to come in, but not really inviting me. I follow him inside, walking through an entryway into the kitchen. He opens the fridge and puts the milk inside before setting the other two bags on the counter beside the sink.

He doesn't look at me, just stops at the counter.

It reminds me of when he was younger and wouldn't make eye contact with me—when there was that strange distance because we had this biological bond but we'd yet to develop a stronger connection than that.

"You changed some of the art," I note as I glance around his place. I notice a piece of artwork above his sofa in the living area. It's black and white, in three panels. It takes me a moment to realize that it's of an octopus.

"Eric, now's not the time to discuss my decor."

I stand on the other side of the kitchen peninsula, which seems like a representation of the barrier that's always been between us, that we've never quite been able to break through.

"I didn't do this to hurt you," I say, keeping in mind

Jesse's text to me earlier when he knew I was heading over to talk to Ty: *Be open with him*. That's something I've never been all that good at.

"Well, you fucking did," he spits out, seething with that same hatred I could feel emanating from him last night. Although, he's not showing it with a tantrum like the one he threw in my condo. It's in his silence, which like so many of his features, is a lot of the me in him.

"I'm not saying I didn't fuck up...or that Jesse didn't fuck up. I should have kept my distance, but the more time I spent with him, the more I realized that I really did share a connection with him. At first, I didn't feel there was any point in telling you. I figured it could be this thing that lasted for a minute and then I moved on, but it wasn't that easy. I'm not asking you to understand, or forgive me, but I'm... I'm here because I love you, Ty."

"You have a fucked-up way of showing it."

I deserve that. I know it, but it doesn't keep it from hurting.

"I knew you had the hots for him," Ty says. "That was clear when I introduced you guys, but with Jesse...that totally threw me. He's never mentioned anything about having feelings for guys before, and I knew him as being with Whitney for five years, so it felt like it came out of nowhere. And then obviously I wasn't exactly excited to find out that you both have been keeping this from me."

I can tell that's a severe understatement.

His jaw is tense as he stands there. The fluorescent lights of his kitchen accentuate the bags under his eyes.

We stare at each other some more. "Seems I'm always shit at finding the right words," I admit.

"Yeah, you could win an award for that."

I chuckle, and he smirks, though quickly forces it into a frown, it seems. Although perhaps it requires less effort than I'm hoping.

"It was a lot to walk into a room with you and my best friend, not knowing what's going on, and then to hear that. It made me feel like the dumbass you guys were keeping it from."

"I can understand, but we didn't mean it that way."

"I'm not sure you *can* understand. I'm not really sure a lot of people can understand that situation."

"Fair enough."

He rests his palms on the counter and pushes his tongue against his cheek as he takes a deep breath, as if he's trying to find his bearings. "It was really fucking selfish of you to do this with my best friend. To fuck around with him."

"I can fess up to that."

He nods subtly, like he's acknowledging hearing the words I'm speaking. "I've been doing a lot of sleepless thinking since last night. Thanks for that, by the way. Not like I have a life I need to keep on top of or anything." There's hate and vengeance in his sarcasm, as though he wishes his words could stab through my heart.

He takes a deep breath before saying, "You want a beer?"

While I'm surprised by the question, I confess, "I could use one right about now."

"You and me both."

He heads back to the fridge and gets two cans out, passing one to me before heading through the kitchen entryway, into the living room.

"Eric, we can be just as awkward sitting on the couch," he tells me. He leads me to the couch, and we sit on opposite sides. He opens his beer and takes a swig, but then as he's about to pull it down, drinks a bit more, as though he remembered the awkward-as-fuck situation we're in and knows he could use the help.

He stares forward, not at me, like he still can't bring himself to look at me.

I open mine, but I hesitate to take a sip.

"Can you imagine the fucked-up reality show we could have about this?" Ty asks.

I chuckle. I get why he and Jesse get along. They have similar senses of humor, and in a lot of ways, it's clear they both use it to diffuse tension.

He stares at his can for a minute before he says, "I can't convey to you how mad I am at you guys, for very different reasons. You, because you had to have known that might fuck with my relationship with my best friend. That it would take that away from me."

"Ty, I could never have imagined this would happen."

"I don't care about your lack of imagination, Eric. It doesn't change that you… But I do get what you're saying. It's something I thought a lot about after I…freaked out…last night. Even though I'm pissed, I know you guys wouldn't have had a reason to tell me that unless what you were doing was fairly serious. And Jesse…" His chin and cheeks quiver as he hesitates, as though he's struggling with what he wants to say next. "Jesse…he's a good guy. He has been that way ever since I've known him. First to be there when a friend needs help. Best listener in the goddamn world. Hell, the guy fundraises for fucking orphans. He's practically a saint."

"Fundraises for orphans?" I ask. I guess I shouldn't be surprised by it, though.

"Yeah, you didn't know that?"

I shake my head.

"I guess I don't see why he would have mentioned it to you. It's for kids in foster care. You'll have to ask him about it. He's kind of an amazing guy, as I guess you've noticed." He seems frustrated by that statement more than appreciative of Jesse's nature. "I say that, but I think that's part of what made it hurt even more. What happened seems so out of character for Jesse…and so selfish of him. But it's also what's making me keep running it all through my head, trying to sort everything out, make sense of what the hell is going on. Jesse's been my friend…the person I trusted…and in some ways, it feels like you took that from me. And I need some time to sort through all that. With both of you."

"I can respect that."

He glances around his condo some more. "I'm not sure what the right question about all this is, but…what, um…do you like about Jesse?"

I don't know how to respond at first. Really, his question surprises me more than anything. It's almost as surprising as him not wanting to scream and shout and kick me the fuck out of his building after everything that went down.

He finally makes eye contact with me, apparently wanting an answer, and I feel I owe it to him. I owe him whatever he asks for at this point. "He's smart and funny. He's worked hard to get where he is in life. And overcome a lot of shit in his past. He's…"

"Yeah, he's pretty cool," he interrupts quickly, almost as if he doesn't want to press further.

We take a few more sips from our beers, almost it seems just for something to do, something to give Ty a moment to process all this shit.

"There's a part of me that feels like I know how this is

supposed to play out," Ty says. "I'm the psycho bastard son who throws a fit and asks you never to see Jesse again. That I kick you out and tell you I never want to see you again. Or that this was all too much."

I'm waiting—hoping—for a *but.*

"But..."

There it is.

"...I think we both know—hell, we all know—life's complicated as fuck. I'm not saying I'm okay, or that I forgive either of you, but I appreciate that you came here tonight to talk to me. And...as weird as this sounds...last night meant a lot to me. I didn't catch you, and you probably could have gotten away with keeping it from me if you'd tried, but you didn't. That took balls."

I'm relieved to hear him acknowledge that since the way he acted last night, it was clear he felt we'd ambushed him, which in a way, we had.

"I'm not thrilled," Ty adds. "I'm not okay with either of you *yet.*"

He stops, but his *yet* gives me all the hope I needed. That there's a fucking chance we can all get through this somehow.

"I need to talk to Jesse too," he adds. "But, well, I guess I don't know where we go after that." He nods before taking another drink. "Alcohol will help."

"Whatever we need to do—"

"Can we talk about something else now?" he asks, desperation in his expression. "I can't handle all this in one night. You seen any good movies?"

The tension has eased up a bit, though not entirely. That would be way too much to ask, but the fact that he's even speaking to me means the world to me.

The conversation shifts to movies, but there's an awkwardness to it. It's not a lighthearted discussion so much as Ty's attempt at moving away from the other conversation. When that familiar silence returns, Ty says, "Well, this is gonna be real fucked up, isn't it?"

"Seems like it."

"But we didn't start off a normal family, so why should we become one now? Do I get to tell Mom?" he asks with a wink.

I laugh. "Oh God."

"She's gonna give you such shit." He rolls his eyes. "The age, my friend... Ooh, I think you should plan to leave town for a while after."

"Right?" I dread the thought.

He rests his hands on his thighs and leans forward, retrieving his can from the coffee table and taking a sip. When he's finished, he says, "Okay, I gotta get some work in for the night."

"Thank you for listening to me," I tell him.

We rise from the couch, and he leads me to the door.

As I open it, he says, "Eric."

I turn around to him. He looks like he's about to say something, but he closes his mouth and shakes his head. "Just don't be a dick to him, all right?"

His words mean so much to me because they aren't the thoughtless, cruel words he was offering in the heat of the moment last night. They're the words of someone who understands what Jesse and I are experiencing.

As he avoids my gaze, I see a kid, much like myself, or what I imagine Jesse was like when he was younger. I see a kid who wants to know his dad, who's hurt and feels so rejected. I've always thought he was pushing me away, and maybe he always has been, but I see something else now too

—his desire to get to know me. That it's still there, even after this bullshit I've pulled. That tears me apart inside.

"Ty, I know I'm a shit dad."

He raises his hand. "This is a conversation that's too much for me right now," he admits, and I respect that. "I say we call tonight a truce and proceed with caution from here."

"I'll take it."

He lowers his hand before adding, "I'm going to be gone for a few days for work, heading back to Chicago. But I'll give you guys a call when I get back in town."

"I'd like that."

"I want to talk to Jesse. I need to talk to him, but I seriously wouldn't mind getting this out of my fucking head for a bit. God, that's going to be an awkward conversation."

"I'm sorry for that."

"Don't apologize when you're not sorry for being with him." He sounds angry and hurt and resigned all at once, but I get that he's torn and conflicted about all this, so I accept that it is what it is.

This next part is hard for me, but I know it needs to be said, that he needs to know because I realized how much I could have missed out on the opportunity to say it when he walked out last night. "I love you."

His eyes stir with moisture before he turns away from me and says, "Okay, that's good. I'll call you when I get back."

He heads inside his unit and closes the door behind him.

Rejection, but very much deserved. This was so much for him to process that I can't blame him for his reaction. He was so amazing about the whole thing, considering how he blew up at us last night.

I'm sad it's all come to this, but relieved because I feel

like I've reached my son on a deeper level than I've been able to in all the years since I've known him. It gives me some speck of hope about what this means, not only for me and Jesse, but for me and Ty.

# 5

# JESSE

I'm on edge as I head into Eric's condo building.

He called me after he spoke with Ty, when I was on my way back to my condo, and asked me to meet him here. I didn't press for details, especially because Eric said he wanted to tell me more about it in person.

How did Ty react? I know, better than most, how much Ty wants a relationship with his father.

As I wait in the elevator, my mind is running through all the possibilities. I don't know how it could be racing as much as it is, considering it's been going nonstop since last night, me wondering if Ty would ever talk to me again.

I told Eric we'd get our Ty back, but I'm scared as shit that maybe we won't, or if we do, if it can ever be the same.

I know better. It can't. Not after everything that's happened. Not with how things have changed. And I know they've changed...forever.

I can't be the one to have totally fucked up Eric and Ty's relationship. Not when I know they both want one so desperately. They're caught between a rock and a hard place. They both desire a relationship, but they haven't found a way to make it work.

Deep down I've known, even before we confronted Ty, that regardless of how upset he was, his desire to know his father would outweigh his rage. Although, maybe I only wished that was the case for our own benefit. Experiencing Ty's hurt last night, that was a whole other thing altogether.

When I enter Eric's condo and head past the kitchen, I round the corner and see him sitting at the dining table, on his laptop. He pushes to his feet but doesn't hurry to me.

I move slowly, cautiously, even though my impulse is to jump him, because even the hours of a typical day are too much for me right now. Every hour away from him is an hour too long.

"How did it go?" I ask, meaning so much more.

"It went really well." But he doesn't look like it went well, and he didn't sound that way on the phone. He looks as though he's pained by something.

"You've got to give me more than that," I insist.

"I went to his place, and I was expecting this big, dramatic scene like last night. I expected him to yell and shout and tell me what a terrible father I was. He was upset and angry, but mostly he was hurt. He was really receptive...too receptive, more than I would have been if I were in his shoes." I see tears welling in his eyes. "I think I've always underestimated him. I know he's a great guy, but this has shown me this side of Ty I never knew existed. His compassion, his understanding, his willingness to listen."

"His love for his father," I add.

"He doesn't love me, Jesse. Especially not now."

"But can't you see that he wants to get to know you? Can't you see that it's always been that way?"

"I saw that tonight. I can't say I really saw it before. At least, not after those first few years."

"He kept asking to get to know you, Eric. He was looking for you."

"He wasn't looking for me. He was looking for this idea of a father that didn't exist. He wanted to get back all those things he missed out on, those things we couldn't go back in time and do."

"Are you sure that's what he was missing out on?" I ask. "Or is that something you're projecting onto him? Eric, Ty wants to have a relationship with you now. That's all he's ever wanted. Yeah, he probably does wish things were different. Do you think I don't wish I could go back in time and have a Christmas like a normal kid? But do you think that in any way takes away from the Christmases I get to share with Stan and Charlotte? Do you think I think any less of them as parents because of that?"

My attempts at soothing Eric don't seem to be working.

"It's different," he says. "They've been great to you. I can't say I've been like that with Ty."

"If you feel that way, you can either keep being shitty or you can actually do something to change all this. Eric, I look at you and see this incredible guy who wants a relationship with his son and who's felt so guilty and so insecure and inadequate for the job of being a dad because of the way it was thrust on him. Maybe you haven't done all the things you should have, but your heart is in it. I know Ty, and I do think that if you actually push and fight for this the way you need to be fighting for it, Ty can have the father he's been looking for."

"I keep feeling it's too late."

"It sounds like you thought it was too late a lot sooner than it was. And as long as you keep feeling that way, it will be too late." I move closer, wanting to set him at ease. "Life is a real shit to some of us, all of us in some ways. Then we make stupid choices on top of that, but the fact that Ty even opened up to you again shows that we can make up for those."

He nods, not like he agrees, but like he wants to stop talking about it, so I take another angle. "Did he say anything else about us?" I ask.

There's a part of me that wants to hear that Ty doesn't hate me, that he understands. That's unrealistic, but I want to believe that if he knew how I felt about Eric, he'd want this for me too.

"He said he knew we wouldn't have even talked to him unless it really meant something to us. That was one of the things that threw me off so much...made me realize he's such a better man than I've ever been."

I move to Eric and wrap my arms around him. In some ways, hearing that—Ty's acknowledgment of our feelings for one another—gives me a sense of relief, like I don't have to feel ashamed of holding him in my arms, which is something I never want to feel ashamed of.

"It's funny," Eric says. "If things had gone differently, according to this script I had in my head, I don't think I would've been as rattled. If he'd blown up and barked at me and swore me off, I would have been angry and frustrated and hurt, but I would've come back here, heartbroken for losing my son, but I would've had you. I would've taken you tonight to ease the pain within me, the despair."

"I would've let you."

"But I feel like what played out just filled me with this horrible feeling in the pit of my gut. I want to be a good father."

"You can be, Eric. It's not too late."

"At the end of the day, I don't know if I'm capable of giving him what he needs."

"I believe in you, and I believe we can find a way to make this work despite how entirely fucked up it all is. I mean, we've lived some pretty fucked-up lives. We're pretty good at handling crazy shit, right?"

Eric chuckles, but it's sort of a bitter realization that I'm not wrong. "Jesse, I can't tell you what you being here has meant to me… You being here is the thing that has given me strength and the ability to face some of these demons I've held on to, that I've avoided and struggled with, things I'm tired of running from. I'm so fucking tired of running."

I place my hand on the back of his neck and massage gently.

I feel his tension dissolving the way it usually does when we're together. He leans toward me, resting his forehead against mine, his breath slamming against my lips as his nose touches my cheek.

"So why don't you tell me about this charity you raise money for?"

"What?" That was fucking out of nowhere.

"Ty brought it up, and it sort of fell on top of all the amazing things about you that I still don't know anything about."

"I wouldn't say amazing. I mean, obviously I care about kids in foster care, considering my life."

"There's nothing obvious about you, Jesse."

My cheeks warm. He's catching me off guard with this. I was trying to make him feel better, and now he's bringing this thing up that I didn't even figure there was any reason to bring up.

"Well, it's this big Christmas party I throw," I explain, since he asked. "We fundraise for kids who maybe wouldn't have a better Christmas otherwise. They're either in foster care or shelters. I had something like that one year when I was in the system, and it felt nice. Like someone really cared, even though I didn't have anyone. I prefer to think I can give that to someone else, you know?"

"You give that to me."

"That's different."

"Not as much as you think, Jesse. Thank you."

"For what?"

"If it weren't for meeting you, I wouldn't be doing any of this—talking to my son, acknowledging my past—if you didn't change the entire fucking game."

"I didn't really change the game, did I? I just made it more fun."

He rolls his head back, pulling away as he makes eye contact. He offers that seductive expression, narrowing his eyes and clenching his jaw—a look he pulls off so effortlessly.

I want him.

He reaches down and grips my ass, cupping it firmly. I can read his expression in his body language so well.

"I guess you can show me exactly how fun this game can be," he whispers. There's this air of mystery to that expression he's wearing, leaving me wondering exactly what he's thinking...what he wants to do to my body.

I'm eager to find out.

# 6

# ERIC

I'm so fucking greedy for Jesse right now. A part of it is the adrenaline stirred during my conversation with Ty. Another is all this pent-up anxiety from my conversation with Jesse last night—about Ty, about my past.

Jesse's body is my escape...and such a good one. I shove him to the side, pushing him back against the wall. Breaking our kiss, I whisper, "It annoys me that you're still in clothes."

His expression relaxes, so different from when he first walked into my place, when he was so concerned about me and Ty. That he cares as much as he does means the world to me. It's one of the things that drives me crazy.

I really get why Ty had a hard time painting this beautiful, amazing man in anything other than a positive light. But I can also understand why Ty struggles—he knows this incredible guy hurt him...so much.

It's hard for me to even understand someone like Jesse. In so many ways, with him and Ty, I'm certain I don't deserve their love, their kindness. I'm the bastard who stormed into their lives, fucked them up.

"Well, *Eric*," Jesse says with that familiar emphasis on

my name that he knows will get me going, stir this passionate desire within me, "I'd be happy to get rid of these clothes."

"I'd be happy if you would shut the fuck up and do it," I growl. It's this primal energy within me that has been awakened, that he always seems to have a way of drawing out of me. It's this hunger...and not having had him for nearly forty-eight hours has been like starving.

He starts to remove his shirt, but I grab the hem and help him pull it off because it's not quick enough for me. As his head comes out of the collar, I see him flinch.

How such a little thing can make me so fucking hard stuns me. It's surreal.

And then his body...oh, his body.

How I've missed every dip, every line, every curve, every tiny strand of hair in his happy trail beneath his navel.

I'm so greedy that I push up against him again, forcing him to the opposite wall, my lips back on his because I can't get enough of tasting his mouth, my hands moving up and down his body. I wish there was a way I could feel all of him at once, not only with my hands, but with my mouth. I want to experience it all in the most selfish of ways.

Close is never close enough.

We scramble to the bedroom, stripping in a frenzy, and I can tell how bad Jesse wants it too. I'm not sure if it's ever been this hot before...or if I'm craving it so much that it feels more intense than usual.

I guide him back onto the bed, and soon I'm on top of him, my knees on either side of his right leg. As I kiss down his neck, he throws his head back as though he's reveling in what I'm offering him. The sort of passion Jesse offers is so uninhibited. He doesn't hold back...or fake pleasure more than he's feeling it. No, Jesse is always totally in the moment, consumed with it as much as I am, absorbed in this hot chemistry we work up between us.

"Eric," he says, his voice low and breathy, which drives me fucking crazy. I lean back, gazing at him, and he seems to almost awaken from this passionate state he's in as he asks, "What?"

"You're just saying my name like that because you know what it does to me."

"Of course I am," he assures me with a playful smile, a smile that's as if he knows exactly what he does to me, a smile as though he understands how head over heels I am for him, that makes me vividly aware of exactly how fast I'm falling.

In the past, I would have stayed guarded and found a way to keep up those boundaries that protect me. With Jesse, all I want to do is find a way to tear those boundaries down...because that's the only way I'll be as close as I want to be to this incredible man.

He leans up and plants a kiss on my lips. He pushes on my shoulder and guides me onto my back. I go with it, don't resist him.

There's always a bit of nervousness that crops up when he takes on this dominant role, but the way he kisses me, and his tender, affectionate caresses assure me that all is well. That he cares about me...that he's listening to me...that he wouldn't hurt me.

"Today was so fucking hard to get through," Jesse says. "I missed your lips. I missed your face. I missed your cock. I missed what you do to me when we're together."

He takes my lips, pushing his tongue into my mouth and sweeping it across my own tongue, tasting me, lapping me up. I wrap my arms around him, forcing his body against mine, enjoying the sensation of his abs against my own.

His mouth breaks from my lips and moves down my neck.

"I need you to kiss me," I tell him.

"Don't worry. I'm not going to stop kissing you. I'm only changing *where* I kiss you."

He trails kisses down my body. When he reaches my cock, he takes it into his mouth, and suddenly all is forgiven as I'm reminded of what progress he's made, how good he is at this in such a short time. I almost envy his skill and dedication to his work. He's become an expert in pleasing me. As soon as I start leaking, he pulls away, gasping.

"I missed that taste," he says, which only makes me painfully hard.

I can feel there's this big, hot load waiting for him, one I'm eager to give him.

He takes me into his mouth again and works up a rhythm.

I stretch my arms out and claw at the comforter as I enjoy the experience...as he shows me what he can do with that mouth of his.

I would think his inexperience, his naivety with how to satisfy a guy, would work against him, but it never does.

Not my Jesse.

There's something about the effort he puts into it, like he's trying so hard to satisfy me...to give me what I need...it's part of what drives me fucking insane.

He slides my cock out of his mouth, grabbing my shaft as he looks up at me. "You mind if I ride you?" There's an innocence in his expression, similar to when we first started messing around.

"Like I would ever need you to ask me that. Of fucking course you can ride me."

His grin nearly makes me blow. "God, you're so fucking gorgeous, Jesse."

He crawls over to the nightstand and slides the drawer open, and I appreciate the way he's comfortable in my bedroom as well as the view of his own rock-solid cock sticking out as he's crouched down on the side of my bed, that body of his on display like he's the star of a fucking hot-ass porn.

When he has a condom and the bottle of lube, he leans back, his abs tensing, revealing their definition. He tears the condom wrapper open with his teeth while he crawls back down to my legs. Suiting me up, he puts some lube on his hands, working some onto his fingers before reaching back and massaging some onto his hole.

"You're quite a pro now," I note.

He tilts his head and offers a cocky smile. "I'm getting pretty good," he says, obviously not believing it, but acting cocky about it, which is how I prefer him anyway.

He straddles my waist, his knees pressing into the mattress on either side of my hips as he lines up my cock with his hole. Gazing into my eyes, he shakes his head. "It's amazing how much I need this thing in me right now."

"I doubt that ass needs my cock as much as my cock needs that ass."

He beams...*glows*.

It's that way he looks whenever I compliment him, which makes me only want to compliment him even more, to make him feel as amazing as he is. And it also makes me want to go back in time and beat the shit out of anyone who could have looked at this kid and not wanted to take him in and give him a home.

How could anyone reject my Jesse?

But here I am, and now I can make him feel wanted and beautiful…like the worthy man he is.

There's a part of me that feels unworthy. Who the fuck am I to have this incredible guy in my life? Regardless of why he's here, I'm grateful he is.

He descends onto my shaft, working it into him, his lips in an O shape as he adjusts to my girth.

As he takes his time, I rub my hand across his abs while cupping my other hand against that firm ass. We work together until he's moving up and down, his eyes closed as he rolls his head back and calls out, "God, that feels good, Eric."

As he becomes more at ease, I thrust, move in sync with him, and he leans down, wrapping either arm around me, around my neck, and offering kisses as I drive my cock into him again and again. We moan together, each of us satisfied in our own way, each of us needing the other.

"I want to make you feel so good, Jesse," I tell him.

His smile tickles my lips as I kiss him again, my hips jerking about forcefully, as though my blue balls have seized control over my movements. Such a forceful intensity, such a powerful impulse urges me on, again and again, until he's gasping, unable to kiss me back because he's so caught up in the sensation.

"Wait, please," he says, and I cease immediately, willing to do whatever he commands.

"Are you okay? What's wrong?"

As usual, my first instinct with him is worry because I would never want him to be uneasy or uncomfortable with anything we shared. I want to make him happy…so fucking happy that he can't stand it.

The corners of his lips curl into his dimples. "Nothing's wrong. I just know how I want to get off."

I love that he knows what he likes best…that he knows how he wants me to take him.

"I'm here to serve you."

"And I'm here to serve that cock," he says playfully as he pulls off me and crawls to the edge of the bed. He's down on all fours, his palms and knees digging into the mattress. He arches his back slightly, his ass lifting, a clear invitation as he looks over his shoulder at me. "This is how I want you, *Eric*."

I offer a soft growl.

He can be so dominant and in control, and then he can offer his ass up as easily. All he wants is to throw himself into the experience, into the pleasure. He can let go and be free.

It reminds me that I'm so not that way, that I have so many hang-ups that prevent me from being this carefree kid who revels in the experience without being caught up in feeling weak or vulnerable…feeling like an object.

I move over to him until I'm on my knees behind him, sliding into that ass once again. He leans back, and I move with him until we're both upright. I hook an arm around him, feeling my fingers against his tight ab muscles, as well as his back muscles against my torso and chest. Jesse turns to me, his lips so close that I can't keep myself from kissing them, despite the strain to reach them.

He grabs his dick and jerks it. "Eric, I can't hold it anymore. You feel too good inside me."

"Do it. Give it to me. Show me your load."

His body quivers and shakes in that familiar way before mine does the same, my thoughts exploding so that I can hardly concentrate on even where I am. There's no sense of place or time, of my past or my worries. There's only my awareness of Jesse and the pleasure he gives me.

## 7

## JESSE

Looks like I'm up.

I wonder if Eric was this nervous when he went to see Ty. Of course, he had to have been even more nervous than I am now. At least I have the benefit of knowing Ty was willing to make peace with Eric. Despite how furious he was with us when he blew up last week, there's obviously a part of him that's willing to talk this out.

"Hey, man," Ty answers when I call him from work.

I'm surprised he picked up. I was going to text him to see if he wanted to get together, but considering what went down, I at least wanted him to know I tried to call.

"Hey, Ty, I wanted to see if you wanted to get together."

"You free tonight?"

"I would be free if I needed to be, Ty."

"Say we meet at my place around seven, if that works for you."

"Deal."

He tells me he'll see me then before hanging up, and that's it. It wasn't unlike a convo we might've had before the fight. We don't typically spend a lot of time chitchatting with each other on the phone.

After talking to him, I don't know how I feel about it, though. I want to talk to him, to get these things off my chest and to let him get whatever he needs to off his.

Despite him sounding okay, and knowing about how Eric's talk with him went, it doesn't change my nervousness about the whole thing. There's that part of me that wants to run and not face this, but that's not an option. I won't be a coward. I did something wrong, and I'm willing to own up to it.

After spending the rest of my day at work, dwelling on this meeting, I head to his place, and before I know it, I'm standing at his door. I think about the key I have on my key ring, one he gave me in case of emergencies. The one I'm not going to be using now.

Strange to think this is what we've come to. Before Puerto Vallarta, I couldn't have imagined anything coming between us like this, not after all the years we've had together.

Now? Now, just fuck.

I knock on the door and wait a moment before that familiar *click* of his lock precedes the handle turning. Hearing the familiar sound of the door opening reminds me of all the times I've walked through that door, some nights stumbling in drunk before passing out on his couch—that couch where we spent entire nights chatting after I broke up with Whitney.

Ty stands in the doorway, in a polo and jeans. His hair's gelled and combed to the side like it would be for work.

I'm used to being greeted with a smile and a warm hug, but there's no hug today. Just that expression on his face, of hurt. Of pain. It's not the anger I saw on it the other night.

"Thanks for letting me come over," I say.

He steps aside, allowing me to enter.

I'm tempted to put my hands in my pockets, but that must be some protective mechanism in me trying to shield me from his scrutiny, his judgment, all of which I deserve right now.

As he leads me into the living room, I notice the print hanging over his couch. "You put up that octopus artwork." It was a piece I'd suggested to him, which wasn't up before PV.

"Yeah, man. I really liked it."

"It looks good in here."

"Amazing, because you have such weird tastes," Ty says, and I'm wondering if he is thinking about how that sounds in relation to our situation. About his father.

Ty takes a beat before blurting out, "Jesse, you did a shitty thing."

"I'm sorry. I fucked up. Like…not in a small way."

"Yeah, this is gigantic. An epic fuck-up, really."

"We just…"

"I heard from Eric about what *just* happened. It doesn't change that it did." He runs his hand through his hair, messing it up. "Where do we start? Trust? My best friend banging my dad behind my back for months without saying a goddamned thing to me?"

I take it, because he's not wrong.

"Betrayed. That's what I feel, Jesse. In case you're wondering. You betrayed me…in a way that feels so fucking cruel. Seriously, did you consider how it would affect me before you started doing…whatever you guys were doing?"

"Yes. I was always thinking about how not to hurt you. I know that the moment I started down that path it was wrong to keep doing anything with your dad behind your back."

His eyes widen, and his jaw tenses. "I would prefer you not call him that right now."

"Sorry. It was wrong, and I know that. I fucked up."

"I hate you sometimes, Jesse."

And now I'm waiting for him to really lay into me.

"Because when I'm waiting for you to fuck up and say the wrong thing...to deny it or make up excuses...you go and prove me wrong by owning that shit." He folds his arms, and his expression twists up. "That's not me excusing it, by the way. It's a fact. And as bad as that, it's as though you weren't even considering my feelings about all this, at any point. Like you didn't care about the pizza nights, or the movies, or the bars, or me fucking dragging on and on about stupid bullshit at work all these years. That always meant something to me, and it's as though you took a dump on it."

"I understand why you're hurt, but I promise you I was thinking of you, and I did feel bad, and guilty, and ashamed, but I couldn't control what happened with Eric."

"You could control keeping your hands off him," Ty says.

"Yes, I could have restrained myself, in the beginning. I was obviously listening to my dick, and I acknowledge that, Ty, and I'm so sorry, but what it became, that was something else."

"Do you love him?" Ty asks, looking directly into my eyes.

"Yes, I do."

He scrunches up his face, then turns like he's about to cry.

"And I'm so sorry, Ty, because it's not fair, and I know that. It's not fair what it does to you. I didn't ask to fall in love. I didn't even think that I could ever feel this way about another person, let alone another man, and I'm so sorry I hurt you."

"Your sorry doesn't help me, and I'm so mad at you... I might have made a scene, but I wasn't being overdramatic when I said you took away my best friend by doing this. Not only because you lied, but because now what the fuck am I supposed to do? You're fucking my dad. And you've been around me when I've said some shitty things about him. I mean, do you tell him that stuff?"

"I wouldn't do that, Ty."

"It's not just that. It feels like you chose him, Jesse. There is a difference between a friend and a partner. When you were with Whitney, did we hang out as much? No. Were you telling me every little secret you had? No, you were telling Whitney, your girlfriend. Who are you going to turn to when you have a bad day? Eric. This isn't as if you've suddenly got a boyfriend that I don't know. And honestly, even then, I think I would feel hurt because it would end up like with Whitney. You'd go off, have your fun, be close to her, and then where am I left?"

This is a curveball for me, and I realize the wounds I've created in Ty's life are about more than me falling for his dad. "Did you feel like I ditched you when I was with Whitney?"

"Not in a big way. You were there. You were awesome. It was fun hanging out then, but it was different, and you know it was different, because the closer you got over the years, the more we had to work harder to see each other and hang out. And I was really enjoying when you guys broke up, because we got to spend time together. We got to laugh, joke around, party, go to Mexico, and here I was thinking that we get to have this awesome friendship again."

"Wasn't it awesome before that? I thought we had good —great times."

"This isn't coming out right. That's what happens. I don't get into relationships. I don't have to deal with that kind of shit, so when you're out spending Friday night on a date with Whitney, I'm at the bar with some other people, not with my best friend, who I obviously wish I was spending time with."

"I get that," I admit. "And I had felt that with you. You'd make comments about it, but I was always like, 'What can I do? She's my girlfriend.'"

"Even if it was just a girlfriend or boyfriend, I would be upset. And now, it's much more. Jesus fucking Christ, this has got to be the most complicated situation ever. What the fuck are we supposed to do? What the fuck is the dinner table going to look like when you're over, and my mother is sitting across from her gay ex-baby-daddy, and his partner, who she's met because he was my best friend, and is now fucking my dad?"

He stops himself.

"Sorry. I'm not saying that to be mean, Jesse. I know it came out that way, but part of me, that's what it feels like."

I'm stunned he's thinking there was something wrong with what he said, and that, along with this entire conversation, gives me some fucking hope that we can really fix this. Hope that I want to believe isn't misguided.

"It didn't sound mean, Ty. It sounded like a legit concern."

We're quiet.

"But at the same time," Ty adds, "as mad as I am at you... and him...and I am fucking mad..." His expression is as serious as it gets, those thick eyebrows arched, his neck and jaw tense. This is what he gets like when he's complaining about crap that goes down at work. He takes a breath, as though he wants to curb that rage. "I don't fault you for loving him. I fault you for getting in it to begin with. I fault him for the same thing, but what can you do? What are *we* going to do?"

"That's a good question. I definitely don't think we have a manual to help us out with this. But I still want to be your friend, Ty."

"I don't think it's that easy."

The despair in his tone only makes the hopelessness feel that much more painful. I can see what he's saying, and it's something I've felt too. No matter where we go from here, it won't be the same. It can't be, but I don't want to lose him. And I feel like a selfish bastard because I want them both—Eric and Ty—in my life. And Ty's expressing my own fear that maybe I can't have that.

"Ty, I care about you."

"I care about you too, Jesse. Otherwise, you wouldn't be in here. But this is such a big *what the fuck?* I don't know. As I told Eric, I'm willing to play it by ear and see how the fuck we manage this, but I'm hurt."

"I'm sorry."

"If only *sorrys* made life easier."

So fucking true.

"I want some space from you guys. I need to fucking process all this, but I couldn't go on without actually talking to you about it. Would have driven me crazy. Give me some time, okay?"

I'm amazed he's this reasonable about it, and I'm more than willing to pay whatever penance is required to maintain what, for me, is a very special relationship.

"I don't fucking know what there is to figure out," he

adds. "*If* there is anything to figure out. But just to get my head on straight."

"Again, Ty, I am so fucking sorry."

Funny that I was the one who was trying to get Eric to cut it out with the sorrys months earlier.

"It doesn't change the fact that I can't order three extra-large pizzas and spend the night drinking and stuffing my face with food while complaining about this shit with my buddy Jesse."

I wish I could hug him right now, but I can tell he's not ready for that, and I don't have a right to ask that of him.

"Don't get me wrong," he continues. "I'm totally going to order the pizzas and drink, but on my own."

I smirk at the joke, and as he sees my expression, he starts to smile too but fights it into a frown.

It's not great, but this is the best we can do right now.

## 8

## ERIC

I jog along the sidewalk on Peachtree Street, moving at a faster than usual pace for me as the sound of Kate Bush's "Running Up That Hill" blasts through my earbuds, pushing me through my final stretch. An intense energy surges through me.

Since Jesse and I spoke with Ty again, I feel more at ease. Not entirely, considering honesty couldn't make up for how we hurt Ty. But like with sharing the truth with Jesse about what happened to me at sixteen, there's this weight that's been lifted off me. Although, with that relief came the vivid awareness that I only muddied my already tricky relationship with Ty.

Life's such a motherfucker.

I try and fight, push through, survive, fuck up. Again and again, I fuck up. I've failed more times than succeeded, and all I know is that, regardless of what bullshit happens, all I can do is keep going.

I finish up my run, working through that strange combination of liberation and guilt. Sweat rushes down my body and crawls across my flesh. I'm huffing and puffing as I make it back to the condo, through the lobby, and wave to Gerry, one of our concierge clerks, as I approach him.

I hope Jesse's here. I hope he's waiting for me upstairs because all I want to do is take his body, feel his flesh against my own. I want to taste his mouth, his cock, his cum.

He had to swing by his parents' place to have dinner with them, but I want him to be back here, close to me.

As Gerry offers me my mail, I ask, "My boyfriend's upstairs?"

"Yes, sir. He arrived about twenty minutes ago."

I feel as if I can breathe...*really* breathe again.

When I open the door and head in, I'm looking around frantically for my guy. I round the corner of the island and see him at the dining room table, typing on his laptop. He's got his earbuds in, listening to one of his podcasts, I imagine.

As I move toward him, his gaze shifts to me, his smile expanding as he pulls out the earbuds and sets them on the table beside his laptop. Rising, he offers me that look that makes me feel like I'm the most important thing in his world in this moment.

It's exactly what I've needed today. What I've been missing.

He's here, and I'm safe...

"Look at this big sweaty man creeping up in here."

That I'm soaked with sweat doesn't discourage him as he hooks an arm around me and plants a kiss on my lips. My dick goes hard, and I cup my hand behind his head, pulling him close, locking lips, getting lost in him. He's easy to get lost in.

As we continue to kiss, I revel in those sensations he has the power to stir within me, how he electrifies me.

Passion ignites within me.

It's that fire I felt the first time we met, with a simple handshake—God, what that did to me. Oh, the things he did to me…and the things he's doing to me now as my dick twitches in my shorts. He must feel it against him because he reaches down and grabs my crotch.

"Mmmm." Our lips click as he breaks away. "There's something I've been missing all day."

"That's funny." I grab his ass. "I've been missing this all day."

Having his firm, tight cheek in my hand arouses me even more, especially as I look at that gorgeous baby face of his—his soft jawline, the subtle dip in his chin, those brown eyes filled with desire like I'm the only guy he's ever looked at like that. And really, considering his limited experience, that must be true…and I fucking love knowing that.

I want to bend him over the table and have him right now, writhing beneath me, greedily taking my cock in his ass, begging me to take him harder, to make him fucking cry out my name.

I restrain myself.

"I better take a shower," I force out through gritted teeth because I'm pissed at the obstacle standing between us right now.

"I'd hate for you to do it all by yourself." He tilts his head slightly, offering an adorable expression that elicits a much-needed chuckle from me.

Ah…that's the spot. That's what I need to get rid of the stress, the pain.

We head into the shower, and I've hardly rinsed off before Jesse takes my lips once again. He presses his hand against the small of my back, forcing our torsos flush as his other hand kneads at my hip.

Heat races from my core to my face as the warm water

from the showerhead slides between us, webbing down our faces, dripping from our lips as I force my tongue in his mouth.

I pull him closer to me, but it's not close enough. I don't know if it's possible for me to get as close to him as I want to be.

He kisses down my face, to my neck, and works his way down onto his knees, leaving a trail of kisses across my body until he reaches my cock. He grips it before sliding it into his mouth—without hesitation or question.

I remember that first time he did that to me, when he was inexperienced but determined to do a good job. Now he's my little pro, and I couldn't count how many times he's had my cock in his mouth, even in these few months we've been seeing each other...fucking each other...falling for each other.

I thread my fingers through his hair, the soaked locks smooth against my flesh as I urge him to take more of me, which he eagerly does.

I know what I want, but there's a part of me that doesn't want to stop what he's doing to me. I whisper, "Stand up."

He obeys, and I push him back against the wall adjacent to us. Reaching my hand down, I cup his balls, his dick hanging out thick and long before him.

He's eyeing me as though he's uncertain about what I'm about to do, but like he's curious, intrigued even.

I slide my hand back farther, pressing two fingers up against his hole, massaging gently, applying enough pressure to tease.

The way the corners of his lips rise assures me of what a good idea this was. That I'm reminding him of those early experiences we shared when he was first discovering how good a prostate could feel. He relaxes against the wall as I continue stimulating his ass.

I kneel and take his cock into my mouth, serving my guy. I want to give him so much pleasure. Not only so he can enjoy getting off, but because I feel as though I owe him so much, because of how happy he's made me ever since he stormed into my life, seizing control of my body and my heart.

His dick keeps getting harder, like a fucking stone. I slide it out of my mouth and pull my fingers away from his hole, licking them before returning them to his ass, working them into him.

"Wait, wait, wait," he says.

I glance up at him, feeling so submissive to him. Like he's dominating me and in control. Part of that is exhilarating, and another scary as fuck.

But scary as it is, I love it. It reminds me of what I want from him...what I want him to do to me...but what I know I can't deal with right now.

"I want you to fuck me, Eric," he says, his expression so fucking serious that I rise and kiss that gorgeous mouth of his once again.

I want to turn him around and fuck him right here, but that's not practical, so I kneel and, grabbing his legs, lift him into the air and throw him over my shoulder, being careful not to hit his head against the glass divider.

He's not a small guy, and it takes a little bit of work on my part. I can tell by the way he's chuckling that he's amused by this game as I open the door to the shower and carry him into the bedroom.

"We're fucking soaking wet," he says as he struggles to speak through his laughter.

"I'll change the fucking sheets." I grab the cover and

throw it aside, then drop him onto the mattress, enjoying the way his wet body glistens in my bedroom lighting. "I don't give a damn what I have to do. I'm going to be inside you."

My determination seems to make his dick that much harder.

# 9

# JESSE

The bed's getting soaked beneath me as I drip all over the sheet.

Eric's jaw tenses, not looking as entertained as I've felt about his own ridiculous display so much as like he's about to take me with a force I haven't encountered before.

I welcome the challenge.

Now that we've settled down from the excitement of last week, since we've returned to our usual schedules and felt some relief since our convos with Ty, it's easier to let go and enjoy a moment like this with Eric.

He grabs condoms and lube from the nightstand before hurrying back over to me.

His frenzy and passion have returned full-force, something I'd been worried about after his confession—after he shared his experience about the loss of control over his own body.

But he doesn't seem to have that on his mind tonight. He just wants me, and I love when his desire is so easy to read.

He throws the condoms and lube down beside me and

crawls onto the bed, pushing down against me. The wet locks of his hair drip onto my face.

As his lips take control of mine, we're reckless in our hurry, struggling to get in sync as our jaws and teeth clash, but soon we're on the same page, and my muscles are twitching and buzzing with a familiar excitement.

Eric is wild, feral, as his lips make their way from mine down to my chin, my neck. His hot breath pushes against my skin, and I roll my head back, moaning. Eric leans back so that he's on his knees, gazing down at me. I feel so vulnerable beneath him, exposed, as though he has absolute control over this experience.

I love it. Need it.

He licks his fingers like he did in the bathroom, and I spread my legs before lifting them back, offering up my ass to him. He slides his fingers within me, taking his time, watching my expression as though he wants to make sure I'm enjoying it.

"Does that feel good?" he asks.

A jolt of energy rushes through me, not from him hitting my prostate, but at the mere thought, some innate part of me craving that sensation that he knows how to activate—the moment when ripples of excitement pulse through me, radiate throughout my body.

"It feels so good," I confess.

He leans down over me, his hand still inside as he presses the other firmly against the mattress and studies my expression.

While he works his way farther inside me, I lean up to kiss him, but he backs away.

"Kiss me," I beg.

He moves forward slowly, taking his time, studying my mouth.

"I will," he says, "but only when I know you need me to. When I think you can't stand being without it."

The suspense is killing me, and as his fingers reach farther back, I finally feel that sensation I've been waiting for, the rush. The thrill of every nerve in my body, the intensity.

Eric growls before saying, "Oh, my beautiful Jesse."

My mouth hangs open as I continue waiting desperately for his lips to lock against mine again, but he stays back, watching me.

I give in because I want him to have me in whatever way he chooses.

I'm his to do whatever he wants with.

He massages gently inside me and leans down, his face near my chest. His hot breath hits my nipple. He knows what that does to me, how sensitive they are. He's teasing me, edging me. I can't stand it, yet it's just right. He offers a soft lick, and I shiver.

He chuckles. "Oh, you like that, don't you?"

"How can you tell?" I tease as I look up at him, this cocky expression across his face, his lip curled into a smirk. He must know the power he has over me in this moment—the power he always has over me in the bedroom.

I'm his servant...his slave...I'm whatever he needs me to be so he can get off.

He finally pulls his fingers out of me and grabs the condom beside me. He tears it open with his teeth, edge of the gold wrapper curling into his upper lip. Discarding the wrapper, he slides the condom on that thick girth...that cock that I need to possess me. Once he lubes it up, I bite my lip, trying to still the impulse to attack him and let him know how much I need him inside me, pleading him to fuck me and fuck me good.

He doesn't leave me waiting long before he's pushing that thick shaft inside me, steadily, taking his time.

"Are you okay?" he asks. I guess 'cause he can tell I've tensed up a little bit.

"I'm good," I say.

His willingness to gauge where I'm at, to make sure I'm comfortable, is one of the things I love about him.

Sometimes I get nervous because of how much I can tell he wants to fuck me. Like he's going to drive that massive thing into me in a way that's too intense. But he never does. It's as though he's restraining himself, holding back that beast within him to make sure I'm okay...building up before he unleashes that fury in a way we both need so badly.

The pressure inside me builds as he strokes his hand across my abdomen, his fingers pushing into the dips between my muscles. When he moves his hand up to my pec, he pulls it back to his face, licking his thumb before returning it to my chest, where he runs the thumb around my nipple, encircling it several times in a way that sends me into a fit of shakes and shivers.

He continues torturing me like this as he pushes his cock back farther to my prostate, sending a rush of sensation sweeping through me. My body jerks—something beyond my control—and I delight in the way these feelings overtake me.

Eric leans down and seizes my wrists, pinning them over my head. He gauges my expression. "How you feeling?" he asks.

I glance down at my cock, which drips precum onto my belly. "How does it look like I'm feeling?"

He assesses this preview of my load and starts to smile, but the smile freezes on his face. "Your ass is so tight, so perfectly tight. I wish I wasn't wearing this condom, that I could come up inside you and force it back farther."

The thought of having him inside me like that... I don't know where this comes from, what animalistic impulse is here, but it excites me. The very thought of being one with him in a way we haven't shared yet, it's intoxicating...maddening.

"Kiss me," I beg him because I can't stand it right now.

He leans closer, as though he's about to satisfy my need, but there's a subtle smirk across his face like he's basking in it as he continues fucking me hard.

Finally, he takes my mouth forcefully.

I'm all his...every part of my body lusting for every part of him, wanting to fulfill that fantasy of having his cum inside me.

Wanting to be totally claimed.

That mouth...those lips...that tongue...his saliva...it's all mine.

Give it to me, Eric. Give it all to me.

He releases my wrists and cups his hand behind my head as if he's trying to keep me close, but if there was a way to be closer to him, I would have found it already.

I take a moment to appreciate our movements before I gasp into his mouth, moaning. He plants his hands down on either side of me and continues his work, stimulating my prostate again and again and again.

My dick swells, my balls throbbing with a painful pressure.

"Tell me again," I say to him.

"Tell you what?"

"About how much you want to come inside me, for me to be yours."

"Oh, Jesse, you have no idea how much I've wanted to be

inside you like that. Feeling you raw. Your flesh, my flesh... you taking my load."

The thought, combined with a particularly powerful thrust against my prostate, is too much for me. I grit my teeth, grunting through them as my body twists about. My eyes seal shut as I endure the intense surge of energy that overtakes me. A rush of cum sprays across my abs, and as I open my eyes, I see Eric leaning back and noticing the mess on my stomach.

A particularly arrogant smile forms across his face. He slides his hand down my body and runs his thumb through the cum. He pulls it back to his mouth and forces it in.

"Jesus," he says as he closes his eyes and appreciates the flavor.

He's mine. All mine.

I'm so fucking possessive of him, especially knowing how he lapped up my seed.

He leans back, hooks his arms under the crooks of my legs, and offers a series of powerful movements before he tilts his body either way, his abs shifting as his expression tenses up.

He's coming, and I'm so fucking satisfied knowing that I'm giving him that pleasure...that my ass can do that for him.

His body remains tensed up while mine relaxes as I feel totally relieved to experience this much pleasure with him.

He leans back down, lying across my body as I enjoy my awareness of knowing the condom inside me is full of him... and wishing it was, like he wanted, up inside me.

He purrs softly, "I think we both needed that." He licks the side of my cheek and offers a soft kiss.

"I think now I know what I need even more."

"What's that?" he asks.

"I want that," I tell him, "you inside me and coming. We talked about being exclusive and getting tested, but we should do it. Then you can really give me that."

Eric grins. "So you're really a dirty cumslut?"

"Is that a problem?"

"Not as long as you're my cumslut."

I burst into laughter.

There's something so fun about fucking around with Eric. It's fun and sweet and hot...so fucking hot. And it gives me hope that we'll find a way through all this bullshit that's been bothering us. This bullshit that Eric still has to work through.

# 10

# ERIC

He lies beneath me, breathing so hard, reminding me of my own breaths when I was out for my jog. Damn, this has all been one hell of a workout.

I can see the need and hunger in his expression like when he was begging for me to kiss him. His damp locks of hair cling together as he gazes at me through those chestnut-brown eyes of his—those eyes that I could look at all day.

The thought of being able to act out that fantasy we both shared about me filling him up—to know that he's mine, totally mine—excites me.

I want Jesse, all of him, to myself. And I want to be his.

There's an intimacy we've shared, not only in the span of the time since we've gotten to know each other, but even in the days after everything we shared that special night when we talked to Ty, and then I talked to Jesse...when I gave him a part of me I've never given to anyone else. And when he received it with such grace and kindness.

I rest my hand on his face and run my thumb across his smooth flesh. His fair skin is in such good health.

"What?" he asks, surely noticing something's captured my attention.

"Nothing. I just realized that your face...remembering when you'd fucking burned it in PV."

"Oh, yeah. That really pissed you off."

"Pisses me off when you do anything to damage this beautiful body of yours."

"You're laying it on thick tonight, aren't you? Beautiful?"

"Yeah, beautiful," I say before slamming my lips back down against his.

As he kisses me back, he rests his hand on the back of my head and pulls me down to him.

I cherish this delicious moment with him...how good it feels to be lying against him. He's brought so many amazing things into my life. And more than anything, made me feel like I'm not alone. I've never felt that with anyone else.

When we finally manage to pry away from one another, we dry off and change the sheets together.

"I could get used to having you in my condo," I tell him as we spread out the comforter.

He's got a towel wrapped around his waist, hiked low. The arches of his cum gutters dip down and disappear behind the towel, hiding some of my favorite parts of him... not that I'll complain about the ones I can see.

"I like my condo too, though," Jesse says. "You need to come over and see my place sometime."

I hadn't really thought about that. We've always messed around here.

"You want me to come to your place?"

"I'd really like that," Jesse replies, this charming-as-fuck smile on his face, an eagerness in his eyes as though he's a kid who wants to show me his new toy.

Considering how he says it, I'm surprised we haven't done it already. Although, I have to remind myself this is all so new for both of us, despite the fact that a few months have felt so long...so wonderfully long.

"I guess we'll have to spend some time at your place, then," I say. "And get tested...so we can...*fully* enjoy each other."

It's just seeing his place and breeding him, but these little things represent where we are now—this juncture and what we clearly have agreed we're interested in pursuing together—the reason why we even told Ty about what we've been up to.

Once we've made the bed, I move around the mattress, approaching him, taking a moment to appreciate everything about him before I steal another kiss. I run my thumb across his temple, through his hair, around his ear.

"What?"

"Just excited about having you beside me tonight."

"I've been beside you for the past few nights," he reminds me.

"And that's how I like it to be. In the arms of the man who's falling in love with me."

"Oh, I'm falling in love with you? Is that the story?" Jesse asks in that familiar playful way he has.

"I've got it pretty bad too. More than bad. Maybe if you stick around, we can figure out who has it the worst."

"I don't know if you're going to win that game," Jesse warns with a knowing smile.

"Well, I don't lose easy."

This time, I'm not sure which one of us initiated it, but our lips are locked and his tongue is sliding into my mouth.

We hop into bed, and it's not long before our arms are around each other and the smacking sound of our kisses fills the room.

This is so different than the lust we managed to work up when we first began all this.

We fuck again because I can't help myself, and after we finish, we're lying side by side, gazing at each other. I notice a change in his expression and sense he's concerned about something—that he's not only reveling in the pleasure of what we've enjoyed with one another tonight.

"What is it?" I ask.

"A lot has come up, Eric, and I want to make sure we're moving in a positive direction. I was giving you a little space. I felt like we all needed a little mental break after what went down last week, but please tell me you're planning to talk to someone. Like your therapist. Or if not them, someone here in Atlanta. I've been looking up places in case you need—"

"What?" I ask, a little annoyed since I feel he's shaken me from what was a magical evening.

I can see his worry, his hesitation, his nervousness. While I don't pride myself in making him feel that way, I can't change how ornery I feel in this moment.

"Eric, I wasn't meaning to push. I want you to talk to someone. I thought it might be easier if I found something nearby. And as I said before, you can go by yourself, or I can go with you. I don't care. I don't want you to put this off or try to act like this is something you can do on your own, because it's not. And it shouldn't be."

This pain in my chest knots up, stinging, burning. It's like he's betrayed me by bringing up something so painful for me, but I know he's only talking to me about this because he cares. I have to remind myself of that because, in a way, it feels as though he's assaulting me with it. He's fighting defenses that have been there for so long.

"Hey, hey," Jesse says, resting his hand on my side. "Eric, I'm trying to help. You're not on your own anymore."

It's what I've already been thinking, yet hearing him say it, there's something so powerful about the words.

"Let me help you with this," he adds.

He's disarmed me, and the same walls that were so quick to come up when he suggested this, begin to lower once again. I don't know if it's because of his sincerity, or maybe his innocence, the authenticity behind his intention. Whatever the reason, I relax into it. It's not comfortable, and there's still this part of me that wants to turn this into a fight, but the only fight I need to be having about this is with myself.

I move closer to him, hooking my arm around his body and pulling close so our torsos press together.

"Thank you," I force past my lips. "I know you mean well, but it's hard, Jesse. This isn't something I've ever shared with anyone else. I don't share things. That's not how I live my life. You're the first person I've actually wanted to tell, and I guess now I know why."

"Why?"

"Somehow it seems I knew you were the only person who would be this incredible about it. Thank you. I have an appointment with my therapist next week, if you want to come to San Diego with me. I don't know if you'll be able to get time off work."

"I'll find a way, Eric. This is important. And I know it won't be easy for you, which is why I want to be there. Please let me be involved in this."

A warm sensation crawls through my body, mixing with a tingling in my chest—such pleasant sensations that have replaced the tension he stirred by mentioning talking to someone about this.

It's not going to be easy, but when has my life ever been easy? I'm good at facing challenges. I need to remember that can be true about this too.

"Thank you for being so special, Jesse." I pull him close for another kiss, feeling like the luckiest man alive for being able to have this incredible guy, not just in bed with me, but as he said, falling in love with me.

Who am I to deserve his love, his respect, his appreciation, his generosity?

And yet, there's also this fear within me that if I don't seize this moment and appreciate it for everything it is, then like so many other things that have been good in my life, it will turn on me, twist into something dark, and I'll lose him.

~

I'M impatient as I sit in my primary-care doc's office, waiting for the results of my STI panel. Jesse and I set up appointments separately, with our respective physicians. He got his yesterday, and I'm taking care of mine today. I'm ready to put an end to boundaries, to be with him without being inhibited by that thin piece of latex that feels like just another obstacle to being as close to him as I can possibly be.

I want to claim his body, and I want him to claim me, despite the issues that prevent me from sharing that with him. That's a fantasy, for now at least. It's one of the reasons why I want to get better. Because I'm so fucking eager to share that with him.

While I'm looking through my phone to pass the time, I check out my calendar for the following week and notice my therapy session, the one I've invited Jesse to come with me to on Thursday.

Looking at that on a normal day would make me nervous. I've never enjoyed having my therapist there, listening to me, scrutinizing my life and my choices. It's always been difficult knowing I was keeping my secret from her, thinking so many times that I could find a way to bring it up, that it would probably help me to be able to actually vocalize it, but never having the strength.

I know why I have the strength now.

Because of Jesse.

He gave me that confidence to speak words I couldn't have spoken with anyone else. I'm pleased he'll be there for me this time when I need to speak them again.

At the same time, when he pushes, there's a part of me that tenses up. But like with so many things, Jesse has this way of tearing through those mental barriers I throw up.

*Fuck you, Jesse, you've made me a goddamn wreck.* I can't look at that face and those eyes, at the subtlest movement of the corners of his lips, without being totally enamored, totally obsessed. Within the short time we've known each other, Jesse has already stolen my heart more than he can realize, more than I want to admit.

The nurse practitioner retrieves me from the waiting room. We meet in one of the patient rooms, where she tells me I'm negative. I'm not surprised, but I'm pleased I can offer Jesse that reassurance. I want him to know I respect him and his body and I want to keep him safe.

I text him immediately to give him the news, and we meet up at a nearby restaurant for lunch.

Sitting in a booth across from one another, there's this sexual tension that lingers now that we know we can finally consummate that element that has my dick rock hard right now.

And here we are, eating sandwiches, when the only thing I want to be eating is that ass of his…and his precum.

"Do you have to go right back to work?" I ask.

I'm being so obvious. No games. No tease. I want what I want, and I'm not ashamed.

"Oh, so you want to take me back to your condo and make good on this, don't you?" Jesse asks, that teasing expression on his face.

God, he's edging me with just a look.

"It's taking me a lot not to leap up and jump across this table, take you right now."

"Is it because I'm so irresistible?" he asks as a joke, but I immediately blurt out, "Yes."

He turns serious, and we stare at one another. I wonder if he's thinking the same thing I am, wanting me the way I'm wanting him.

I dig my fingers into the table. It's as though I'm trying to control my body to keep from leaping up, taking him right here and now, like some sort of fucking animal.

If only Jesse knew what he did to me. If only he understood the level of arousal he could trigger in my mind and my body and every nerve that knows how good it can feel to have his skin pressed against mine, those parts of me that I can feel aching for him, pining in an almost dangerously potent way.

"Does this mean you can get off work?" I ask.

"You don't have plans tonight. We were going to make dinner," Jesse reminds me.

"Yeah, but I have a feeling I know what else we're going to be doing instead," spits out of my mouth.

"You want to go on a date?" The way Jesse says it, it's as if we're in high school and I'm standing at a locker, Jesse leaning against the one beside me, trying to be as charming as ever and totally winning at it. I'm flustered and surprised by his question. I start to say something but stutter over the words, and he seems to know that he has this advantage over me because his smile broadens. He leans forward. "Come on, Eric. Go on a date with me tonight."

And goddammit, I know he's going to make me wait, but he's worth the wait.

# 11

# JESSE

I drive up the porte cochere of Eric's condo building and park in a fifteen-minute parking spot before texting to let him know I'm here. Admittedly, I feel kind of silly about tonight, sitting here dressed in a button-up and slacks, looking as though I'm getting ready to take Eric to the prom.

He's wrong if he thinks I didn't want to take the rest of the day off and spend it at his place, fucking, letting him fill me up, taking complete control and having his way with me.

But that isn't how I want our first time sharing that to play out.

I want it to be special because this moment of tearing away that boundary represents the level of trust we have for one another.

And I do trust Eric.

I want him to be the man who gives that to me, just like I wanted him to be the first man inside me.

When he walks out of the revolving glass door, he's wearing a button-up and tie, dressed up, like I asked him to when I texted him during work while I coordinated our date.

A date, a fucking date. Nice to have those, considering we spent so much of the early part of our relationship having to keep it all secret.

When he gets into the car, he's smiling.

"I don't think I've seen you this giddy before," I tell him. "Is it because of the date or because you're gonna get to come up inside me later?"

"A little bit of both," he says as he adjusts the seat.

"You look sexy, by the way. I think I like you best when you dress up."

"I'm pretty sure you like me best when I dress down."

I laugh. "But seriously, you look really hot." He eyes me peculiarly for a second, and I say, "What? I can't compliment my date?"

"Oh, I'm your date now, am I?"

"Yeah, that's right. My date to wine and dine."

"I do whatever I got to do to get a piece of ass," Eric says. But I can tell by the expression on his face he's only giving me a hard time.

"Eric, there will be plenty of opportunities to give me a hard time later," I retort, and he laughs.

"You're feeling particularly clever this evening."

"I have a good feeling about tonight. I give good date, that's all I'm saying."

"Oh, I bet you do," Eric says.

I start the car, and as I'm driving out of the porte-cochere exit, I turn on the radio and push Play on my iPhone, which is resting in the dash mount.

Kate Bush's "Cloudbusting" starts up.

Eric bursts into laughter. "You fucking charmer."

I remember when the noise of Kate Bush, which Eric

calls music, first assaulted my ears. It's just as bad now, but it's worth every second as Eric sits beside me, mouthing the words, shaking a little to the music, reminding me of how our spark lit up on that dance floor in PV.

"Just so you know," Eric says as we're on our way to our destination, "I'm not letting you pay for everything. You can call me your date because you asked first, but we're going to split this fifty-fifty. I'm a modern woman."

He earns a laugh for that, and when I look to him, he offers a wink. I imagine his scruff against my face, against my body as he trails kisses down it. Like at lunch today, he oozes charisma and pure animalistic desire, which was one of the things that first ignited that lust between us—something I still can't shake my nerves of.

As we arrive at the restaurant I booked reservations at, Eric snickers.

"What are you laughing about?" I ask him.

"I'm assuming you intended for me to be amused by the fact that you're taking us to a Mexican restaurant."

"It's gourmet Mexican. Only the best for my guy. I'm thoughtful like that. I told you, I give good date."

"It was very thoughtful to choose something that would remind us of how we met," Eric says, but he's not joking or giving me shit. He's being totally sincere, which is nice.

We walk to the restaurant together, and the host seats us at a balcony table I picked out on the second floor, which looks out over Midtown.

"This is a nice place," Eric says, glancing around at the decor. "Did you and Whitney ever come here?"

I scoff. "I'm not going to take you to some place I took Whitney. I used to actually see it on my way to flag football down the street."

"I guess that's where you and Ty would meet up," Eric adds, as the mention stirs for him what it stirred for me.

This is a reality we can't escape from—we had our fantasy already when we got to enjoy our time in Puerto Vallarta, and now we face the music and push through real life, where consequences for actions are all too real.

The waiter approaches and takes our drink orders. As soon as he leaves, I ask Eric, "When do you think Ty's going to want to talk to us again?"

He shrugs.

"I keep checking my phone," I say. "Keep waiting to get a message or a phone call. I know it's only been a few days, but that's a long-ass time considering we used to message each other all the time." That familiar guilt rises within me. I shake it off. "Once we can all talk, once we're all able to be around each other, I have to believe we can work through this."

"I appreciate this, Jesse. It means a great deal to me how much you care about my son."

"Ty's always been a good friend to me. He's been there through some of the shittiest things I've gone through in my life. Hell, he was there when my granny passed."

"What?" Eric asks.

"Stan's mother. She was a beautiful person, and a big part of our family when I was growing up. It happened while I was in college, while Ty and I were friends. She had a stroke...and that was it. There one minute, gone the next. The day I found out, I told him about what happened, and he dropped everything. Showed up at my place not an hour later and gave me a ride to my parents', then hung around with me and my parents, letting us talk about Granny, get that off our chest. He ordered us pizza and got everyone laughing. That was how he was. I think that's one of the first moments where I realized what a truly good person Ty is. He likes to act very laid-back and like he doesn't give a fuck about anything, and he doesn't let a lot of people in, but he's not the only one who does that."

Judging by the way Eric's gaze sinks to the table, he caught my reference to his own nature.

I shake myself out of my state, feeling guilty for hogging the conversation, and like maybe this isn't the sort of thing to discuss on our date night.

"Anyway, I guess we'd better look at the menu," I say, which we do before the waiter arrives and takes our orders.

There seems to be something on Eric's mind, because he keeps quiet. I figure it has to do with that stuff I shared with him…dumped on him, really.

"Sorry. I wasn't meaning to make tonight about Ty. I was—"

"I'm glad you brought him up. And that you said all that. That's not the Ty I know. Not the Ty he lets me see. Even with what happened when I went to talk to him, that shocked me. I didn't realize that Ty could be that kind of man. In my mind, the way he lashed out that night when we told him what happened between us…that's what I expect from him."

"Well, Ty's full of surprises," I tell him.

"Apparently."

"Yeah, my granny, Whitney…he's always been there."

"Were you really broken up about Whitney?"

"Why? Do I not act like it?"

"You don't talk about her as though you were in love."

"No, I wasn't in love. I knew what we had wasn't that, but I cared about her. I still care about her. Our breakup…it was like losing my best friend. Five years we saw each other, and then she wanted to move on, so all those things we did together, all that fun we had, in a moment it was gone.

"I have to admit, I felt...abandoned. That was the hardest part. I was planning on lying around the condo, sulking over it, but Ty called me to hang, and when I said no, I guess he could tell something was wrong, because he showed up at my dorm room with a Meat Lover's pizza and a couple of beers. He said, 'If you just want the pizza and not the company, then you'll have to order your own.'"

Eric smiles.

"We spent the night throwing back beers and joking around," I continue, "him getting my mind off it. And it really helped...more than he could know. Then he didn't let me sit around moaning and groaning. He got me involved in the flag-football team. We'd go out drinking and on the girl chase."

"The girl chase?" Eric asks. "Really? How did that work out for you?"

"Eh, not too great, because I was never really on the prowl, and honestly not that great for Ty either. We usually wound up shit-faced and Ubering back to one of our places. We'd order Chinese, and one of us would crash on the couch."

"Okay, I know we've never talked about this, and you don't have to answer, but I'm not going to learn you ended up making out with my son at some point, right?"

"Oh, God, no. There was definitely no hanky-panky going on between me and Ty."

"You did not just say hanky-panky."

"Yes, I did," I confess.

"And here I'm supposed to be the old guy?"

"Get out your driver's license, and we'll see who the old

guy is. I'm going to say hanky-panky if I want to say hanky-panky."

Eric laughs, and I'm glad I could break the tension that's been building from talking about Ty.

We let the conversation shift to more pleasant topics, catching up about work, about the new people I've met at the office, their friendliness, some of the characters that amuse me on a day-to-day basis, Sam included. Eric talks to me about some investments he plans on making this year based on things his accountant told him.

When the waiter arrives with the bill, my credit card on top, Eric glares at me.

"What?" I ask. "You didn't really think I was going to the bathroom, did you?"

I'd slipped away for a few minutes to take care of it behind his back because this is me taking him on a fucking date, whether he likes it or not.

As I sign the check, Eric says, "You little bastard."

But that smile forming across those beautiful lips assures me he's pleased with my sneakiness.

"This has been a really nice date. I appreciate it, Jesse."

"Our date isn't over yet," I tell him, and surely he must detect the mischievousness in my expression.

## 12

## ERIC

Jesse has this sneaky expression on his face as he drives us to the next part of our date.

I don't do surprises.

And there haven't been many people in my life who've tried to surprise me, but Jesse is always full of surprises.

I'm trying to consider what he could have planned next.

When we pull into the Midtown Arts Plaza parking lot, I eye him.

"So we came to see a movie?" I ask.

"Of course we did," Jesse replies, though it's clear by the way he says it and that sly expression on his face that he has something else up his sleeve.

We head to the theater, and Jesse hands the usher our tickets before we get in the concessions line.

I look at the different movies playing. Never heard of any of them, but there's one that's a French film, so I figure that might be his surprise. "Aww, you bringing me to a foreign film?" I ask with a wink.

"Who's to say?" he responds, trying to remain mysterious

as he grabs a medium bag of popcorn, a Coke for me, and bottle of water for him from the cashier. He passes me my Coke before guiding me to the hall of theaters.

As we pass a room with the marquee for the French film, I find myself annoyed that I haven't figured this out yet.

"What are you up to, Mr. Morgan?" I ask him.

"Good things come to those who wait."

"Now you're talking about what we'll be doing after the movie."

He chuckles before guiding me to a screening with an empty marquee.

As we enter the empty theater, Jesse says, "Ah, this is going to be a tough choice. Did you have a preference of where you wanted to sit? We don't have many options here."

He has that sneaky expression, perfected with that smirk he's wearing, one I could fix by sticking my dick in his mouth.

We pick a row in the middle, and I plop down, wondering what this little prick has in store for us.

Jesse gets out his phone and texts, being careful to keep me from seeing who he's texting.

"I get to find out what the surprise is eventually, right?"

"Give me a second, Mr. Impatient."

"Okay, one second on the clock, Mr. Morgan."

As soon as I say that, the lights along the walls of the theater dim and the credits for the movie begin, no previews.

These credits are so fucking familiar. God knows how many times I've watched this movie.

"*The Silence of the Lambs*," I say. "You fucking bastard."

His eyes sparkle with the blue glow of the movie screen. I can tell he's so proud of himself for having orchestrating this.

"How did you ..."

"A friend of mine works here. We met on the volleyball team Ty and I play for. You're not the only one with big connections around this town," he teases. "You like it, right?" There's a sort of desperation in his tone, as though he was really hoping I would.

"Like it? This is...so fucking thoughtful, Jesse. All of tonight has been."

His smile returns in an instant. I love knowing I'm the one who keeps him smiling.

As the movie plays, we both find ourselves quoting different pieces to one another, laughing, not having to worry about bothering anyone around us. It's just the two of us, in our own little world...the only world I'm interested in existing in.

During Clarice Starling and Hannibal Lecter's second meeting, Jesse slides his arm around me, then sneaks his hand onto my shoulder. I'm about to give him shit because that's such a high-school sort of move, but I enjoy it too much to give him shit about it. There's something about Jesse spending the night trying to put moves on me that feels so special. So right.

The way he gets to me fucks with my head, because how can some kid have this power over me?

Although, as much as I call him a kid, he's far more than that. He's more mature than most of the guys I'm friends with who are my age.

After the movie ends, Jesse and I head out of the theater. Jesse shakes the kernels at the bottom of our popcorn bag before ditching it in a nearby trash can.

"That was a lot of fun," I tell him. "And I appreciate it. I've never really had anyone take me out like that before."

"What?" he asks, genuinely surprised.

"No, I'm usually the one who's taking other people out on the date. This was a refreshing experience."

"Not even Casey? Come on. That's bullshit."

"We went out, of course, but he never took me out. I was always the one finding the restaurant, paying the check, making the moves on him."

"Well, that's too bad because you deserve someone to do all those things for you, Eric."

He takes my hand and holds it, and I hadn't realized it until that moment, but we've never held hands in public before.

I fucking love it.

I wasn't like that with Casey, at all. And if I'd ever reached for his hand in private, he would swat it away and tell me not to be too sweet.

Jesse isn't anything like him.

No, I've never met anyone like him before, no one who could do what he does to me...who can continuously catch me off guard...who can make me want to lower my usual defenses.

Nice as it is to have someone else take the reins, it's also kind of terrifying to know I'm not in total control. But I've done that for too long, and it's too much. It's time to let someone else help for a change.

He was right about that, when we were crouched down in my condo, his arms around me as he dished out my own advice to me: *"Sometimes we all need a little help."*

We both share that.

He needed help when he was a kid, before Charlotte and Stan were in his life. And I had to have it when I fled mine and reached out to friends who supported me and helped me set up a life for myself. I had to find hospitable, kind people in a sea of darkness during a time where I struggled, where I was in so much pain.

We walk to his car, still chatting about the movie as he drives us out of the parking lot. "Okay, so that scene where Jack Crawford is like freaking out about Clarice," Jesse says, "that's weird, right? Like a plot hole."

"What do you mean?"

"She calls Crawford and tells him that she has this lead, but then he's telling her she doesn't need to investigate it because they've got the guy. So Crawford and his guys break into this house, and we find out they followed a bogus lead, and he's freaking out, saying 'Clarice,' like he knows she's in danger. But why would he think she's checking out the lead when he told her not to? And how the hell would he know she's in the serial killer's house when she doesn't even know?"

"You've clearly given this a lot of thought," I say.

He tucks his head down for a moment, as though he feels embarrassed for how he launched into that commentary about what sounds like a plot hole—one I definitely wouldn't have picked up on.

"Yeah. I find myself trying to make sense of it whenever I watch it, and then that moment happens, and it's clearly a big deal, but I don't understand...at all. Bugs the crap out of me every time. He has no idea where Clarice is, but he's absolutely certain she's in trouble, or at least that's how it looks. And she is in trouble, but how would he know that? As far as he's concerned, didn't they talk about her not looking anymore? Even if she was about to go find the killer, how would he know that her lead was going to lead to the right one?"

"That sounds reasonable. I'd have to rewatch it to decide for myself."

"I don't know, maybe I'm completely wrong, but it bothers me." He chuckles before it becomes a full-on laugh. "Sorry. That's weird, right?"

"That's adorable is what that is. I love that you've put that much thought into it."

He flashes his ever-so-charming smile again, as though he's putting it on display for me.

He's passing Piedmont when I say, "You were supposed to turn back there."

"We're not going back to your place, Eric."

"What?"

Once again, I'm thrown. I was certain of how tonight would play out, at least after the date. We would go back to my condo, where we've shared night after night, and we would consummate our feelings with something that has been burning on my mind since I got my results for my tests back.

My balls feel heavy, as though they want me to come inside Jesse even more than I do.

"We're going to my place this time," he says. "It's not all fancy like yours, but I like it, and I want you to see it. It's very...me."

I'd taken for granted that we always meet at my place, but now that he's mentioned it, I'm eager to see it. I want to find out more about who he is. I want to know Jesse as well as I can possibly know another person. I want to be in his life in the way I almost thought wasn't possible when we first started messing around in Puerto Vallarta.

We pull up to his condo building, and he drives us through the relatively small complex before parking in a space in the lot. He guides me through the building, to his unit.

I'm stunned by how eager I am, how excited to see this part of his life.

As soon as I enter his place, I'm taken aback. Jesse's tastes are pretty modern, like mine, but where my style is clean and...safe, Jesse is a little more adventurous. The walls and cabinets are white, his cement floors painted light gray with a lacquer finish. The open-design layout is mostly whites, creams, and silver, but he's not afraid of the occasional pop of color—like with his red sectional sofa in the living area, which is just past the kitchen area to the right of the entryway. His walls are decorated with artwork—black-and-white prints and some more abstract paintings. I don't have a lot of artistic flair, but Jesse obviously has his particular tastes—another thing to add to my list of things I'm learning about him.

As we pass his kitchen and head toward the living area, I notice the white quartz top of the island. It's obviously something Jesse selected, considering it's unlikely this is a standard selection for any condo building in town.

He stops in the living area and turns to me. "You look shocked."

"I wasn't expecting it to be so bold," I admit.

"In a good way?"

"Yes. I like it. You clearly have your own style and aren't afraid of getting a little daring. And your tastes are fairly... expensive. I recognize several of the manufacturers you carry, actually."

He laughs. "Did you think I was living in a poor house?"

"No, I just assumed you would have been a little more modest."

Jesse shrugs. "I don't know. I spent so much time early on bouncing around to different houses, I figured I wanted to have a place...a home...that looked like a home. And I care about making it one I enjoy living in, even if I have spent all my time at your place recently." He winks. "Now come on. I want to give you the grand tour."

I follow his lead, and he walks me around his unit, paying special attention to the artwork he's collected throughout the years and why each piece captured his eye. He guides me up a short stairwell to the second story of his condo before he leads me into his bedroom.

There's a framed picture on the nightstand. It's of him and his adoptive parents, I assume. I walk over to it. "Is this Stan and Charlotte?"

"Yeah, that's them. You'll have to meet them sometime. They'd really like you."

"Looks like I'm about as old as they are."

"They're a little older, but not by much." He chuckles as though that isn't such a great obstacle to him. "And all they want is to meet this special guy I met and am going crazy over. How do you feel about that?"

"You going crazy for me?" I say, knowing he was really asking about me meeting his parents.

"That too."

I smile—something I do so much more with him in my life. I also cry more too, apparently, but that's a whole other thing.

Jesse moves toward me, slowly. He scans me up and down. "What do you say, Eric Westright? Are you ready to meet my parents?"

Everything about us feels as though it's happening too fast. Like we're on this freight train that's heading right for a cliff, but if we go off a fucking cliff, I hope we go off it together. Jesse makes me want to be a better person, a different person, to push past all my insecurities and fears and worries.

I wrap my arm around him, pull him close to me. "I would love to meet your parents," I say, "but right now, I know one thing I would love to do even more."

He kisses me, and it reminds me of how much of the night has been spent without his lips against mine…and I feel this almost rage swell within me at the thought that I've been deprived of his delicious mouth for too long.

I shove him back on the bed.

He goes so willingly, gazing up at me eagerly. "Tired of talking?"

"I love talking to you, but my cock has its own plans."

"Well, I'd love to hear its suggestions," he says before I pounce on top of him.

This night has been so amazing, and now I want to scratch this itch, the one that's burning within me as though I've never fucking gotten off with him.

I want his body, I want to be inside him, and the way he claws at my clothes, the way I claw at his, I can tell that neither of us can stop the passion we ignited any more than we could after the spark we shared the moment we first met.

He might be the biggest mistake I've ever made. Thank God for mistakes.

## 13

## JESSE

He kisses the hell out of me, working so frantically to get my clothes off that I'm sure he's going to tear the buttons off my shirt. When we've undone the placket, I struggle to get out of the button-up, and Eric starts laughing as he unfastens his tie and slides it out of the collar, throwing it back behind him. He appears so cool and collected while I feel like a fumbling mess.

"Look at you acting like a needy bottom," Eric says as I manage to get out of the shirt, as though I was imprisoned in it.

"I am a needy bottom right now. *Your* needy bottom." I throw it aside and lean up, wrapping my arms around him and pulling him down onto me. "Why do we have to be wearing so many clothes?"

"The clothes were your idea," Eric reminds me as he unfastens my belt.

"I figured it would make it hotter, but I'm frustrated that your cock isn't inside me already."

He grips the ends of my belt and lowers the connected end against my cheek, down between my pecs, to my abs.

"Well, considering you've been cockteasing me all day, I'd say now it's my turn. I think if you want my cum, you should have to beg for it...like you begged for that kiss."

"I beg best on my knees."

Eric tosses the belt aside and unfastens his fly.

I crawl onto all fours on the mattress as he drops trou. I take his cock into my mouth. He's already dripping with precum, which I lap up eagerly. I glance up and see him removing his shirt as I let his girth fill my mouth.

He kicks off his shoes and lets his pants and boxers fall to the floor, stepping out of them, but I do a good job of maintaining my rhythm, serving him.

As he runs his hand through my hair, I pull his cock mostly out of my mouth, so the bottom of its head is resting on my tongue, which I slide side to side.

He runs his hand down to the back of my neck, clawing.

I lean my head back so that beautiful dick is right before me.

"Like I said," Eric mutters. "Fucking cocktease."

"You love it, though."

"You have no fucking idea how much."

With that compliment, I decide he's earned some relief, so I take his cock into my mouth again.

How didn't I ever know that a man could taste so good?

How did Eric take me from casual interest and curiosity in guys to this sex-obsessed slave to his cock?

I get lost in trying to make him feel good, trying to give this my all, when he grabs either side of my head gently and says, "Stop, stop, Jesse. You're gonna make me come like this."

I obey and pull back, letting his shaft fall from my lips as I gaze up at him.

"And I don't need to waste any cum in that perfect

mouth of yours. Not tonight."

He leans down and claims my mouth, resting his hand on the small of my back and guiding me so that I'm upright, still on my knees.

"Take these pants off," he commands.

"Yes, sir."

I start to remove them when Eric says, "No, no, Jesse. Slow down. Let me enjoy the show."

I freeze.

I was planning to strip out of them like I typically do, but now he has me intrigued, especially with the way he's looking at me.

"What do you mean?"

"I want you to put on a little show for me. Earn my cock in your ass."

I blush. *Eric fucking Westright, you are fucking breaking me...in all the right ways.*

I want to make a joke because the request sounds awkward, but I don't want him to feel self-conscious for asking. Plus, it sounds hot as fuck.

I unfasten my fly, feeling a little weird about giving him a show, but as I start to pull down my pants, I realize I'm moving too fast and decide I need to go for this...own it. It's not about me being in my head. It's about doing it for Eric. Giving him what he wants. Showing him I deserve him inside me.

I turn around on the mattress so that my ass faces him, and I reach down and hook my thumbs into the sides of my pants, sliding them down, slowly...hearing him growl softly.

I continue pulling them down, but I realize it's going to look silly if I start having to fight my way out of them once they get to my knees, so I lean forward on one arm and continue working them down my thighs, taking my time as I glance over my shoulder and see Eric watching me, stroking himself as he enjoys the view.

He crawls onto the bed and leans down, taking a bit of my right ass cheek between his teeth and nipping. I don't know what it is about something so simple that drives me insane, but it does.

Eric grabs the sides of my pants and boxers and pulls them the rest of the way down before adding them to the pile we've created on my floor. He leans back down and kisses the back of my thigh, working his way up to my ass.

A series of tingles races through me as he moves up my body, my back...to behind my ear. A moan escapes my mouth.

He presses his hand against the back of my neck and slides it around to my throat before whispering in my ear, "Now who's the one blue-balling?"

I feel...empty. Like I fucking *need* a cock in me—Eric's cock.

"Tell me what you want me to do to you," he says, whispering the words against my neck as he slides his face down toward my shoulders.

"I want you inside me, Eric."

He growls as he slides his face back up my neck, back behind my ear. "Now you're just trying to make it harder on me, and it's working." As he speaks the words, he presses his pelvis down against my ass so I can feel his erection.

He pulls back up on his knees and slides his arms around my thighs, lifting and then rolling me onto my back. I chuckle at his forcefulness, at how he's basically flinging me around in bed, but when I see that stern expression on his face, pure desire for me, for fucking, for fucking me...I'm not laughing.

"You better get some lube," I say, because by the looks of

him, I would think he might try to jam that thing in me dry, and fuck no, that's not happening.

He steps off the bed and heads to the nightstand.

"Bottom drawer," I tell him.

He opens it and grabs the bottle but inspects something else. "Only Magnums for my Jesse, I guess."

"Only Magnums for either of us, really. You want to put one on for old times' sake?"

While we haven't been together long, the amount of sex we've had, especially while we were in Puerto Vallarta, and the amount of condoms we've torn through, has been epic.

"That's so not happening," Eric says as he comes back to the bed, crawling after me and lifting my legs up until his lips are right where they belong, on my ass.

As if I wasn't hard enough already.

His skilled tongue works my hole, and my thoughts spiral out of control. He pushes his fingers into my ass, working them with his tongue. Oh, he's trying to drive me insane. He knows how needy my ass is...needy for him, and he's toying with my emotions as he gives me this incredible massage.

It's funny to think that before I met Eric I never would have imagined wanting to have a guy like this, but I feel this craving, this desire to have him slamming into my prostate. I wonder where this comes from, this intense need rippling through me.

Another moan escapes my lips before he stops pleasuring my hole and moves up my body, offering kisses, licks, the occasional soft bite, gripping my flesh, making me feel his need for me. When his mouth is against mine, I enjoy his taste and the sound of our smacking lips as he takes hold of my wrists and then pushes me onto my back, pressing his weight against me as he pins my arms down at either side.

He kisses across my face, down my neck. His movements wild, frenzied. The smell of his cologne and minty breath fill my nostrils. "Fuck you, Eric. Fuck you and this goddamn power you have over me."

"What are...you talking...about, Jesse?" he asks between kisses, as though he struggles to pull his lips away from my flesh even for moments. He looks into my eyes as he adds, "You're the one doing this to me, driving me crazy, surprising me at every turn, making me need you in a way I've never needed anyone else or felt his want, his need for me."

He releases my wrists and kisses down my body until he reaches my cock, which he takes into his mouth, offering me that familiar, delicious sensation.

He's so good at what he does.

It's expert, it's impressive, it's mind-blowing. I'm left twitching and turning, struggling because I've been enduring this horrible pain in my balls since I heard about Eric's test results.

Now the pressure in my balls is almost unbearable.

I'm climbing so fast. I hope not too fast.

"Eric, stop edging me," I tell him. "Get inside me. Take me the way I need to be taken."

He doesn't resist. He grabs the bottle of lube he threw down on the bed at some point after he retrieved it. He lubes up his cock, which looks harder than it normally does.

He throws the lube back on the bed before gripping the bottoms of my thighs and pushing them back, like he wants to make that ass that much easier for him to access. I hold my legs in place when he turns and retrieves a pillow from beside the headboard. He pulls it over, and I lift my back, allowing him to slide it under me, which we've done occasionally when we've fucked in this position. It's one of those things that reminds me of how much he cares about my comfort, that he's not just greedy for it himself. But I enjoy that part too, when I feel like he's selfishly fulfilling himself with my body, that I can give him that.

He lines up his cock with my hole.

The anticipation is killing me the way it's been killing me all day as this image has possessed my thoughts, the idea of having him inside me, of it being flesh against flesh.

He smiles, and I imagine it's because he's as excited about this as I am.

He begins pushing. The pressure building feels different than it does when we fuck with condoms, and the way he slides in is different too.

He takes his time, and once he's inched his cock in a bit, he leans down and rests with his elbows on either side of me, his face right before mine as he gazes into my eyes, his mouth hanging open as he makes it farther within me.

I'm doing that to him. My body is giving him this pleasure.

God, I love knowing that.

"How do you like it?" Eric asks. "Does it feel good?"

"Really good. I didn't realize it would feel different."

I mean, I could imagine, considering how different it felt not to wear a condom on my own dick with Whitney, but being on the receiving end is a whole other thing.

Eric's grin broadens. "I can't tell you how much I love this tight ass." He rocks his hips back and forth, the sensation urging me to throw my head back and relax into the experience.

I sneak a peek back at Eric, who watches me as though he wants to see what he can do to me.

"You're so beautiful," he says as he pushes farther into me, and I feel him hit my prostate.

As I gasp, his lips slam down against mine, and he fucks me…hard. I wrap my arms around him, pulling him close.

"Do you want me to spill my load inside you?" he asks.

"Yes, Eric."

I'm needy for Eric, for his cum, for that release.

He's the man who changed the game.

Even when I'm at the office, I'm daydreaming about spending more time with him, thinking about his face or his smile, that scruff, his tattoo. There's torture in daydreaming about him, though, because he's so complex, and so many things about him turn me on that I'm left in agony at my awareness that I can't fathom every facet of him all at once.

I'm getting close when he slides out of me and urges me onto my knees, facing the headboard. I grab the top of the wooden frame as he enters me from behind. He hooks an arm around me and kisses right behind my ear.

"You know this position is my favorite," I tell him.

"You have a lot of favorites, don't you?" He licks his thumb and brings it around, encircling my nipple with it.

He's exciting so many different nerves in my body, sending these waves of pleasure racing through me, coursing through my veins. My nerves are hypersensitive, my balls aching as though I'm some sort of prepubescent teen.

As his cock continues striking my prostate, I can feel that pressure mounting. I groan through gritted teeth, my body trapped between feeling tensed up and so at ease at the same time.

"Kiss me, please," he says, his hot breath slamming behind my ear.

I strain to turn, and our lips collide. He cups his hand behind my head to help keep my head in place, pulling me closer. Even like this, with him bare inside me, it's never fucking close enough.

"I'm going to come inside you, Jesse." His voice is a whisper as he removes his hand from my nipple. He licks his hand before bringing it around and jerking my shaft.

My body twitches, the sensations that race through me combining with how he's worked me up so far, everything so fucking stimulated, all my nerves ready to erupt with that rush of ecstasy that isn't ever just about getting off. Hell, I've gotten off plenty of times on my own and with someone else, but what Eric and I create...it's a fire that burns to my core.

"You're going to make me come..." I say, breaking our kiss to get the words out. He massages his thumb against the back of my head.

"Tell me you want this. Tell me you're mine," Eric says.

"Eric, I'm yours," I confess because it's true...because I've given up. Eric has me, all of me, and I need this certainty far more than he does. "Make me yours," I plead, hearing that desperation in my voice.

His face tenses up as he offers a series of jerks, his arm wrapping around me. He continues stroking my cock as his lips slam against mine. We call out together, and I feel in his movements, from all the other fucking we've shared, from getting so good at reading that body of his, that he's about to spill his load within me.

When he does, it's too much for me, especially with him stroking me in that expert corkscrew motion. My load spills out across the sheets, and soon we're both a mess of spasms, a collision of frenzied passion.

As I take a breath to recover from the workout, there's relief in knowing what we just experienced together and that he's inside me, the way I want him to be.

# 14

# ERIC

I lie next to Jesse, his body spread out across the mattress, totally exposed.

I appreciate every line in his torso, between his muscles, as well as the impressive bulk in his chest and biceps, and that little curvature in his lips.

He looks satisfied with what we've shared.

We've been lying here, basking and reveling in that experience.

I feel more content than I've ever felt with anything we've done together because I got to have Jesse in a way that felt so much more intimate than ever before. It was about more than filling him up raw. It was about this place we've reached in our relationship, what that moment represents for us.

"That was incredible," he says.

"*You* were incredible," I say quickly, because I'm still thinking about every movement, every whimper, every moan...about my fixation on this amazing guy.

I've had a lot of sex in my life, but Jesse...he's the only

one who takes it to something so far beyond fucking. It's wild and intense, but so intimate too.

As I roll over to him and rest my hand on his stomach, I gaze down into those eager eyes, which look at me as though he wouldn't mind me taking him again.

I'm as obsessed as ever, and there's no one I'd rather be obsessed with than my Jesse.

Of course, I can't seem to just enjoy an amazing experience, since my thoughts turn elsewhere.

"I want to give you that," I tell him. "What you gave me. I want you to experience it."

His gaze lowers. "Eric..."

"I know you want that too, Jesse. Don't tell me that you don't. I've seen the way you look at me, felt the way you handle me. I know how much you would enjoy that."

"I enjoy being with you." He sits up and turns to me. "Spending time with you, in and out of the bedroom, though I have to admit I enjoy the bedroom a lot."

I can tell by the way he smiles after, he wants me to laugh, but I can't.

"Jesse. It's not just that I want to give you something you want. I want it too. I wish you could understand how badly I want it, and I feel twisted up inside about it."

"Eric, there's plenty of time for us to figure that out. We can walk instead of run. You deserve help with this, and you deserve someone who can take their time."

There he goes again, saying the thing that is surely part of the reason why he's the one I want to share this with. Intellectually, I appreciate the words, but at the same time, I'm running through all the issues that stand in our way—that he could be with someone younger, less fucked up, someone who doesn't carry around all this baggage.

"You're a kid," I remind him, and in a way, I'm reminding

myself. "You shouldn't have to deal with any of this. You should be out, banging every guy that moves, sticking your cock in them, letting them stick their cocks in you."

"Are you talking about what my life would be like if I stepped into a porn?"

"I'm being serious, Jesse. I appreciate when you lighten the mood, but I feel like there are a lot of serious discussions that need to be had."

"There are, and we've had some of them, but we don't have to have them all at once, and we're not going to magically get on the other side of this, so why not appreciate this time we do have, where things aren't so shitty, where I shared something with you that felt really incredible to me."

Of course he would do this. As soon as I called him a kid, he proved me wrong. He's not the naive, innocent thing I sometimes mistake him for because of his age. There's wisdom in that little head of his—wisdom I know is the reason why I'm really here...why we're here, together.

This is why I'm so intoxicated, not only by his body, but by his mind.

I don't just want to be coming in him. I want to be in his head, in his thoughts, at one with those, getting to know those in a way I've never desired from another person.

Jesse rests his hand on my side and slides it to my back, sneaking his arm around me. He scoots across the mattress, pushing close to me, his thick cock alongside mine.

"Come on, Eric. Didn't you have a good night? Didn't you enjoy that?"

"I enjoyed all of it," I admit as I reflect on this thoughtful, carefully planned evening we shared. "I enjoyed dinner, the movie—"

"And then giving me your load?" Jesse interrupts.

"You make it sound so dirty," I tease him. "But yes, I think I enjoyed that best."

He's finally gone and done it, broken through once again, and a smile tugs at my lips.

He takes advantage of his victory and moves in for a kiss.

A stir of passion rises deep within me, fire shooting out, erupting through my veins, seizing control of me. I pull him closer to me, slipping my tongue into his mouth. He's such an interesting combination of push and pull. I'm fascinated by Jesse in all his intricacies. In his willingness to take the lead whenever he damn well feels like it.

I hardly realized how hard I was getting until I feel him slide his hand between us, against my crotch.

"I think someone's ready to go again," Jesse says.

"I plan on going again a lot tonight with you."

"I like the sound of that. What do you usually do when you go again? Should I go clean out?"

"How do you fucking do this?" I ask, because I can't help myself. His expression sobers as he seems thrown by my remark. "You go from being so sly and cocky to innocent and naive in a moment. You show whatever vulnerabilities you have, don't try to act as though you know more than you do."

"I'm not ashamed of being dumb about things. I can't know everything."

"I agree. In some ways, I think your ability to be okay with that is part of what makes you stronger than most. You don't feel like you need to know everything. Or as if you have to hide when you don't know something. You don't even play games."

"That's not true. I love games. I love teasing my Eric."

"Only the fun kind of games, though. You're not trying to fuck with my head...not in the wrong ways, at least."

"I have this sneaking suspicion you're talking about Casey…?"

"I was actually referring to most of the guys I've dealt with in my life, but he definitely enjoyed games. He was constantly trying to make me feel like I wasn't good enough, like I had to earn something from him, but you aren't that way."

"I'm sorry he made you feel that way, Eric. But you've already earned what you need to from me, by being you."

I chuckle.

"That wasn't me being funny."

"I know…that was me being awkward."

"Well, you shouldn't be the one feeling awkward, considering I still don't know what the fuck I'm supposed to do about my ass right now."

I'm in awe of him in this moment, and he says, "That one was a joke, so you can laugh at that. And answer my goddamn question before I have to start Googling on my phone."

I laugh again. "If you keep being this sexy, you won't be cleaning out at all tonight, since I'm going to take you again and again."

"So we can do that?"

"Yeah, it actually makes it a lot easier for us."

"Oh, really? Well, I'm glad to know access won't be an issue."

"You can't know how appreciative I am that you're in my life now."

"Well, Eric." The mischievous look in his eyes suggests he's deliberately using my name to remind me of this power he has over me. "I'm just as happy that you're in mine. And I'm eager to explore this with you."

"Oh, Jesse, Jesse." I run my hand through his hair,

slightly wet from our fucking, and move a little closer, leaning in, smelling him, because God, I love the way he smells. "You're so fucking addicting," I tell him.

He smirks, offering me that ever-so-sexual look as he whispers, "Then why don't you let me give you another fix?"

Before I know it, his mouth is back against mine. He wraps his arms under mine and pulls me back on top of him. And there's the eruption again, and the sweet promise of that same satisfaction that I was offered this evening, that I've been craving.

I rub my hard girth against his pelvis. I need release. I need to be inside him again, coming in him again and again and again. I don't know how I'll ever get enough of him. I don't know how I'll manage without this chemistry of having his body against my own, this burning, hot lust between us that seems to get more and more out of control the longer we're together. What started as a spark has become a raging inferno, ravaging my whole world.

## 15

## JESSE

Eric leads the way down the plane aisle, me following in tow, holding my carry-on in front of me. As we pass first class, I reflect on our debate when we were booking the tickets. Eric typically flies priority, but since I didn't want him buying my ticket and I refused to fly first class, he conceded. I can tell by his uneasiness as he puts his bag in the overhead compartment by our seats that he would have been perfectly happy to upgrade.

Eric waves for me to get in, but as I scoot to the window seat, I turn back, catching Eric's uneasy expression. "Oh, did you want to sit by the window? Sorry. I assumed by the way you offered that you preferred the aisle." I start to get up.

"No," Eric says as he forces his way into the row and sits in the aisle seat. "This is your first time going to San Diego. I'd rather you get to see it when we fly in."

"It's really thoughtful, but there's no reason you shouldn't be able to sit where you normally do, considering you're already not sitting in first class, Mr. Bougie."

"Whatever. Sit down and be quiet." I enjoy the playfulness in his tone as I obey his command.

However, he seems tense...more tense than he should be from giving up a window seat.

"Are you nervous about flying?" I ask.

He leans close to me and whispers, "I'm nervous about being in the economy comfort. I don't want to sound like an asshole, but I don't enjoy being around a lot of people...not close, at least. I get a little claustrophobic."

I'm left wondering if this is somehow related to the abuse he experienced as a kid—if it acts as a trigger for him. Now I really feel like a shithead.

"Eric, if you would've mentioned that it was about that and not just you wanting to be fancy, I wouldn't have fought you so hard about it."

"No, it's fine. I need to push past my comfort zone, and I took a Xanax. Waiting for it to kick in."

I take his hand and squeeze gently, and his grip quickly relaxes.

"Guess that Xanax is kicking in," I tease him.

He smiles, though I can read the discomfort on his expression, which is so different from how it's been the past few days, since our date night.

We've been fucking like rabbits, like we did when we first started fucking in PV, but barebacking has been so much better. I love us being unrestricted and free with one another. Even as I'm sitting in an airplane, I can't keep some of these interactions from creeping into my thoughts and making my dick hard.

This new chapter in our relationship has me thinking even more like a horny teen than after meeting him. I want Eric so badly it hurts. It hurts because I know I can't spend every waking moment with him. We both have lives and careers, and this trip forces me to bear in mind that there are going to be times when Eric won't be in Atlanta. Because really, his life is in San Diego.

We've been lucky that hasn't presented an obstacle for our relationship so far, but similarly to PV, I'm aware that, in some ways, what we've been doing is a bit of a fantasy...that we'll have to find a way to sustain this relationship long term.

Once we're in the air, I watch Eric as he seems to grow more comfortable, perhaps because his Xanax really is kicking in.

I pull my earbuds out of my pocket while Eric pulls out his. We sift through the movie selections on the screens mounted on the seats before us.

"What movie are we gonna watch?" I ask.

"What?"

"What movie are we gonna watch? I assume we're gonna watch something together."

"At the same time?" He appears totally thrown by my suggestion. "Do you do that?"

"You don't? Not even you and Casey?"

"We would just watch whatever we were interested in. We didn't really have similar tastes, so..."

"Are you kidding me? It's so much more fun flying when you watch movies with someone. I mean, we don't have to watch every movie on a flight like this together, but one would be nice. Come on, watch a movie with me, Eric."

He beams. "You have a way with words, Jesse."

"What do you mean?"

"That reminded me of the way you asked me to be your boyfriend, which wasn't much of a question. You basically bullied me into being in a relationship with you."

"You did have an opportunity to say no."

He laughs. "That wasn't going to happen."

I'm an idiot for how giddy I feel when he says those words. Obviously, he wants to be with me and he's in this relationship as much as I am, yet confirmation means so much to me, especially considering how guarded he typically is.

I know that's why he made such a big deal the other night about how candid I am about things I don't understand or have questions about. He's not the type who likes to let people know when he's down or what his weaknesses are, which is one of the reasons I'm appreciative he's letting me come with him to this therapy appointment.

Who knows how that will play out? I fear he might not let me actually go to the appointment with him...or if he does, not bring up this issue that's been weighing on him for so long.

I hope he will, for his own sake.

Although, even if it's not this time, I need to keep being there for him...to help him get to the place where he can do this.

The more research I've done about all this, the easier it's been for me to remind myself that he's not alone in this... that so many have had to walk a similar path and face these demons. And that it's not a race to figure it out.

We scan through the available movies on the flight, naming our options and reading synopses, searching for one neither of us has seen, since we agree it'll be more fun to experience it together for the first time.

Hell, I do enjoy sharing first times with Eric.

There's this 2008 French movie called *Martyrs*, and while it's older, the synopsis catches our interest.

"Sounds pretty cool," I say. "Although, I'd hate to bore you with subtitles."

"Shut up. You know I love me a subtitled movie. Let's try it and see if we like it."

We agree, and start the movie on each of our screens.

The film opens interestingly enough, but what I figured would be a quiet psychological thriller is a giant mind-fuck that has us nearly crawling into each other's laps as Eric grabs my arm during particularly suspenseful scenes, whispering, "Holy fuck, holy fuck, holy fuck." At one point toward the end, we're both muttering our *holy fucks* together.

I glance around to make sure no one is noticing our freak-out, and the rest of the plane doesn't seem to get how the director of this film is terrorizing our brains.

"Are they seriously about to..." Eric has his hand over his eyes but is peering around his fingers.

So many times I want to turn away, but my eyes are glued to the screen, and despite Eric's attempts at shielding himself from the horror, so are his.

"Why are we doing this? Why are we doing this?" Eric asks.

"Because you haven't said to stop yet," I say, and I have to admit, there are times when I kind of wish he'd bailed.

As the final scene comes to a close and fades to black, Eric whispers, "What...the...fuck?"

The credits roll, and I feel out of breath, like I do after a night of Eric working my body out.

"That was kind of amazing," I mutter.

Eric eyes me peculiarly. "I worry about the thoughts in your head, Jesse, if you thought that was amazing."

"You should be worried...because that was...*epic*. I haven't had that kind of movie-watching experience in a long-ass time. And I was thinking it was going to be boring as fuck based on the synopsis."

"I thought I was going to have to get up and go to the bathroom to throw up."

I chuckle. "All the gross stuff we watch, and this freaked you out?"

"It was that one scene toward the end where they had her tied up, and then they were going to…"

He doesn't even want to finish his sentence, so I start to do it for him. "You mean when they—"

"Don't say it, don't you fucking say it."

"Okay, okay," I say.

We chat some more about the movie, which we're both still recovering from. Then we switch it up and watch some other movies. I pass out during the second one since it's not nearly as interesting, but Eric wakes me up and urges me to look out the window when we get near San Diego.

After we land, we catch an Uber, and Eric gives me an oral tour as we head through the city.

I don't think I'm as interested in the city, though, as I am in the fact that it's Eric's city. I imagine him walking to the Starbucks on the corner or stumbling out of a bar he mentions he and his friends hang out at. This is where Eric's life is…where so much of it has taken place.

"This is my condo building we're coming up on," he says, indicating a high-rise alongside the beach.

"Oh, Mr. Bougie indeed," I say, and he snickers.

As soon as we enter his unit, I realize how true that nickname is.

"What do you think, Mr. Morgan?" he asks.

"Mr. Morgan and Mr. Bougie? Hmmm…fitting," I say as I look around at the decor—far more extravagant than his place in Atlanta.

Sunlight pours in through stacked windows on the other side of the room, which overlook the oceanfront, apparently, by the view, perfect for a sunset. A black-leather sectional sofa sits in the middle of the room, facing a dark-brown wooden coffee table and the mounted big-screen TV. Behind the sofa, an empty space allows room to walk around to the dual balcony doors. He's got print artworks, some microphotography. There's a photo behind the sofa that takes up most of the wall—a black and white that it takes me a moment to realize is actually San Diego.

Unlike his Atlanta unit, where the kitchen is to the left, here it's on the right, but with a similar large, rectangular kitchen island in black marble. Complementing the place are various side tables with accessories I'm sure he and his designer picked out just to his tastes.

These are Eric's tastes, I tell myself. This is the sort of world he's used to living in. This is part of the man I want to come to know so much better.

He gives me a tour of the place, the way I gave him the tour of mine. He guides me upstairs, through a massive library and office space, and then he takes me into the master bedroom, where I hope we'll be spending plenty of time while we're here. He leads me onto the balcony in his room. It overlooks his impressive view of the ocean. I press my hands against the concrete rail, shaking my head before turning to him and folding my arms.

He stands at my side, the wind catching his bangs.

"What?" he asks, but judging by his expression, with one eyebrow raised higher than the other, he must know what I'm thinking.

"You were all surprised by my place, and this is incredible. Not the kind of place I was expecting from a guy who likes his ten-piece nuggets meal at Wendy's. I think I've been had. But seriously. It's very nice...insanely nice. I'm constantly surprised that it's easy to forget how much money you really make."

"How much money do you think I make?" Eric asks me.

"A lot more than me." I glance back through the floor-length windows. "I'm basically in the poor house compared to you. I'll be collecting food stamps by the time I get back home, especially taking a vacation right at the beginning of my job."

"You didn't have to come here," he says, his tone unexpectedly serious.

"No, no. That was a joke. I wanted to come. This is important, and I have plenty of vacation time. I'm not concerned. Most of what I do at my job I can do remotely anyway."

He approaches, his gaze drifting to the floor as his arms make their way around me so naturally...which is good because that's where they belong.

"Well, I am glad you're here," he says.

"I appreciate you letting me be here for you, Eric. Speaking of which, how do you feel about tomorrow?"

"Nervous. Worried. It still doesn't feel like it's going to happen."

"But you are going to tell her, right?"

He looks uncertain, as though he's considered bailing.

"I'll do my best," he says.

"That's all I ask, but you owe it to yourself." I rest my hand on his bicep, running my thumb along where the hem of his sleeve meets his skin. "Let me know what I need to do. If you don't want me to go back in the room with you, and I need to wait until you're finished, that's fine. I don't care. I want to hold your hand through this as much as I can, but I'm not interested in doing anything that'll make you uneasy."

"I appreciate that, Jesse. More than you could possibly know."

We gaze into each other's eyes as he moves forward slowly, and then once again, like so many other times, I can't help myself. My lips are back on his, and his hands are clawing at my back.

I relax into it, but he leans back. "Enough of that," he says, a wicked grin spreading across his face. "I haven't shown you the best view of the bedroom yet."

He squats down, wraps his arms around my legs, and hoists me up, throwing me over his shoulder as he carries me back into the condo.

We take advantage of this opportunity, enjoying each other, enjoying the evening in bed before we make dinner together and have an incredible evening with me appreciating how much he fits into this place.

At the same time, there is that worry that maybe I'm the thing that's a little out of place in his life.

# 16

# ERIC

I tap my foot anxiously as I sit in the waiting room of my therapist's office. Jesse sets his hand on my leg, and I turn to him as he offers a warm yet subtle smile. He's trying to reassure me, I figure...trying to let me know he's here for me. He can't realize how much I appreciate that he's come all the way to San Diego to do this with me.

Because as put together as I'm trying to act about all this, the idea of facing these demons again, with someone other than Jesse...is fucking terrifying. There's a strong part of me that would rather pretend that night—and my confession of that night—never happened. After all, that's what I've programmed myself to do all these years.

When the receptionist asks Jesse to sign a consent form and for my payment, I find myself fumbling, struggling to pull it from my wallet.

I'm a mess.

I'm on edge, nervous, and I hardly got any sleep as I dwelled on the fact that this wasn't going to be easy for me. I feel as if I could totally slip, lose control and have some sort of breakdown in an instant. It's as though I've spent my life keeping a series of rubber bands tense, in the right place for me to function, and if I release them, they will snap away, maybe break, and the Eric I know will be gone.

"I'm here," Jesse reminds me, and I need his reassurance, more now than ever, especially when he's the only one who knows my secret.

I take deep breaths, the way Michelle's taught me to, but only within the context of what she's always believed has been general anxiety.

The door to the back office opens, and Michelle steps out. "Hi, Eric," she says, and I grab Jesse's hand and push to my feet, pulling him with me, partly because I fear if I don't bring him with me, I'll make him stay here…and partly because I really need him in this moment. But the way he joins me, without question or hesitation, gives me strength I know I wouldn't have had if he weren't here.

As we head toward the hallway leading back to her office, Jesse rests his hand on the small of my back. It's such a simple thing, but it's little movements like that, like when he set his hand on my leg, that soothe me. They remind me I'm not on my own.

It's comforting and terrifying at the same time because now it's not just my own mouth that the truth can come out of, but Jesse's as well. Even though I know he would never say anything, that he would never violate my trust that way, it doesn't keep the fear—irrational as it is—from being there.

Of course, since my experience with my uncle, I've had a lot of irrational thoughts I can't seem to shake. They creep up on me at the most inopportune of moments, like when Jesse was going down on my ass when we were camping a few weeks ago.

Michelle greets us, very friendly and polite with Jesse as

she guides us into her office, which is spacious, with a few plants and a sofa and a cushioned chair. She asks us to sit as she takes a seat in the cushioned chair beside the sofa we sit on together.

"How have you been, Eric? I was surprised to see you wanted to have someone join us today. Since you brought Jesse, we can set aside where we left off in our last session and come back to it later. Was there something in particular you were interested in discussing?"

The truth isn't written all over my face? Surely, she has to be able to see exactly what my issue is. I've always felt like in some ways it was somehow marked on my body and people could sense what happened to me. That any slight weakness I revealed to Michelle told her too much, even though she's never given me any reason to believe she's caught on to my real issue.

Jesse keeps his hands to himself. Maybe because he doesn't think holding my hand is appropriate right now, but really, that's what I want—what I need.

"Maybe we should start with Jesse," I say. "He's my boyfriend."

"Congratulations," Michelle says with a smile. "It's great to meet you, Jesse. It's been some time since you've discussed seeing anyone, so I'm glad to know you're at a place where you're comfortable entering into a new relationship. How long have the two of you been seeing each other?"

"A few months. We met in Puerto Vallarta in January."

This is something I knew would have to come out as well—that I've seen her since Jesse and I started seeing each other and haven't mentioned the whole I've-been-screwing-my-son's-friend issue. I may be self-aware enough to know I need a therapist, but that doesn't mean I'm any good at actually getting help for my issues.

"I remember when you went on that trip," she says as though I haven't left out an important element from all that. "How is everything going between the two of you? Is there anything you'd care to discuss?"

"It's a little more complicated than just us seeing each other."

Jesse takes my hand, and I inhale for some much-needed air before getting this out of my system. "Jesse was down in Puerto Vallarta in my condo with my son. Not *with* my son like that. He was there as a friend." Goddammit, I can hardly get to the real issue if I'm fumbling over stupid shit. But I press on, explaining how things started up, letting the whole deal unfold until the final confrontation with Ty and our subsequent chat that went so much better.

"Oh? Can you tell me anything else about that?" she asks, though I can tell she's clearly trying to act very cool about the situation.

"So one thing led to another, and then..."

She waits for me to finish my sentence, but I don't.

"I'm sure that was a relief, getting all that off your chest with Ty. Jesse, how about you? How have you felt about everything that's happened so far?"

Jesse's eyebrows rise as he seems surprised that Michelle's directing attention his way. "Well, I knew it wasn't going to be a great reaction, but...um...it was time. We'd been sort of lying to ourselves about how far we'd gotten, how much we'd felt for each other, and by the time we got to that, it was a little too late."

"And how do you feel about where things are at between you and Ty?" she asks.

He thinks long and hard before responding. "Not great." He chuckles, but clearly not because anything's funny. Because everything about us is so fucked up.

"I want my friend back, but I want Eric too...and that's complicated."

"It sounds like you're both feeling frustrated about where things are at with Ty. Eric, I'd like to talk some about what you want out of your relationship with Ty and also what you want for Jesse's friendship."

"If only it were that easy. Jesus, I feel like I'm so fucking confused by all this that I can't even get to that part of it." I try to humor her, though. At least give her something to work off. "Us to all be one big happy family, I guess." I roll my eyes because those words sound so convoluted. I take a long sigh, reflecting on her question. "I want a relationship with my son. And I think I have more reason to hope for one now than I ever have before. And I want him to be happy. I don't want to be the reason he lost his best friend."

"From what you said before, it sounds like Ty is interested in working through things with both of you, so how are you planning to approach your individual relationships?"

"I don't know yet. Seems like I really fucked up."

"It presents some challenges, naturally. How do you feel about those?"

"Can we cut it with the rational conversation bullshit? I'm in a relationship with my son's best friend. How is that supposed to make things easier for us?" I shake my head. "I mean, come on. You can just admit that this is a messed-up situation."

"Eric, this is a difficult subject to discuss, and I can tell you're frustrated and annoyed right now, and maybe feeling concerned about judgment from me. But I can assure you that I have seen weirder situations than this, and I'm here to help. Now, I'm going to ask a question, and you answer honestly. And I've asked it before, so humor me. Do you believe Ty wants to have a relationship with you?"

I hesitate, but Jesse spits out, "Yes."

Michelle's gaze shifts to him. "That was a very assertive reply. Why do you say it like that, Jesse?"

"I've known Ty for a very long time, and he's mad, he's hurt, but he cares about his father and his relationship with his father."

Jesse's said that so many times since I've known him, and as much as he speaks the words, it doesn't change that I feel like it can't be true, that there's no way Ty could behave as he does around me—keeping his distance and, every time I push, pushing back harder—and really want a relationship.

"Eric," Michelle says, "how do you feel when Jesse says that?"

"I don't know that I entirely believe it's true." Although, as I reflect on it, I know how crazy I must sound. "At the same time, I can't imagine why Ty would have even talked to me after all this happened if he didn't."

"Yes! Let's explore that some more. How do you feel this lines up with some of the thinking errors you've identified in our work together?"

I'm irritated that she's bringing up these stupid thinking errors that we've discussed plenty of times before. I know this is the whole point of therapy, but I don't have to like it. "Maybe *mind reading*, a little." I acknowledge, especially when it comes to Ty, that my biggest fault has always been assuming I know what he's thinking, how he's judging me for anything I do.

"It's just, Michelle, how can he ever really forgive me for this?"

She's about to say something, but I beat her to the punch. "I know that's the whole issue with mind reading.

I'm assuming he can't forgive me for this. Maybe because I don't feel like I would ever forgive someone who did that to me."

It hits me hard, and it's something I recognized as I sat on Ty's couch with him, chatting after all the bullshit.

"I don't think I could do that," I say.

"It does sound like you are engaging in some mind reading, and that's definitely something I want to explore further with you, but just as much, I think this goes much deeper, dealing with a core issue you have with feeling like you're not worthy of love, specifically Ty's love in this case. You haven't been willing to do much work on this in the past, I know, but this is the hard work of therapy. If you're open to it, I have some homework that might help, which you can bring in for our next session. Your responses will help us come up with a plan with realistic goals and steps toward helping build your relationship with Ty. We can dedicate the next few sessions to this, if you'd like. In the past, you haven't been very receptive to this approach, but I do believe it's something that will be really useful for you, especially with how you approach your career goals."

She talks me through my homework, more bullshit worksheets. While some have helped me in the past, I don't always see the value in them...or maybe I just don't want to because they make me so goddamned uncomfortable. After some more discussion around how to approach my situation with Ty and how I can respect Ty and Jesse's relationship, I'm starting to get uneasy, fidgeting around in my seat since we haven't even gotten to the very reason I'm really here today.

"You seem agitated right now, Eric," Michelle says. "Is there anything else you'd care to discuss or is there something about what we've talked about that's making you uneasy?"

Jesse takes my hand and squeezes gently, urging me on —something I need right now.

I look to him. I can tell he's not going to push too hard, but that he knows it's what's best.

"There is something," I admit.

Michelle perks up. "Yes? I'm listening."

"I... I..." I stammer because I don't want to get this out. There's still this part of me that would love nothing more than to keep this close to my chest. I feel safe when it isn't out in the open where I can become vulnerable or someone would know my weakness, my pain.

"I had an experience when I was younger, a very painful experience."

I'm dancing around it, but it's the only way I feel I can get there. I open my mouth but stop myself. I stare blankly forward. I can't go further with the story. This isn't like that night when I was in Jesse's arms, when I felt like I could say it. This feels oppressive, painful, as though my entire world will be ripped apart if I speak the truth.

I try to speak again. Nothing comes out, and I curl forward, shaking slightly.

Jesse hooks an arm around me over my shoulder, pulling me close to him. I want to break down. I want to cry, yet that's weak too. Michelle's acting so calm and patient, and finally says, "It's all right, Eric. Let's focus on using some calming breaths. Whatever you have to say, it stays right here."

"Would it be better if I leave?" Jesse asks.

"No, I need you here. Please don't leave me." It reminds me of when he almost walked out of my condo, that feeling, the idea of not having him in my life, so painful to my very core. The thought of losing him—the thought of not having him here to help me—I can't bear that. It's even worse in this moment when I feel like if I totally lose it, the one person who will be there to make sure I'm all right is Jesse. I almost wish he would say it for me, but I know that's a coward's way out.

I won't be a coward, not anymore. I survived saying it once. I can say it again.

*Say it, goddammit.*

"I was attacked by my uncle when I was very young…sixteen."

Michelle waits a moment…and then another, surely expecting me to go on, but does she realize what a big step that was for me?

"I'm so sorry to hear that happened to you, Eric. Can you tell me what you mean by attacked?"

It's as though she's patronizing me, not meaning to, but dancing around it like she already knows, so I spit out, "He put his cock in me."

The moment I say that, my face flashes with heat, and I hide it in my hands.

I don't want to look at either of them. I turn to Jesse. I want to curl up into him, I want him to hold me, and he pulls me close, and as he does I fall against him, my head against his shoulder, shaking, trembling. I need him right here, need him close.

"God-fucking-damn it," I mutter against him.

"Eric," Michelle says. "I'm so very sorry this happened to you. Thank you for sharing what was clearly a very difficult part of your life."

"I'm sorry. I didn't mean to say it like that."

"That's all right. Sexual assault happens more than most care to acknowledge. And even using the terms *sexual assault*...or *rape* can be very difficult for people, especially survivors."

I don't know why I'm so determined to say it. She already fucking knows the truth, and it still feels like pulling teeth to try and get that word out of my mouth because of what I associate it with, because of the stigmas and my own feelings of what that means—that I'm weak, that I'm still that fucking kid who couldn't beat the shit out of my uncle and keep him from doing what he did.

"I was...*raped*." The final word is strained, a whisper almost unable to escape my lips. It's out there now, and the tears well in my eyes because I feel once again so vulnerable.

"Thank you for sharing that, Eric," Michelle says. "This sounds like something that's been weighing on you for some time. Am I right in assuming that you haven't told very many people about this experience?"

"Not until Jesse," I admit.

Haven't done a lot of things until him.

"Well, you're safe here, and it's very clear that you have a good support system from someone you obviously feel you were able to trust with this."

She talks to me about how it's not my job to explore it all in this moment, and that any area of it needs to be explored as I feel comfortable with that. She offers me various reassurances. I can tell she's trying to soothe me, especially as she guides me through a relaxation exercise to help relax me from the discomfort that confession activated within me.

"Eric, I'm really impressed with you for sharing this today," she tells me after I've started to calm down. "Unfortunately, trauma, which is what I would call this, isn't my area of expertise. While I can certainly help, you could benefit from working with a practitioner who specializes in trauma, especially as I see how much it's affecting you. Would you be open to a possible recommendation to another therapist?"

Great. She can't even fucking help me. Although, I have to admit, telling her, and hearing her calm reaction, have felt like relief. It's not as intense as that ease I felt when I spoke to Jesse about it that first time, but the relief is still palpable.

"I would be open to that," I say. "But honestly, I would prefer to see someone in Atlanta right now. I want to spend as much time as I can there. With Jesse and for Ty."

"That's totally understandable and makes this a much better option anyway because the sort of intensive work you would need to do shouldn't really be done long-distance. If you are comfortable with it, I'll look to see if I can find a good recommendation of someone in Atlanta who specializes in trauma-based treatment? I want to consult some of my colleagues to make sure I can connect you with someone who can help you. In the meantime, we could schedule teletherapy sessions together so that we could discuss things that way, for a while at least to keep exploring other areas that you're working on...like with Ty."

"I would like that a lot," I say, feeling relief that she's working with me, helping me find a practical solution.

We chat some more. She keeps asking me how I'm feeling, checking in to make sure I've come back into my own. I manage to even ease up a little.

"You've taken a big first step," Michelle says as we come to the end of our session. "Don't underestimate that, Eric. That can be one of the hardest things for a rape survivor to do."

I note her use of the word *survivor*. I've heard that

before, but for some reason, every time I think *rape*, I think *victim*.

"That said," she adds, "I would like to bear in mind that, even though your pain is very real, that event is not the sole defining moment of it by any means. I want you to walk away from today's session knowing that, at the very least, you're on the path toward healing and living a more fulfilling life."

I nod.

Mostly I don't believe it...mostly I feel like I'm that sixteen-year-old boy sitting here in her office, and like a failure because all these years, when I have been thinking I've been in control and powerful and taking over in the business world, I was still a kid, running scared, afraid...and so fucking hurt.

## 17

## JESSE

I keep quiet after our session with Michelle. I don't want to push Eric because I can tell he already has a lot on his mind, that he stirred up plenty within the past fifty minutes. It wasn't only about the serious shit he got into at the end of it, but about all that stuff we've had going on with Ty.

I offered to drive Eric's Audi, but he insisted. Maybe it'll at least distract him. I worry whenever I offer to help him, he feels like it's because I think he's weak, which isn't true. I want to help him, and I want him to know I'm here if and when he needs me.

He drives us to a restaurant we agreed to have lunch at after the session, a pizza joint not far from his place. We're still quiet as we order our drinks and food.

He fidgets with his hands, knotting his fingers up and pushing at his knuckles.

"You okay?" I finally ask.

Even that seems like it could be too much, considering how he's behaving.

"I'm fine," he spits out in a way that assures me he's

anything but fine. He must sense that his response is a little harsh because he shakes out of whatever state he's in and says, "Sorry about that. I'm thinking about a lot of things."

"That makes sense. It gave you a lot to think about. Both of us, I guess. There are some things she was telling you about Ty that got me thinking. Not that I want to make it about me... Shit."

Foot-in-mouth syndrome much?

Eric snickers. Although, he doesn't seem amused so much as appreciative of some morbid aspect of all this.

"Did you think this is how you'd be spending your trip in San Diego?" he asks.

"Whatever. This is one aspect of it, which, by the way, is why I wanted to come here to begin with. And we have other shit we're doing this weekend. I'm excited about meeting your friends tomorrow night."

"There you are with your subject changes," Eric notes, smirking, though there's still sadness in his expression.

"The great thing about a subject change is that it gives you an out." I'm teasing him about a conversation we had when we first met, but it's really why I mentioned his friends...in case he wanted to avoid altogether talking about what we discussed with Michelle.

"I'm sorry, Eric. I'm trying to be helpful. I don't ever seem to know what the right thing to do is."

"You're doing the right thing, Jesse, by being here with me. There's a lot going on in my brain right now, and I need to process it some more. I'm glad she offered to look up someone in Atlanta, and then the Skype thing will help there too. I want to spend more time with you guys. Try to mend my relationship with Ty and also keep pursuing what we have."

His words remind me that even though I may be dumb

as fuck about how to handle some of this shit, at the very least, he gets that we're in this together.

"I always find this part of therapy such bullshit," Eric continues. "Worksheets, exercises. Calling it *homework* like I'm in fucking school. I'm not saying I've never benefited from any of it, but that doesn't change life. Doesn't change the things that have happened or that I've done to hurt other people. I'm going to try, but I don't know… It's all so stupid. Then we have this fucked-up mental-healthcare system where I'll see Michelle every week, and she'll give me a number to some other therapist I might be able to make an appointment with…a month, maybe two months from now, if I'm lucky. And then it'll still be weekly or even biweekly sessions. So when does that actually add up to anything that's worth a damn? Two, three, four years from now?"

"Eric…"

He runs his hand through his scruff, then wipes it across his face as though he's fucking tired. I don't think he's tired from today so much as depleted from the things that have happened to him in his past.

"It's okay, Jesse. As I said, I'm going to do this. I feel a little frustrated with how shit like this works. I finally can voice what happened to me to a professional, and what did she really do?"

"She listened," I say, defending Michelle. "And she offered some practical solutions."

"Yeah, I know. In my mind, I should be able to go to a therapist, say what's wrong with me, and they give me some magical fix like a Xanax. Instead, I get this bullshit, and at the end of the day, no matter how many thinking-error exercises I do, I'm still fucked-up me."

"Well, fucked-up you isn't so bad," I say. "He is who I fell for, after all."

"Your mistake," Eric teases, and I laugh.

His gaze shifts to me, and for the first time since the session I see warmth in his expression.

"Say it again."

"What, that I'm falling for this fucked-up version of you?"

"Yeah, that's the part."

He reaches across the table, holding his hand out, and I take it. He rubs his thumb across the back of my hand.

"I'm falling pretty goddamn fast too," he says. "For this crazy kid who has a thing for guys with serious issues and baggage."

"Nah, just *this guy* with issues and baggage," I tease.

He grips my hand tighter. "What do you say when we finish eating, we head back to my place, change, and go to the beach for a bit? I'm not gonna let you miss the beach while we're out here, away from landlocked Atlanta. And really, any excuse to get you to take off your clothes is fine by me."

"I like the sound of that."

The waiter arrives with our pizza, and when we finish eating, we head back to the condo. We don't mess around. In fact, Eric keeps a little distance from me, not nearly as affectionate as he can be. It's rough because I enjoy feeling his arms around me, love when he makes like he can't keep his fucking hands off me. But I get it. Like other times when we've stirred that memory, we don't fall back into each other's arms and start fucking the hell out of each other. He needs to relax, come back into his own again.

And despite the fact that it can be a struggle, I can be patient. I don't mind waiting, especially when I know how incredible it is when he is comfortable with me...and how hot the sex can be.

When we arrive at the beach, we spread our beach towels across the sand.

Eric tosses off his shirt before he digs into his bag and retrieves the sunblock. Looking sexy in his shades and navy trunks with a white stripe along the side, he opens the bottle before saying, "Okay. You know the drill."

It reminds me of when he was so concerned about my face in PV, and when he rubbed me up and down with sunscreen when we had our camping outing the other week.

I remove my shirt so that I'm only in my swimming trunks.

I wonder if he's ready for this. If he's going to just rub me down in this sort of cold, unfeeling way because of everything that's happened.

He steps behind me and starts rubbing the sunscreen across my back in circles, moving slowly...like he's being careful to make sure not to miss any spots. He tends to my shoulders and arms, and I feel him move close to me as he slides his arms around my sides, to my abdomen, moving his hands about freely. I can tell he's not trying to apply sunscreen anymore as he pushes up close to me, his hard erection against my ass.

His face slides beside my own, and I feel his nose against the side of my face.

"Thank you, Jesse. For coming here and doing this with me. I know I'm not good at showing it right now, but I really appreciate it. I appreciate you."

I half turn, so that I'm looking at his shades, which doesn't work for me. I grab them and slide them up his face, resting them against his bangs so I can see those sparkling blue eyes. I have an ocean I could be looking at, but I want to get lost in those eyes. No matter how many times I see them, it's never enough.

"You're better at showing it than you think."

He tugs me closer to him, so that my back is flush with his chest, and he kisses me.

The beach isn't empty, far from it, but he doesn't seem to care about making a scene. I don't either, not when I'm with him. I feel that familiar passion as I taste his mouth, but there's also something so intimate about it. Like I can feel his appreciation in that kiss.

As I get lost in it the way I tend to get lost in those blue eyes of his, I find myself moaning. He growls softly before kissing the side of my face—a much softer, more meaningful kiss. It makes me feel special.

He pulls back and glances around before he notes, "Looks like we have some fans."

I scan the beach and discover a few people watching us from their towels, including a couple of guys, who are all-smiles and whispering to each other.

I laugh.

"Too bad they miss all the best parts," he says with a smile, and even though I know he's still rattled from the day, he's coming back into his own...coming back to me.

# 18

# ERIC

I'm excited but a little nervous.

Excited because I'm eager to introduce Jesse to the gang. I want him to meet these incredible people in my life, and I want them to see Jesse, this man I've been fortunate enough to have discovered. But that doesn't keep me from being a little on edge, since they can be fairly intimidating...and not always the most welcoming of people. They haven't always gotten along with all the guys I've brought around, Casey included. And I've also never seen Jesse handle a situation like this.

I wonder how he fares when he's in a group setting. I imagine he's as personable as he usually is, but it reminds me that I still have a lot to learn about Mr. Morgan.

We walk into the back room of one of the bars we meet up at, not far from my place.

A few overhanging light fixtures illuminate the pool tables beneath them. It's not the best place to play pool, considering there aren't many good cues along the wall, and I'd say it's fairly questionable how level the tables are, but it's good enough for us.

Jax and Dexter are by the pool table, Dexter preparing to strike the cue ball, and Jax gripping his cue stick, rolling his eyes because I assume Dexter is taking his sweet time—something we're all too familiar with. Remy and Allison sit on bar chairs at a small table, chatting, Allison giggling at what I assume is something funny Remy said. Because the whole reason she's always been hooked on him has been his sense of humor.

Baxter and Will typically hang with us, but they weren't able to make it tonight. It was a lot different trying to get our crew together when we were in our early twenties than it is nowadays when we all have our own busy lives.

As soon as we walk in, it's like everyone's spidey-senses are activated, because they glance up and their gazes shift right to Jesse, whom I went ahead and gave them a heads-up about coming so they wouldn't give me as much shit about springing a guy on them.

Although, this isn't just any guy. This is Jesse.

"God, I gotta swing by more often. You guys have aged so much," I tease, and everyone bursts into laughter, breaking up the awkwardness of Jesse's presence. "Guys, this is Jesse. Jesse, this is the rest of the Bastard Motherfuckers." I say that with the utmost affection, and as I repeat the name, my friends offer warm smiles as they seem to be reflecting on all the good times we've shared.

Allison hops off her chair and heads over. She runs her hand through her dark locks, nearly as dark as mine. She pulls that hair back behind her shoulders. "About damn time you made it back to your home." She pulls me in and offers a hug before turning her attention to Jesse. "I hope you don't mind hugs, Jesse. Because at this point, we're pretty much related." She winks.

"I'm totally fine with hugs," Jesse says as he embraces her.

As she pulls away, she says, "I can't believe you've been hogging my man all to yourself. You're cute, so I'll forgive it."

The other guys head over and greet us, welcoming Jesse with their own hugs, being as open and friendly as I hoped they would be, even more so than they were with Casey.

"You play any pool, Jesse?" Dexter asks before pushing his glasses up the bridge of his nose.

"I'm not terrible."

"He's on your team," Dexter tells Jax.

Jax laughs. "You motherfucker. I'm always with the newbie. Come on, I'm good enough to make up for both of us."

Jesse laughs off the teasing, and I sincerely hope he gets that it's our way and that none of the guys mean anything by it. Casey sure as fuck never did.

"Eric, that means you're on my team," Dexter says. "We've got to break the couple up because you guys have been holed up for too long anyway."

"Are you okay with that, Jesse?" I ask him.

"Only if you're okay with me kicking your ass."

"Oooh," Dexter says. "Maybe I should have picked you for my team after all."

We play a quick game of eight ball. And by quick, I mean the quickest because Jesse's a lot better at this than he let on. So much so that Dexter's cursing me because I didn't warn them about my boyfriend's impressive billiard skills.

As Jesse hits the eight ball in the corner pocket he called, Dexter shouts, "You've got to be fucking kidding me. I was at least hoping that first round was beginners' luck. You could have told us you were some sort of billiards Olympian."

"Why?" Jax asks. "So you could have hogged him all to

yourself? Serves you right. Don't worry, I believed in you from the get-go, Jesse."

"You are so full of shit," Jesse says, all smiles.

"Eh, true…but now you're my magic eight ball. Plus, you basically duped me too. Here I would have been betting for more than a couple rounds of shots if I'd known you could kick ass like this. Dexter, get out your wallet."

"Go to hell, Jax!"

Dexter turns to me as I lean back against the wall. "Eric, can you please teach your boyfriend some of your business skills so that he gets he has to take advantage of opportunities like this."

Jesse laughs, and there's this sort of cockiness in his expression, one I'm already familiar with. He knows how much ass he's been kicking during these games, and he seems to be enjoying the satisfaction of proving them wrong more than any money he could have been making off them.

"Someone gonna set her up for another game?" Jesse asks. "I won, so…technically, losing team has to." He eyes me, grinning, and I laugh.

God, I fucking love this kid.

Jax shakes his head and turns to me, saying, "Eight Ball is as bad as you are."

We all laugh together before we begin another game.

When we finish, Jesse claiming victory once again, I step out and let Remy jump in for me while Allison and I grab drinks at the bar—an excuse to catch up.

Since I arrived with Jesse, she's been eyeing me with this expression I can read all too fucking well. She's beaming, her smile ear to ear as though she has this secret about me.

"What?" I ask before taking a sip of my rum and Coke.

"Don't you *what* me. You are stupid in love. If I was in love as you are, I would be embarrassed."

"You are that in love with Remy, which is even more embarrassing."

"I know, that's why I have every right to give you shit about this, considering how much you gave me all those years."

I roll my eyes.

"He's adorable, Eric."

She glances back at the pool tables in the other room, and I do the same.

Jesse's joking around with Jax, who hooks an arm around Jesse and pulls him close before rubbing his head like they're old pals.

"Fits right in, doesn't he?" she says. "You always said we were all good at judging a person's character, yet you couldn't seem to believe us with Casey."

"I figured you were all jealous that you couldn't have me all to yourselves anymore," I say, slightly teasing, and at the same time, there's truth to my remark.

"Admittedly, that was true. But I have a feeling if we're going to lose you to someone, it should be this one."

"You're not gonna lose me. You're gaining a son."

She laughs. "Oh, I'm your guy's mother now? I love it. I knew I was getting old, but Jesus Christ, not that old. And speaking of old, talk about robbing the cradle. Do you always have to snatch the young ones?"

"This one isn't like the others, at least isn't young where it counts. He's different...he's special."

"I can sense that. He has this way about him. He doesn't seem like the kind who's always had it easy."

"No, he hasn't. I think that's why we've gotten along as well as we have."

Despite all this chatting about Jesse, there's a part of this that's itching on my conscience—a part I can't keep from

Allison anymore. "I do love him, but...our situation is a little fucked up."

Her expression sobers. I better be out with it. So I start with PV, and the connection...and then move into the deception. She does what she's always done best and listens. "And goddamn if Ty wasn't the best about it, but...we're working on things."

She rests her hand on my shoulder. "Well, you're not going to win a Father of the Year award, that's for sure."

And I can't help but laugh.

"It's shitty, for sure. I remember when we were younger and you were this stressed-out, brooding, mysterious guy who liked to keep a lot of things in, and...right now, you seem very open."

"I don't feel very open. More like there's some shit going on in my life that reminds me of exactly how closed off I am."

"You've always had that stuff. But I don't know, something's different right now about you. There's this mood to you that I can't quite read. I have a feeling it's a good thing, though."

"Maybe you're reading that I'm taking steps in the right direction, or at least a better direction. Although, as you now know, I'm making a hell of a lot of mistakes too."

"We're in our forties, Eric. We've all made a hell of a lot of mistakes to get where we are, but look at us now."

"I thought you were trying to cheer me up, not remind me of how wrecked our lives all are."

"Shut up," she says, gently slapping my shoulder. Then her expression turns serious again. "I'm worried about Ty being hurt in all this, but I also want my best friend to be happy."

"Welcome to the club of a fucked-up situation."

"Another crazy, hilarious story the Bastard Motherfuckers will be telling in a few years."

"I don't know if it'll be all that hilarious."

"We'll see," she says. "Hang in there, Eric. Even though you might have royally fucked up, I have a good feeling about this guy. I don't want to condone how any of it went down, but if it took me making a massive mess of my life to be with Remy, I'd take it because whatever it would have taken for us to end up together, it would have been worth it."

Her point rings so true to me. It's something I've been working to accept.

"But again, don't disregard Ty's place in all this. I know you love him, and he needs you now more than he's ever needed you before. You need to be there."

"I agree."

"Fuck that," I hear Jax say behind us.

I turn and see the guys heading our way.

"Eric, Dexter's trying to steal my Eight Ball. Can you remind him that he didn't want him to begin with?"

"I think it's only fair," Dexter says. "You played enough rounds with him, and I've lost enough money on these shots we owe you."

Jesse still has that goddamn cocky expression on his face as he approaches behind them. "What can I say?" he asks as he slides between them and puts his arm around my shoulders. "I have a feeling I might be a little tipsy tonight with all the shots I'm owed," he tells me. "You gonna take care of your man?"

"I always take care of my man."

"Yes, you do."

I kiss him, and it gets the guys going, and as Jesse and I part, I can't help it—I'm smiling...insanely big.

Stupid in love, for sure.

While Dexter orders some rounds of drinks, ones he and I owe to Jesse and Jax for their victories, Dexter asks me, "So what are we going to do about your birthday next month, mister? Because I have a feeling you're not gonna be in town."

"Birthday?" Jesse, now seated on the stool on the other side of Allison, perks right up.

"Yeah, birthday boy," Allison tells him. "Mr. Forty-Three coming up on May tenth."

Jesse wears a sneaky expression on his face, like he's already plotting something.

"Jesse, forget she said that."

"Is he trying to keep his birthday from you?" Allison asks. "Don't worry. He tried to do that to us too. But we tipped a bartender a long time ago to tell us the birth date on his license."

Jesse laughs.

"Mr. Mysterious," Allison teases again. "Don't you worry, Jesse. You stick by me and I'll give you all the dirt on this one."

It's funny because as much as Allison knows about me, there are things I've shared with Jesse now that feel like they would be more dirt on me than anything she might have. At least, things I wouldn't want anyone else knowing.

We hang out with the Bastard Motherfuckers some more, laughing, joking around. Jesse's relieved me of any of that nervousness I had at the beginning of the night about him possibly not getting along with everyone.

We throw back some drinks before the group agrees to call it a night. Before heading back to my condo, Jesse and I chat with Allison and Remy as they grab an Uber.

"Well, that's the guys," I say as we head along the sidewalk. I hope Jesse had a good time.

"They're really cool, Eric. And I appreciate you letting me meet them. That meant a lot to me that you shared that part of your life with me. I know they mean a lot to you from things you've said to me in the past."

"They do mean a lot to me. Everything really. I didn't have a family, so I made my own."

"Is that where the group's name, Bastard Motherfuckers, came from?" Jesse asks.

"That's something a guy shouted at us when he was wasted one night and Allison beat him at a game of darts. The gang all had to get the guy under control and into a cab. The name sort of stuck."

"I like it. It seems to fit you guys nicely, from one bastard to another group of bastards," he says, reminding me of his own circumstances, which are far more fitting than any of our situations. "Speaking of which," he adds, "I'll be eager to introduce you to my family too. You need to come over for dinner at some point."

I tense up at the thought. "God, I wonder how that will go down."

"Are you nervous about how my parents are going to feel about you?" Jesse asks.

"Scared shitless."

"Eric, you surprise me sometimes with the things that make you nervous. You're a very confident guy, and to think that my totally innocent, playful family intimidates you is kind of amusing."

"I'm intimidated because they sound like really good people, and I would hate to think that they would think I'm anything other than good for you."

Jesse takes my hand and stops me on the sidewalk so I'm forced to turn to him.

"Eric, you're a good guy. And Charlotte and Stan are great at reading people, so I have no doubt that when they meet you, they'll see what I see in you and they'll trust my judgment."

"Funny, I was thinking the same thing earlier about my friends."

We gaze into one another's eyes. There's a lightness about this moment, a sort of appreciation for each other, and I love the way his face looks in the dim orange glow from a nearby street lamp. Although, I do notice a small darker spot just below his hairline. I lift my hand and run my thumb over it.

"Ooh, stings," Jesse says. "A little sunburn I got yesterday while we were at the beach."

"I wasn't doing a good enough job taking care of you. I was distracted, and I guess I missed that spot."

"It isn't your job to make sure I don't get a little sunburned. I'll live."

Even though I know he's right, I feel like I hurt him, and I never want to hurt him. I want to care for him the way he deserves to be cared for.

"Eric, I've been taking care of myself since I was a kid. It's not your job to protect me. Your job is to kiss the shit out of me."

I don't resist his suggestion. I hook my arms around him, pulling him close. My lips crush down against his, and he pushes his tongue in my mouth. He rests his hand on my face, then slides it to the back of my head.

Since we met with Michelle yesterday, I've struggled with being affectionate with him. Just needed to take a break. I was fine when we were at the beach, but after, I felt like I wanted to push everyone and everything away, including Jesse. It's not the first time, and it won't be the last. But in this moment, I don't want to be without his touch…his taste.

I can't stand how much I want to get him back to my condo, out of these goddamn clothes, rocking my fucking world.

We wind up in my bed, stripped naked. I have my arms hooked under his as I roll back so that he's lying stretched out on top of me. He pulls away from our kiss, gazing down at me with a look I love. Like he's claiming victory over me the way he was with the guys at the pool table.

"Jesse, Jesse, Jesse," I whisper as I rest my hand on the back of his neck.

He smirks. "You can keep saying it. I like when you say my name too."

I laugh before rolling again so that I'm on top of him.

"Aren't you frisky tonight?" he asks.

"I was thinking that I don't owe you a drink for those wins tonight. You deserve a good victory fuck."

"Now that is something I could use." He grins as I take his mouth once again.

And I can't wait to get my cock inside this beautiful man.

*My* beautiful man.

## 19

## JESSE

"Oh," Charlotte says, her jaw dropping as she sits next to Stan on the couch. I sit in front of them, on the ottoman, fingers interlocked, nervous as fuck about how this will go over.

"Charlotte, you okay?" I ask.

The expression on Stan's face isn't much more reassuring.

Are they upset? Disappointed?

I didn't figure either of them would be happy when they found out the news about me and Ty's dad, but it had to happen at some point, and if Ty showed us anything, it was that it's better sooner rather than later.

I started at the beginning, obviously leaving out the parts about having banging-hot sex, but telling them about the spark, which steadily evolved into so much more. I focus on the connection I discovered, but admitted we didn't tell Ty until it was too late for both of us. We'd fallen too hard, too fast.

While I'm not exactly comforted by their response, it's about what I was expecting.

Stan bites down on his lip and nods, a familiar habit of his when he gets to thinking hard about something. "It was one thing discovering you're bi," he says, "but you have to admit this is...something else altogether."

"It's difficult," Charlotte adds. "It all sounds really bizarre, but also...knowing Ty makes it even stranger. He's never been anything but friendly when all that stuff happened with Granny. And then whenever he's come to dinner. I know how much your friendship with him matters to you, so I have to believe you have very strong feelings for Eric if you're willing to put that on the line."

"Surely Ty knows you care about him, though," Stan adds. "Regardless, if when Granny was around my best friend had told me he was dating her, it wouldn't have gone over well, especially if they'd kept it from me. I don't know. I'm trying to put myself in a similar situation, and it doesn't turn out well."

"Thanks, Stan," I say.

"Sorry. I didn't mean it like that. I meant I understand you're all in a really unusual situation."

"Yeah, it's not ideal," I admit. "But it's where I'm at, and I'm trying to figure it out."

"How is Ty now?" Stan asks. "Are you guys talking?"

"He needed some space, and I've been giving it to him."

"And are *you* okay?" Charlotte asks.

I see the concern in her expression, the genuine worry about me. They both know how close Ty and I were...how much that friendship meant to me. Seeing their concern about us outweigh their judgment about what Eric and I are doing means a lot to me, more than they can know.

"I'll be okay," I reply. "I'd feel better if Ty reached out to me again. Last time we talked, it was an okay conversation.

He wasn't thrilled, but he's a lot more understanding than I thought he'd be."

"You guys will work it out," Charlotte says, the perpetual optimist.

Admittedly, I'm having a harder time understanding how that'll happen, though I have to believe it's true. I have to believe somehow it'll all work out.

Stan leans forward on the couch and sets his hand on my shoulder. "It's not great, but we support you. We're here. We love you. And seeing as we've never met Ty's father, we would really like it if you would bring him by at some point for dinner."

"Really?"

"Of course," Charlotte says. "You're a very responsible person, Jesse. And it's clear based on everything that's happened that you care about him…a lot."

"So see if you can drag him to dinner so that we can do the typical interrogation of your latest love interest," Stan chimes in.

"I don't do an interrogation," Charlotte says.

"I wasn't talking about you."

She laughs, a loud, boisterous laugh, and it's clear Stan's humor has lightened the mood.

They assure me they love me and trust my decisions, and then we eat dinner before I head back to Atlanta.

I'm relieved to have told them. Eric and I need to be out about this now so that we're not left feeling like we're sneaking around anymore.

When I get back to Eric's condo, I head in, searching for the man who's the reason I had to have that conversation with my parents…the man who's the reason I've done so many things I never imagined I'd do—kissing a guy, letting a guy inside me.

I find Eric in his office, earbuds in as he sits at his desk, typing away on his laptop. The way he punches at the keys, vigorously, like he's pissed about something, makes me wonder if he's had a good evening.

"Hey, sexy," I say, not sure if he'll hear me.

He shakes his head as he turns away from the screen, pulling the earbuds out. He can't seem to stifle a smile as soon as he sees me, and his eyes light up. I see him relax, like my presence has pulled him out of whatever stress he's dealing with.

He pushes to his feet and approaches, his lips curling into a grin, like I made his day by being here, which would be funny as shit considering he knew I was going to be here tonight.

"How was dinner with the parents?" he asks as he reaches me and slides his hand around my waist.

"I told them about us."

His expression twists up. "You...told them? What do you mean? About me being an older guy or about...?"

"Everything. About you being Ty's dad."

"What did they say?" he asks, his expression rife with worry.

I chuckle because I know my answer is going to surprise him. "They want to meet you."

His jaw tightens and his arms lock in place.

"Relax. They don't bite, Eric."

"No, I haven't had to do the meet-the-parents thing in a long time." He takes a breath, as though he's trying to process it all. "Now you've told them, the awkwardness is out of the way. It's bizarre how many people we have to essentially come out to about what we're doing."

"Tell me about it," I say. "It's fucking exhausting, but...I don't mind telling people that I'm falling for a pretty incredible guy."

Eric smiles again. "Only pretty incredible?"

"Eh, I say that to keep that asshole boyfriend of mine from getting a big head."

"That's clever," Eric says. "I'd be careful with that Mr. Bougie asshole, if I were you. He doesn't need an ego boost."

"Well, Mr. Morgan enjoys giving him ego boosts nearly as much as he enjoys talking to him in third person. Hell, Mr. Morgan enjoys giving him pretty much anything else he wants. I think Mr. Bougie's kind of spoiled."

"Mr. Bougie likes being spoiled." He kisses me after he says that, and as if I wasn't already enjoying the relief of talking to my parents, the relief he gives me with his lips and tongue is so satisfying.

When he pulls away, he offers that soft growl that gets me going.

"So how about your day?" I ask. "You seemed pretty intense typing away when I got here."

"I'm losing money on this company I invested a lot into. The CEO is making some crap decisions, and I need to meet with him to talk about executing some of the plans he's made about pitching changes to the board. Fun times."

"I'm sorry."

"It's fine. That's my life. In better news, Michelle's assistant called with the name of a therapist here in Atlanta who specializes in the sort of trauma I need help with."

I can tell he's still struggling with saying sexual assault or rape. I can't fathom what that must be like to carry the pain of something so traumatic around for so long, to have been terrorized by it since he was a teenager.

"I would love to come with you, if you'll let me," I offer.

"Absolutely. It's the first Wednesday in May."

"That's sooner than you thought," I say, recalling his complaints about the mental-health industry.

"I'm kind of relieved to do it sooner rather than later. After everything that's happened, I'm ready to deal with this."

"See? My parents don't think I've lost my mind, and you're able to schedule a therapy appointment earlier than you thought—it's been a pretty fucking amazing day."

Eric laughs.

"Speaking of May," I add, "we need to come up with a little special something for your birthday weekend."

"Ugh, that."

"Yes, that. It's your birthday, and I'm gonna celebrate my boyfriend's birthday. You take that weekend off. Why don't we do something crazy? I was thinking maybe camping."

Aside from the incident that transpired last time we went camping, we had a great time. I'm eager to get back to that...and in a way, maybe make up for the trauma he experienced with me before.

His expression relaxes once again. "Now that's something I would be fine with." He thinks for a moment. "Any chance you've ever gone rock climbing?"

"I've gone indoor rock climbing."

"Well, that's good enough. We should do a little rock climbing at a place I go to about three hours north of here. Have us a fun camping outing. I think we could both use that."

"My first time outdoor rock climbing. Hmmm... All my first times with Eric Westright?"

"I like being your first times," he says before offering a kiss.

I hear a familiar sound coming from one of his earbuds. It's a chime. As soon as we part, I glance down.

"You're listening to *Rocks and Hard Places,*" I say. It's my favorite podcast, one that I know I must've bored him to tears talking about since we first met, particularly when we were confined to the condo, working jigsaw puzzles as I annoyed him with my ramblings about the latest episodes.

He blushes and glances at the floor before his eyes return to mine.

"I wanted to get a little more informed about some of these subjects you like to bring up."

"Which one are you listening to?"

"That woman, Mags, is talking about this Newport sex scandal."

"Oh, yes. About the undercover operation to bust up gays in the navy?"

"Yes!" he says, those thick brows of his pulling together. "It sounds like something out of a slapstick comedy. These allegedly straight guys were letting other guys blow them so that they could find the secret gays and—"

"I know. I listened to it back when I was still with Whitney."

"And you didn't even get a little chubby?" he asks, resting his hand on my crotch as one brow arches higher than the other.

"I jerked off after listening to it," I confess. "I'm bi, not oblivious."

He smiles. "What are you going to do now that I'll be able to carry on discussions with you about these podcasts you're so into?"

"Me? You're the one who has the misfortune of *not* being the victim of my seminars about them. Poor you."

"I always enjoy when you talk about things you're interested in, Jesse." He's sincere about that, no teasing, no jokes.

He strokes my crotch some more, and I keep getting harder. "Do you have much work to do?"

"I could stop now, especially if my alternative is getting to throw my boyfriend on the bed and do whatever my greedy hands desire."

"Here I was thinking we needed to finish that jigsaw puzzle," I tease.

"Jigsaw puzzles can wait," he says, before cupping his free hand behind my head and reeling me in to him.

And while it might've been an awkward-ass afternoon, I have a good feeling it's gonna be a much better night.

## 20

## ERIC

Jesse sits beside me in the waiting room of this new therapist's office.

With his hand on my leg like when we went to Michelle's office together, I can feel his support, which is nice, because I feel like the others waiting with us are judging me...as if they know why I'm here and that I'm some pathetic bastard who can't keep his shit together. Of course, there's no way they could know what I've been through, and I have to keep reminding myself of that.

"You sure you don't want me to go back there with you?" Jesse asks. He's asked a few times this morning, something I haven't minded because I've been considering it myself.

"I'll be fine. I need to do this one myself," I say.

As much as I love having Jesse here with me, and as helpful as it was that first time, I feel that this is about pushing myself to take on these sessions alone. At the very least, this time I could write down some of the details on the questionnaire I filled out, which will keep me from feeling like we're beating around the bush.

When the therapist, Troy Slaughter, fetches me from the

waiting room, he guides me through a back hallway, introducing himself and being friendly and cordial, talking about the nice weather we're having.

I can tell he's trying to set me at ease, which seems like a vain pursuit, considering I'm going to be totally on edge talking about this, regardless of how friendly he might be. Although, I guess it's better than the alternative.

Eventually, we're sitting across from one another in his office, me on a sofa and him in a chair across from me, similar to the way I talk to Michelle.

Troy reviews some of my paperwork as I shift around and the sofa pleather squeaks under my ass.

It's weird having someone reading the details of my past on some sheet of paper with "sexual assault" listed with a check mark next to it.

"If you could give Michelle Warner my thanks for referring me, I'd appreciate it," he says. "So you're coming from San Diego? Are you moving to Atlanta? What's the reason you wanted to see someone here?"

"This is where my son and my boyfriend live, and I want to spend more time here."

I leave it at that. I'm here to talk about my uncle, not my fucked-up relationship stuff. I have Michelle for that.

"Do you want to tell me about why you're here today?" he asks, setting my paperwork on his lap.

"I wrote it down."

He smiles warmly. "Yes, I have read it, but if you could humor me. It's usually better to hear it in your own words."

I take a deep breath.

I'm quiet for a moment. Once again, I'm in the position of having to tell someone else about my past, and I know how liberating it can be, but I also know how vulnerable that place is, and I don't want to feel that. It's painful, and it makes me feel like the very thing I've been fighting my entire life—weak. I'm not weak.

"I had an experience," I say, still dancing around the subject…which is just the way I am with this. Hell, I've been dancing around it for so fucking long, I'm not surprised. "When I was sixteen, I was staying with a family member, an aunt, my dad's sister, and her husband…my uncle…" Even though I'm trying to get it out, I'm finding little ways of delaying the inevitable reveal.

*He already fucking knows. It's on that goddamn paperwork*, I remind myself.

But I struggle to push forward.

"My uncle," I repeat. I have to fight. I'm stronger than this. I can say it. "He…assaulted me…sexually."

It's the best I can do right now.

Troy's quiet for a moment. "I'd like to hear a little bit more about what happened, if you're comfortable with that. It would help me get a better sense of your experience."

I remember spitting out those harsh words in Michelle's office, about my uncle's cock. It was so fucking crude, but for some reason, it was the only thing I felt like I could say at the time.

"My uncle pulled his pants down…and held me down as he took advantage of me."

"He sexually assaulted you?" It seems so fucking effortless for Troy to say. The words slide right past his lips in a way that almost makes me feel ashamed of how difficult it is for me.

"Yes. Yes, he did," I confess, and I feel a sort of numbness, as though my mind is drifting away from my body. Finally, I push past my lips, in what feels like it requires far too much effort, "He raped me."

There's that same relief again that I've felt whenever I've

said it, but at the same time, there's the vulnerability that comes with it—and that feels like fucking weakness.

The goddamn double-edged sword.

"It sounds as though you've been carrying this for a very long time," Troy says. "Have you talked to anyone about this?"

"My boyfriend, and my therapist in San Diego, but only recently—within the past few weeks."

"You've been keeping this to yourself since you were sixteen up until the past few weeks?"

"Yes."

"That's a long time to carry something like this around. A very long time, but it's not unusual at all. So I want you to know that you're not alone in this."

"I'm not weak."

Don't even know why I said that. The words spit out.

"I'm not some statistic. I'm a person this happened to."

Immediately after I say the words I wish I could suck them back into my mouth because I feel like they've already told too much about me, about what he's surely looking for to be wrong with me.

"Well, I think that says something about how you feel about sexual assault. Eric, I would really like to work with you on this, if you'll let me."

"I want to get better."

"I'm glad to hear that. You're not alone in this experience by any means, and there is help. I've worked with a lot of patients who have been even more secretive and carried it much longer and who are living very healthy, meaningful lives now, beyond the trauma. I want to go ahead and encourage you and let you know that it is possible to find a way to live and manage the stress that comes along with that. It may not always be easy, and in the beginning the solutions we have to help you will be difficult, but it is manageable.

"I use what's referred to as cognitive-processing therapy, a combination of cognitive-behavioral therapy and some exposure therapy. For the remainder of our session, I'll explain the details of the program, and we'll work out a plan specifically catered to how we can best serve your situation."

He discusses the program, the details involved, and talks to me some more about my goals in all this. I tell him about my situation with Jesse, specifically my discomfort with bottoming, since that's really what I want to find a way to work through.

I feel on edge, alert, wary. There's a part of me that wants to run, to not have to deal with any of this. That feels like it would be better if I pretended everything was fine. I know that isn't the solution, and I know that if I want to have any sort of a fulfilling relationship with Jesse, I have to push myself through this, and I do want that. I've never wanted that more in my life. The thought of what we share, what we have shared, what we could share, is what gives me hope in all this.

I want it for myself. I've wanted that for a long time, but Jesse has inspired my interest in caring for this aspect of myself, not just the businessman and success.

No, I want something so much more. I want to share so much with him...to be the man he deserves, yet even as I sit here talking to a shrink about something that is so incredibly painful for me, I'm not sure how that's possible. It seems like a pipe dream, yet I wonder if I'm only telling myself that because I don't want to deal with the consequences of having to finally face this.

"Before I let you go today, I have some homework for you. It's not difficult."

So not what I wanted to hear, but it's part of this whole system that I have to accept and push through.

He retrieves a worksheet from his desk cabinet and approaches me before handing it to me.

"Very simple. Write a page of what being raped means to you." He explains it further, and it seems like such a stupid exercise, and while all this stuff he's discussing involves dealing with my fucked-up brain, I want to know how this will help me with Jesse.

"As far as your goals with your relationship with your partner," he says, taking a seat in his chair once again, "you might consider a colleague of mine who has a studio not far from here. It might sound kind of strange, but if you're open to it, it's a mindful yoga program to help people who have experienced sexual trauma. There's been some growing research around it, and it can really help deal with the physical aspects that present themselves in the bedroom. This work we're doing will help there as well, but I've found that combining this with something like mindful sex therapy can really speed up the recovery process."

Speeding up the process sounds nice.

"I'll give you the number of my colleague, and if you're interested, you can reach out to her directly. If it's something that would make you or your partner uneasy, it's not something you need to push, but I think you could find a lot of value from her methods."

It sounds like work...a bunch of work that may or may not be of any value. However, at this point, I'm desperate. I'll try anything.

When our session comes to an end, I head out of the office, and there's Jesse in the waiting room, with his earbuds in. I imagine he's catching up on *Rocks and Hard Places*. As soon as he spots me, he hops up from his seat. He's wearing this concerned expression as though he wants to be here for me.

There's some relief to having at least a bit of homework and a recommendation for this yoga bullshit that could help, but nothing beats knowing that I have this incredible guy here for me, who cares about me.

I schedule my next appointment, and then we head to the car.

Jesse doesn't press or ask questions, and when we get inside, he waits a moment as he sits behind the steering wheel. I can tell he wants to ask something, but he's hesitant. I don't like him feeling as if he needs to walk on eggshells around me.

"How do you feel about the session?" he asks.

"It was nice talking to someone and coming up with a plan. This guy, Troy, he's very friendly. He listened. I was expecting a little more judgment when I said certain things. I guess it's his job to not look like he's judging, but since he sees this so much, I think it didn't really surprise him...what I said. If anything, it sounded like my experience was one of many he's encountered, which was a relief too." Jesse reaches his hand over the console between us, sets it on mine, gripping gently. "He said you could come to some sessions if you want to, and we can talk about us as a couple."

"I would love to do that with you, Eric. We have a lot of things we have to get sorted out."

Guilt rises in me.

"Jesse, I just... Talking to him, I realized we're looking at something that's maybe six months...if not longer. How could you want to sign up for this?"

That's something that keeps confounding me, that as I try to rationalize why Jesse's still here, I keep getting stuck.

"It destroys me," Jesse says, "that you're sitting here next to me and you don't understand you're worth fighting for. I'm here because that's how amazing of a person you are. Although, in some ways, I get it because I remember being in that shelter...talking to Stan and Charlotte, realizing they were considering adopting me. I couldn't understand how I could add any value to their life, but now I get that I do, and they've never made me feel like it's different than that. Eric, if there's anything I plan on doing, it's showing you the value you bring to my life. I'm not just talking about that big dick you have, either." It's an obvious ploy to get me to laugh, and it works. "You're a special guy, Eric, and I'm happy I get to be the person to help you figure that out."

He leans into me but stops short of my lips, as though he's waiting to make sure I'm comfortable with that right now, that this is what I want. "You can kiss me, if that's what you're wanting to do," I tell him.

"Well, I want to do a lot more than that right now, but I guess this will have to do."

His lips are on mine in no time, bringing me that familiar relief, that fire, that passion that has a way of distracting me from all the bullshit. I grab the back of his head and pull him closer till he's crawling toward me. Close. I can tell it can't be a comfortable position he's in, but he doesn't seem to let that stop him.

"We need to get home now," I tell him as I pull away from his lips.

My cock's throbbing, full, and I want to be inside him, coming, filling him up, letting him know how absolutely beautiful and incredible I think he is. Giving him as much pleasure as I am physically able to.

He pries away from me and puts his seat belt on.

"You don't have to tell me twice."

Clearly he's just as fixated on the end goal as I am as he backs up in the parking lot, offering me a quick glance—that reassuring glance that reminds me once again that I'm so fucking lucky, and simultaneously scared as shit that it'll all be ripped away from me somehow.

THE WEEK DRAGS ON, and on Friday, I get a text from Ty.

It's the first time he's reached out to me since our chat. He wants to get together for dinner this weekend. It's a relief, and I'm excited when Saturday night arrives and I'm sitting in a booth in a restaurant near his condo—somewhere we've met up several times before.

There are so many thoughts racing through my head, but my biggest worry is that anything that comes out is going to be me continually telling him, "I'm so fucking sorry."

When he arrives, I stand up to greet him, but he slides into the other side of the booth. He's clearly trying to keep his distance, and I understand that.

I slide back into my seat. "How've you been?"

He nods repeatedly, refusing to make eye contact with me as he tells me about his week, not in any great details. Just glossing over it. He mentions his work in Chicago and this promotion he's up for.

"And how do you feel about that, in terms of getting your CPA certification?" I ask.

"I want to go for it. Mom's not going to be thrilled, but I really want this, and I've been thinking about what we talked about before."

I blurt out, "You have?" I'm shocked he gave a damn about anything I said.

"Yeah, I think I can do it." Though the way he says it, I can sense his doubt.

"You can do it," I tell him.

His gaze meets mine. This is the first time he's looked at me directly since he arrived.

He sizes me up. It's not the sort of thing I would have said to him before, in many ways because I've always felt like I don't have a right to say anything about his life.

He doesn't make a big deal about it, though. Just changes the subject and we move on to more mundane topics before he asks, "Do you really think I can do this, get my CPA certification?"

"Why wouldn't you be able to? It's hard work, studying."

"Yeah, but I will have to either get time off work, or find a way to navigate with classes. I might have to be without my job for a while. I mean, I can make do with the money I've made, but it's scary stuff."

"It's a great opportunity if you're willing to take the risk. Sometimes you have to take risks."

Like I did with telling Jesse about my experience. Like I've done my entire life to get everything I have.

"No, you're right," he says. "I haven't taken a lot of risks in my life. I know that, but I really think I'm at a point where I actually know what I want. I think you know I really haven't ever figured that out."

"I'm impressed you realize you want this. It's amazing, Ty."

This reminds me of that conversation we had when I told him I was proud of him. Feels like we're actually starting to talk to each other.

"So, doesn't someone have a birthday coming up?" he asks with a smirk.

"Ugh, don't remind me. Big four-three."

"If you wanted to get together next weekend, that'd be cool."

The way he says it, it sounds as if it's not a big deal, but his expression suggests otherwise and makes me feel guilty about the plans I have.

"I have some plans with Jesse. We were going to go camping and rock climbing."

His gaze shoots to the table.

"You should come...if you want to," I blurt out, without even thinking about it. But as soon as I speak the words, I realize how nice that would be and how that's likely the last thing in the world he would want right now, especially after everything that's happened.

He's quiet...so fucking quiet that it's unnerving.

"I don't have anything going on that weekend," he says. "I would actually really like to go, if you guys wouldn't mind." Once again, Ty's stunned me. "But only if you guys really want me there. I'll grab my tent from Mom's."

"I have a tent that's big enough—"

"Eric, that's weird."

I chuckle. "Okay, yeah. I wasn't thinking."

"Baby steps," he says, his expression stern, as though he's reminding me that he still has every right to be upset with me.

Baby steps doesn't sound like such a bad idea, and I'm appreciative as hell that he's even offered, though terrified that if I get too excited, he might bail.

"It sounds like a fun birthday weekend," he says, forcing a smirk.

But that's enough to keep this hope within me alive.

## 21

## JESSE

Eric pulls the car into a spot in the lower parking deck of Ty's condominium before texting him to let him know we've arrived. I would have texted, but I figured that might be weird considering neither of us has texted since that night we talked at his place about my relationship with Eric. I'm respecting his desire for space. Not that it hasn't crossed my mind countless numbers of times to reach out, not really to reconnect, but out of habit... out of the need to spend time with my friend again.

"How do you feel?" I ask Eric. "Because I'm nervous as fuck."

There's something bittersweet about this moment. Yeah, I'm thrilled to see Ty again, but it's hard not being able to talk to him about everything that's going on in my life or being able to talk to him about this CPA stuff Eric was telling me about. I don't get to have that, and for a very good reason: because I was an asshole.

Ty steps out the cream-colored metal door a few feet in front of us, in cargo shorts and an orange polo. He's grown his facial hair out a bit, but it's trimmed, unlike the last time

I saw him, when it was pretty unkempt. The straps of a duffel bag and tent case are slung over his shoulder. As he approaches, he wears a serious expression. This isn't the fun-loving, easy-going Ty I'm used to seeing making a face or goofing off whenever I pick him up from his place. The look on his face reminds me more of Eric...a resemblance I haven't really seen until this moment.

Eric hops out of the driver's side, popping the trunk to let Ty unload his tent and bag before sliding into the back seat.

"Hey, man," I say, turning to him, forcing myself to spit it out so we can move forward as best as we can.

In the past he would have said, "Hey, brah," or start forcing me into some elaborate friend-handshake, but instead he says, "Hey, what's up?" while avoiding my gaze.

Eric gets into his seat and drives us off.

The car's quiet since the episode of *Rocks and Hard Places*, which Eric and I were listening to, cut off as we were coming up to Ty's place. We were so caught up in our discussion about the hole in the ozone layer, we hadn't put anything else on.

I play around with Eric's phone and put his music library on shuffle. But even Fall Out Boy can't spare us the lingering uneasiness.

I wish he'd be out with what he's upset about...yell at me. Hell, if he would shout...maybe punch me...that might make me feel better. Although, I know that even a hit to the face wouldn't magically change where we're at. It can't undo the damage or heal Ty's pain.

There aren't any quick fixes for this. It requires time and patience, and we're fucking lucky as hell that Ty's this receptive already, considering we're a little over a month from that painful discussion when we finally faced the truth about what Eric and I were doing...and our feelings for one another.

I try not to look at Eric too much, but I occasionally glance his way to catch his reaction, to see how he's handling Ty being in the same car with us. I want to crack a joke, say something to lighten the mood, but I show reverence for the silence.

After a bit, Ty starts whistling, something he does when he gets nervous. Eric turns down the music, as though he's intuited this and wants to step in to soothe him.

"How's your mom doing?" he asks.

Ty stops whistling and gets quiet.

"When you went and got that tent, I assume you talked to your mother?" Eric adds.

"Yeah, yeah," Ty replies. "She's doing good. You know she's been seeing this new guy, and I don't know, they seem to be getting on pretty well."

"That's good. I'm glad to hear that."

"Eh, you shouldn't be. I don't really like him that much. He's kind of a jerk. Mom seems to have a talent for finding them."

I can't tell if that's an intentional dig at Eric or not.

"I meant that she's dated a lot of jerks recently," Ty clarifies, his words rapidly shooting out of his mouth, as though he realized he hadn't meant it as a dig at Eric.

"No, I understand that," Eric says. "She obviously has a thing for jerks." Eric smiles as he looks into the rearview mirror, and Ty laughs. I do the same as we all seem to fully embrace the peculiar situation we find ourselves in.

Great. Now only two and a half more magnificently awkward hours before we get through this.

Eventually, we all start loosening up a bit more as Ty complains about work stuff. I recognize several of his coworkers' names from issues he's had in the past. As he finishes sharing his own grievances, he asks how my job is going, and I offer up my own complaints before Eric has his turn. When we're all finished dumping on our jobs, we start making fun of some of the billboards and strange shops we pass.

"These Chick-fil-A ones get creepier and creepier," Ty says, noting one with these cows holding a sign that says: WE SEE U BURGER EATERZ.

The song on Eric's playlist changes, and I immediately recognize the voice as soon as she sings the first note. Kate fucking Bush.

"Oh my God," Ty says. "My ears, my ears. They burn."

I glance to the back seat, watching him cover his ears and close his eyes like he can't bear the sound.

"See?" I tell Eric. "I'm not the only one who thinks this is a bunch of crap."

He smirks as though he enjoys us giving him a hard time about Kate Bush. Then he shakes his head. "You guys are so unappreciative of genuine talent and an actual musical artist."

"I can't believe he listens to this crap," Ty says playfully.

"And what would you have me listen to?" Eric asks.

"I don't know. Something from the Billboard charts of this century. Why don't you have any Dua Lipa on here? Or Imagine Dragons? Or Bruno Mars?"

"I have Imagine Dragons, thank you very much," Eric says, defending his tastes. "And for your information, this song you're disrespecting is 'Hounds of Love,' the title of her hit album, which was extremely popular at the time it came out. It included a track called *The Ninth Wave*—the songs that were on it possibly being some of the greatest songs ever produced."

"Don't listen to him," Ty says. "He said that to me so many fucking times, and it doesn't change how her voice grates at my ears."

I'm all smiles as I glance back at Ty, who's looking directly at me for the first time since we began this trip, a broad grin across his face. He's looking at me the way he would have looked at me back before all this happened, when we would be sitting around and telling jokes. It reminds me of how he got me and my family laughing that night when he was there after Granny passed, and then when he did the same for me with Whitney.

I hardly have time to appreciate the moment before his face twists up as he seems to realize, as I do, that things have changed...and we can't go back.

Despite some lingering uneasiness from that moment, the vibe remains laid-back.

I hadn't figured how good it would be for us to have a long drive ahead of us to North Carolina, but it seems to give us all some much-needed relief. The atmosphere has lightened up and the conversation flows freely, with fewer pauses and tense moments. I can tell we've all relaxed a bit.

When we finally arrive at the park where we're having our rock climbing/camping outing, Eric finds a spot, we grab our gear, and head into the woods. Eric and Ty work together, showing me how to create an anchor for the climb on the boulder Eric's selected, one he's climbed up a few times, evidently. After we finish setting up the ropes, we harness up and inspect one another for safety.

"Jesse, you're up. I'll belay you," Ty says, this mischievous expression on his face as he winks, as though he's letting me know he's ready to watch me plummet to my death. Not that I think Ty would ever do that, but I hadn't considered that maybe, after all that's happened, us relying on one another to keep each other alive isn't the best idea.

Eric and Ty check my gear before I begin my ascent up the rock.

I get a few yards up before I hear Ty groan. "Oh my God, Jesse! This is taking you forever. I'm going to get up there, crawl like a spider-monkey to the top, and ring a fucking victory bell."

"Shut up!" I call back. "I'm figuring out where all the good places to grip are to make your job easier."

I glance over my shoulder and see him smiling like he was in the car.

I enjoy this sort of competitive spirit we've shared in the past—like when we'd tease each other during flag football, volleyball, basketball, or any of the sports we enjoyed together.

I'm still chuckling as I reach for the next crack where I try to get my grip, but I lose my footing and slip down, scraping down the boulder.

I curse when I feel the rope tug, and Ty calls out, "Belay on!"

I pull close to the rock and regain my footing, clinging on before turning back and looking down at Ty.

"Um...you're supposed to call out 'watch me' or 'falling'!" he reminds me, and I laugh. "You're fucking lucky you have an awesome belay partner." He winks, and it feels like he's more like his usual self...the awesome guy I'm used to hanging out with.

The guy I miss.

I finish up, and then Ty and Eric take turns on the boulder. When we're done, we pack our gear and pull out our anchor before packing back into Eric's car.

"We gonna head over to the campsite?" I ask.

Eric has this suspicious expression on his face. "Nope. We have a little stop to make first."

I narrow my eyes, curious as fuck. "I have a feeling I know what you're up to."

"Am I that obvious?"

"Well, we are at the lake."

"Boat, boat, boat," Ty chants from the back seat.

Eric rolls his eyes. "I guess I'm not as good at surprises as I was hoping. You two are spoiled."

Ty keeps chanting, and I can't help but laugh.

When we get to the boat Eric has rented out for the day, Ty hops in the boat and takes a place in the back, spreading out, stretching his arms to his sides.

"Don't worry. I'll do all the work," Eric says, as he grabs the cooler and carries it into the boat.

The attendant helps us get out of the dock, and Eric drives us to a cove like he did the last time we came out here together.

"Let's do this," Ty says before removing his shirt and shorts, but leaving his trunk boxer briefs on.

"Hold up," Eric says. "You're not getting in without some sunscreen on."

I'm a little weirded out, especially considering our previous experience with sunscreen in our relationship. Eric reaches into his bag and retrieves a spray bottle sunscreen before turning and winking at me.

Clever bastard, but thank God he is. That could have been creepy as fuck.

Ty sprays himself, and Eric gets his back before Ty jumps into the water.

"I have a feeling you had this detour in mind before we even got here."

"I did want to have an amazing birthday weekend, and I do love me a boat outing."

"I'm enjoying them too."

I hear a splash, and Ty comes up from under the water. "Stop goofing off and get in here, you guys," Ty calls out. "It feels amazing."

I'm sure it does. When we were here a few months earlier, it was already feeling good, and now the weather is so much warmer.

We strip down, and Eric and I spray each other with sunscreen before we jump into the water with Ty and swim so that we're all in a circle.

"It's a good day for this," Ty notes. "Good thinking, Mr. Big Four-Three." He winks at Eric before eyeing me strangely.

I'm trying to read that expression before he splashes me.

"Motherfucker," I say before splashing back.

We go back and forth for a bit before we stop, both grinning ear to ear. It's more like something we would have done before all this shit blew up.

We swim around a bit before climbing back onto the boat and drying off. Ty and I stretch out in either corner of the back of the boat.

Ty's blond locks are soaked, clinging to his forehead as water streams down his face. He runs his hand through his hair. Eric grabs some snacks out of the cooler when Ty tells me, "Oh, you know that CPA thing I was telling you about? I think I'm actually going to go for it."

"Eric was telling me." As soon as I say the words, I regret them, especially as I notice the change in Ty's expression.

"Of course he did," he says. It's like we've both been confronted with the reality of the situation...that even though we haven't seen each other, we have this link, and it reminds me of what he talked about after that first blowup, about how now, when he tells one of us something, it can get back to the other one.

"I hope you don't think Eric told me something he shouldn't have."

"No, no," Ty says. "That's not something he would have any reason not to tell you. It wasn't a secret. Forget I said anything."

I figure he was going to tell me more than that, but now he's shut down.

Fuck me.

It's hard watching this, knowing Ty's not trying to be a dick, but that it makes him uncomfortable for the reason it would make anybody uncomfortable.

As Eric approaches, he glances between us as though he can tell something's off.

"Protein bar for you," Eric says, handing me the one I requested. "And granola bar for you." He starts to hand it to Ty, who rises from the seat we share. "I think I'll take another dip." He takes the granola bar and tosses it onto the cushioned seat before stepping onto the side of the boat and diving into the water.

"Ty okay?" Eric asks.

"I'm an idiot, is all."

I really hope I haven't ruined Eric's birthday trip because of that. Not only because of him, but because Ty seemed like he was having a really good time before I put my foot in my mouth. Just a reminder that things aren't okay...not yet. Hell, maybe not ever.

## 22

## ERIC

After we finish up at the lake, we head over to our campsite. We have three tents to set up, two of which I brought, one for me and one for Jesse. We're not spending the night together while Ty's here, something Jesse agreed with when we discussed him joining us on my birthday weekend. We both agreed it wasn't appropriate considering everything that happened.

Despite our conversation about this being the best solution, I didn't really consider how awkward it would be for us all to pitch them together. I notice Ty's gaze drift between me and Jesse as we're all pitching our tents, as though he's realizing it's a strange thing for a couple to be doing. Still, it makes me feel a hell of a lot better.

I could tell there was some awkwardness between Jesse and Ty back on the boat. Not sure what it was about, but it seems to have smoothed over. Hell, Ty is even giving Jesse a hard time about struggling to set up his tent.

"No, you reversed the poles. I've done that a few times too," Ty explains before helping him out.

He's a fantastic kid, who could have done with having a

better father figure in his life...and I mean me, not that ass Tricia was with when he was growing up.

Once we've set up our campsite, I take over the barbecue with steaks and mixed vegetables and potatoes wrapped in aluminum foil—all of which I prepared this morning before putting them on ice.

"You need help with anything over there?" Ty asks as he picks some cubed watermelon out of a container, something we picked up at the store on the way to his place.

"I'm all good here. If you guys want to grab some wood for the fire pit, now would probably be a good time, before it gets dark."

"I got that," Ty says. "My seedless watermelon companion and I will be back in a bit."

He takes off with the watermelon container, and by how quickly he volunteered, I figure he might need a mental break from us. Since this trip began, I've been questioning every expression, every action, every slight comment he's made. Just wondering what he's really thinking while all this is happening...if he's judging us, hating us. Although, if he was hating us, he wouldn't be here. That's something I find I have to keep reminding myself of.

When he's out of earshot, I head over to the picnic table, where Jesse's seated, pulling out the plastic knives and forks and plates to set the table for when dinner's ready.

"How do you feel?" I ask Jesse.

He glances in the direction where Ty went, says, "Pretty good. Obviously I've been freaking out a little bit all day, over stupid shit, but this is definitely better than I could have imagined it would be."

"I agree."

"It's these little things that are throwing me—stuff I wouldn't have thought about. I said something back at the boat, about him getting his CPA certification. What you were telling me the other day. He wasn't mad, but it reminded him of...what's all going on, and the things he kind of mentioned to me when we had our talk after we told him what we were doing. Like...I might be his friend, but now if he says something to you, it might get back to me before he tells me, which I'm sure is strange for him."

"I hadn't really thought of it that way. I was telling you because—"

"He wasn't upset, Eric. It surprised him, and I think he was even surprised that he hadn't considered I would have already known. Don't mention I said it."

"No, of course not."

"It was stupid of me."

"Don't be too hard on yourself. Let me be the one who's hard on you."

I'm trying to cheer him up, and it seems to work as he offers that dimple-filled smile I love so much. "Fair enough."

I return to the barbecue to finish cooking.

Some time later, Ty returns with several sticks, which he tosses into the fire pit. While he works to get the fire going, Jesse and I set the table with the food. When we finish eating, we set up foldout chairs around the fire pit. While the sun finishes setting, Ty and Jesse talk about one of the podcasts they both listen to before they get into movies and Ty starts talking about a graphic horror film he watched. "It was gore and more gore," Ty says.

"That sounds horrible," I say. "It reminds me of this movie..." As I'm about to talk about it, I realize it's the one I watched with Jesse. I'm not sure it's a good idea to bring it up, but I've already mentioned it, so I might as well be out with it. I feel like honesty is the only way we're all going to get through any of this. There's no need for secrets. That's what got us into this mess to begin with.

"It's called *Martyrs*," I continue. "Jesse and I were watching it on a plane," I say, trying to make out like it's not a big deal.

The excited expression Ty had while talking about the movie he saw turns serious. "Where did you guys go?" he asks, and I can hear the hurt in his tone.

Shit.

"San Diego," I reply.

"You guys went to San Diego together?" Even in the dimming daylight, I can see his face turn pale. He shakes his head. "No, it's cool. That's cool."

By the way he says it, I know it's not cool at all.

"It was just the other week," I assure him, but I don't know how that's supposed to help.

"No, of course you did. What movie did you say it was?"

I can tell he wants to change the subject. Subject change. Easy way out, as Jesse would tell me. In this case, it's a godsend.

"*Martyrs*," Jesse says. "It's really good. Fucked up in all the right ways." He sounds like he's taking full advantage of the subject change, trying to pull Ty's attention away from the fact that we went to San Diego together.

"It's insane," I add. "I was definitely judging Jesse for liking it."

Ty smiles. "Yeah, Jesse can be kind of…dark with his movie tastes. I wanna hear about this movie."

"You have to watch it," Jesse tells him. "It's crazy, and fucked up, and there are, like, five plot twists."

"Not that many," I chime in.

"There were a lot."

"Now I have to watch this," Ty says. "I wonder if it's on Netflix."

He pulls out his phone like he's going to check and see, and we chat a little more before Jesse says, "Okay, let me go grab my charger from the car. Get some juice in it before it dies."

"Good time for me to get my earbuds to listen to some music." Ty follows.

I'm a little disappointed. I figured Ty might want to talk to me some while Jesse slipped away, but I can totally understand why that's not the case.

Ty rifles through his backpack for a minute. It takes him some time, leaving me wondering if he might have forgotten his earbuds.

I look toward where the car's parked and see a faint glow, and as Jesse comes into view…I realize I've been had.

I turn back to Ty, who pulls a wrapped package out of his bag and brings it over, a sneaky smile across his face. The closer Jesse gets, the more candles I realize are lit on the cake. "Christ, that thing's a goddamned fire hazard!"

"Well, I wanted to make sure to give you the forty-three you deserve."

As he nears, I notice he's holding a present of his own, but I hardly have a chance to acknowledge it before Ty starts singing "Happy Birthday." Jesse joins in, his voice atrocious as he continues making his way to me.

He holds the cake before me, and as they finish singing, I can't help but take the cheap shot. "Who are you to judge Kate Bush?" I ask him.

"Shut the fuck up and blow out your candles," he says with a wink—the kind of wink that reminds me of how crazy I am about this guy.

I blow, which takes some fucking time, so much time

that there's quite a bit of wax on the cake by the time I'm done.

"When were you guys plotting this scheme?" I ask.

"Jesse got the cake," Ty says as he rises from his foldout chair and approaches with his gift wrapped in paper with "Happy Birthday" printed in cartoon-looking letters all around it. "And we talked about springing this on you after dinner. Here you go."

He hands me the present as Jesse sets the cake on the picnic table behind me.

Jesse returns to the fire and sits in his foldout chair, watching as I open Ty's gift.

I tear through the paper, open the box, and pull out a picture frame. And as soon as I see the image, of Ty and me, my heart...oh, my fucking heart.

"Ty..."

"It's dumb. I found it a while ago, and—"

"What is it?" Jesse asks.

"It's the first picture we ever took together," I say, recalling the day we met.

My hair was longer then, and Ty's nearly a buzz. I wore my leather jacket and a pair of jeans while he was sporting a tee and shorts for the pic. Seeing those bright smiles across our faces tears me up inside, because fuck, we were so happy that day. We had hope...that we'd found something special. Of course, goddamn, I sure wasn't the dad he'd been imagining I was. But look how far we've come.

As I look up at my son, his gaze shifting away from me, I'm reminded that I still have hope, because he wouldn't be here tonight if I didn't...and he wouldn't have given me this picture if he didn't.

It's not over yet.

"Thank you, Ty," I say.

He shrugs. "I just found it when I was looking through stuff, and you know, whatever."

I know this isn't any more of a whatever than him joining us today. And it reminds me of what a bastard I've been all these years.

"It's perfect," I assure him, and he makes eye contact with me again, smirking.

"I want to see," Jesse says, rising from his chair and walking around me to get a view of the picture over my shoulder. "Look at you guys!"

"Right?" Ty says. "That hair on Eric. Oh my God. Dated."

"Whatever, I was cool back then," I insist.

"I'll give you that much. Jesse, he showed up in a rental car that first day. This...piece of crap, but the moment he got a place here, it was Harley-Davidson all the way. Do you still have that bike, Eric?"

"I do, actually," I confess.

"I remember thinking you were so fucking cool when you'd show up on that, swing by for dinner. Mom always gave you shit about how you could hurt yourself."

"I haven't gotten to see this bike," Jesse says, eyeing me suspiciously.

"I get it out from time to time, but nowhere near as much as I used to. I think I value my life a little more nowadays, and Allison and Tricia gave me hell about winding up in a body bag one day, enough that maybe it finally sank in."

"Yeah, Mom was about as thrilled about it as she was when she found out about the tattoos," Ty adds. He directs his attention to Jesse. "She used to tell him he was a bad influence on me. That I was going to wind up with them all over my body because he made me think they were okay."

"She's always lived more conservatively, with most things," I explain to Jesse.

"That's an understatement," Ty adds. "Overcautious and paranoid are probably better words for her."

"I feel like I'm supposed to step in and defend her," Jesse says. "She's always been very nice to me."

"We'll see about that now," Ty says, glancing between us and laughing, and Jesse covers his face with his hand. "Whatever, man. You gotta let me take these shots when I can."

"Totally fair."

"Okay, okay, Jesse's turn. Show and tell," Ty tells him.

"You just want to upstage me with that incredibly personal gift." Jesse passes his gift to me, and I open it, pulling out a vinyl of Kate Bush's *The Kick Inside*, her first album.

I'm stunned that he would have come up with something so thoughtful. Casey never would have given me anything like this. Hell, no one would have.

"It's an original version of it," Jesse adds. "I wish I would have known you would be ranting and raving about *Hounds of Love* today because I would have totally looked for that."

"It's perfect," I tell him. "Both of you guys. I can't imagine having gotten better gifts. Thank you."

"We're kind of amazing," Ty says. "Now let's make some s'mores."

We do just that and get to talking before Ty decides he has to see some of this *Martyrs* movie. He pressures me into turning on the Wi-Fi hotspot on my phone and pulls it up on Netflix on his tablet as we all lie on a blow-up mattress in my tent.

Because of all those twists Jesse mentioned, I almost forgot about the beginning of the movie, and I get to be horrified by it all over again, listening to Ty as he keeps shouting, "Holy shit!" It's all too similar to my own experience of watching it for the first time. By the time the movie's over, we're all caught up in this mind-fuck the movie's put us through.

"Great. Now I'm going to be thinking about that all night and not sleeping," Ty says as the credits roll.

"It's really good, right?" Jesse says.

"He's right, Eric. It's really good," Ty replies, backing up Jesse.

"You guys don't like Kate Bush, but you like this? I will never understand either of you."

I enjoy them ganging up on me, though, especially since it gives me a glimpse into the friendship they shared before all this crap went down.

We head back to the fire and make some more s'mores, and I'm appreciating how at ease we are compared to when we first got into the car together.

Once we've finished the chocolate bars off, I realize the fire is getting low, so I say, "I think I'll go get some more wood."

"Eh, I think I'm about to call it a night, but this was really cool," Ty says. "I'm glad we did this." I can hear the sincerity in his tone.

Again, I'm reminded that he's a much better...much bigger person than I've ever realized. I don't know how he's my son, because God knows I would never be so understanding.

As he heads for his tent, he calls out, "Night!"

He unzips the door and then turns back, glancing between Jesse and me, still sitting in our foldout chairs. "By the way, this tent setup you two got going on is cute and all, but you don't need to be sleeping in separate tents. I'm not a kid, and I'm not stupid either, so be grown-ups and sleep together. Like, not in a dirty way, but you know what I mean."

He starts to whirl around but then swings back to us and says, "I do appreciate the gesture, though."

As playful as he was acting before, he's clearly serious about his appreciation, and I'm glad he at least recognizes we were trying our best to be respectful of his feelings about all this.

He heads to bed.

Jesse's eyes are on me, and I see in his expression what I'm sure he must read on mine as well: hope.

Maybe he was right. Maybe we'll get our Ty back after all.

## 23

## JESSE

*I'm a little busy at work this week, but we need to get together for some volleyball with the guys.*

I read Ty's text, excitement rising within me. Are we suddenly besties again because of the camping trip last weekend? No, but the fact that Ty's even talking to us again gives us hope that maybe there's a way to navigate all this.

After I finish up at work, I head to Eric's condo and make us some dinner. Unlike Eric, I may not be the best chef in the world, but I do my best. When he gets home from the gym, he's sweaty, a big wet stain on the front of his shirt. He looks tired, depleted, but as he approaches me, that smile suggests otherwise.

He takes me into his arms and slams his lips down against mine. I relax in his hold, any stress I was feeling from my workday easing up. When he pulls away, he studies my face.

His nostrils flare, and he glances around the room. "Smells great. What's for dinner?"

"Fettuccine Alfredo."

"I love the way you make fettuccine Alfredo."

"Stop teasing me," I tell him. He's saying that because that's one of the few things I know how to make.

"I wasn't kidding."

"Well, it's one of the many things I picked up during college, learning how to survive."

"You need help with anything?"

"I got this. You shower up and get your sexy ass over to the table as soon as possible."

"Deal," he says. He heads off, cleans off, and then joins me for dinner.

"Ty messaged me today," I tell him.

"Really?"

"He's trying to round some guys up for volleyball, and he wanted to see if I was free. It's a step in the right direction."

"It's more than that," Eric assures me. "Ty's definitely doing a hell of a lot better than I ever figured he could under the circumstances."

"Yeah. I was stunned he was willing to go on that camping trip to begin with, and even when I put my foot in my mouth—"

"We both had our moments of putting our feet in our mouths."

"Fair point. I saw you put that picture in the office. How does that feel?"

Eric's expression turns serious. "I experience a lot of emotions looking at that picture—fear, regret, excitement, appreciation."

"Why did you say fear?"

"Back when I found out about him, at first, I was so scared of doing it all wrong. I'm always afraid I've done it all wrong, and clearly, I have. It was my job to bridge this gap, and I can't say I ever had the confidence that he cared enough to do that, and all this has proven me wrong about that."

"I'm glad," I say. "I know it's shitty, but maybe, in some fucked-up way, all this crap will bring you guys closer together."

I almost feel bad saying that. I'm not reveling in the fact that Ty's hurt by what we've done, yet what happened on that camping trip, how they both seemed to push a little harder to talk than I imagined they would, how they both tried to open up and reach out to one another, makes me feel like they're finally taking steps they weren't willing to take before. In a way, until we started messing around, until the whole thing blew up, I think they'd both given up, thought their chance was over. It doesn't feel like that anymore.

"Did you guys talk any today?" I ask.

"We did. He called and asked how work was going. Evidently, he's having some work shit he has to sort out again."

There's another burning question on my mind, but I'm not sure if I should push and ask, because he hasn't brought it up yet. I feel it's almost negligent for me not to mention it at all.

"You didn't really mention anything after your appointment earlier today," I say. "Did everything go well?"

I was waiting for him, like usual, but I left him to tell me what he wanted, and he preferred to listen to podcasts and talk about those rather than whatever came out during his session with Troy.

"Appointment?" he asks. "You're saying that as though you don't know what it was for."

"No, I'm just—"

"Sorry. I get a little defensive about this. It went okay. He gave me another worksheet, like last week and the week before. I have my homework. Gonna need a file folder for all this stupid shit."

He's trying to blow it off, but I can tell this still rattles him. I only went to one session, last week. Troy says I'll be more involved in the process as his treatment continues, but it frustrates me because all I want to do is to be there for him and help in whatever way I can.

"You don't have to come with me every time," Eric insists. "I know you have a job, and you can't just leave."

"It's basically taking the time off my lunch break. I am hardly making time for that anyway, and I want to be there."

"That means a lot to me, so thank you."

"You seem kind of frustrated about the process. Is there anything you want to talk about?"

"I would rather get through my week and not think about it."

I tense up because I know that not thinking about it, not dealing with it, is what made the problem stretch out. It's the reason we're having to deal with it the way we're dealing with it now, but maybe today isn't the day to push. Maybe today's the day to give him some space.

"Speaking of which," I say, "did you schedule that mindful yoga thing we wanted to try?"

When Troy suggested the idea, I pushed because it sounded kind of cool, and I figured it would be better than us working on it in Troy's or Michelle's office.

His lips curl into a smile. "I did. We have our first session next month. I'll add it to our calendar."

He's referring to the shared calendar on our iPhones, which we've been using to keep track of his appointments and schedules. It helps make it easier for us to find time to spend together.

"The whole yoga thing is a little weird," Eric says. "Sounds kind of cheesy and ridiculous."

"Cheesy and ridiculous could be fun."

"We'll see what this nutjob shrink has to say. I'm curious what the hell it'll be about."

"Everything I've looked up online looks like it'll be just meditating and stretching. Of course, I've never been the best with yoga, so don't tease me if I'm shit." My jokiness doesn't ease him up the way it normally would, so I reach across the table and take his hand. "It could be fun."

"Everything's more fun when you're here," he says, shifting his hand with his palm up so that he can grip mine softly. "Speaking of things that stress me out, I'm freaking out a little bit about next Tuesday."

"I can't imagine what there is to freak out about for next Tuesday," I tease. "Nope, not at all."

"Shut up. No, just to hear that I'm finally going to be meeting your parents does feel like a certain rite of passage for us, with where we're at in our relationship."

I went ahead and coordinated the dinner with them, figuring we needed to deal with it sooner rather than later so it didn't become something that loomed over Eric. He doesn't need any more stresses in his life, especially something like meeting my parents.

"Are you nervous about where we're at in our relationship?" I ask.

"Not about us. The timing of all this feels right. More about if your folks will like me or not. I'm not exactly the warmest person in the world."

"You, Eric Westright? I can't imagine that." He chuckles. "You have a lot going for you, including a glowing reference from me."

"Oh, a glowing reference?"

"Yeah, didn't you see the look on my face when you first walked in?"

He looks as though he's trying to stifle his grin but can't.

"They're going to love you, Eric."

"They already think I'm a shit father for what I did to Ty."

"They're surprised by the situation, but they're not the judgmental type. They want to understand. They want to be on board. So be you, and they'll fall as in love with you as I did."

"Say that again."

"What? That I'm in love with you?"

"Yeah, that."

"Eric Westright, I'm fucking in love with you."

"I'm fucking in love with you too."

We kiss, and Eric really is right. It does feel as though everything's moving just right for us.

## 24

## ERIC

"I've never fidgeted with my hands so much in my goddamn life," I mutter as Jesse and I make our way up the drive.

"Here," he says, handing me the bottle of wine I brought as a gift.

I smile at him, appreciating the grin on his face. "You're loving how uncomfortable I am right now, aren't you?"

"You know how you're always telling me how adorable I am? This is pretty adorable on you right now."

He earns a laugh.

It's not just meeting his parents that has me a nervous wreck. There's a lot of shit running around in my mind, frustrating me, including an exercise my therapist gave me last week, one that put me on edge the moment he told me about it. I'm supposed to complete it by tomorrow, but I haven't mentioned it to Jesse because it's been playing in my head so much.

As we reach the door, it opens before we have a chance to knock, letting me know his parents were clearly waiting for us to arrive, and there they are—Charlotte, with big wide eyes, and Stan smiling beside her.

"Eric, so nice to meet you," Charlotte says. We greet and hug, even though hugs make me a little tense. It's something I push through when offered.

Stan offers a warm handshake. "Come on in, come on in," he tells me. "I'm finishing up the roast."

We head into the kitchen. As we do, I notice their tastes, their decor very traditional, as I would have expected.

The dinner goes well, us laughing, talking, joking. But as we're interacting, I can't help but wonder what they must think about me. They're friendly, but surely in the backs of their minds there must be the judgment that what I did to Ty was so wrong and unlike anything they could imagine doing to their own child. Must be easy for anyone on the outside to judge us, although even as I think that, I recognize they're being as hospitable as anyone could possibly be to me, something I deeply appreciate.

They're kind, generous, warm people. These are the spitting images of the sort of people who live up to the expectations of everything Jesse said—about their kindness, their ability to see the good soul he was, back when no one else wanted him, and I have to admit that even thinking about that, the idea of someone causing Jesse pain stirs a heat and a fire in my chest. The idea that anyone could ever make him feel unwanted, or like he isn't the amazing man I know him to be, horrifies me, and in a way, it's another reminder of how cruel this world can be.

But we're fighters.

That's how we got to where we are today, each of us in our own way, although we have our weaknesses, me especially.

After we finish up with the Morgans' dinner, Jesse and I

head back to the car. He has this uneasy expression on his face as we get in and I reach for my seat belt.

"They loved you," he tells me.

"They were incredible. They were everything you had led me to believe and more."

"Then why do you still seem so off?"

God, he can read me so well. It bothers me exactly how well he can read me, because I don't want him to know, don't want him to catch on to the thing that's really bothering me.

"Does this have anything to do with tomorrow?" His voice has grown softer, like he's trying to sound as sincere as he can so as not to rouse my defensiveness—something I want to push between us to get him to back off.

I release the seat belt and grip the steering wheel.

"I would rather not talk about it, if that's okay." And saying those words, speaking them out loud, reminds me of what a coward I am—what a coward I've always been.

Jesse gets quiet for a moment, and I don't have the heart to check out his expression. He means well, I remind myself, yet it feels like he's punched me in the gut. I'm waiting for him to say something, to push me, and if he does, I'm certain I'll snap. I won't be able to handle it, not tonight.

He reaches across the console and takes my hand. "It's okay, Eric. I'm here for you."

As is his way, I relax, feel less guarded and a little stupider about how difficult I'm making all this.

Jesse turns on an episode of *Rocks and Hard Places*, and we start talking about their discussion about some viruses and bacteria that basically brainwash their hosts, which makes for an easy distraction.

Still, I can tell, even as I am able to finally look at his expression, he's holding back. He wants to help me, but I'm not ready—not yet.

When we get back to the condo, I shower up, my mind fixated on the thing that has added to the stress of meeting his parents—this meeting with the therapist tomorrow, a meeting I'd rather cancel than do this stupid exercise. *It's useless. What's the point?* I keep telling myself. *It's not going to help anything to relive it.*

These are the same excuses I've told myself since it happened—the ones I have for not sharing my story except for one night when I was so weak, I couldn't hold it in anymore.

In this moment, I regret sharing it with Jesse. Not because he was the wrong person—or that he's been anything short of amazing since I told him—but because it feels like he's the only thing that makes me want to fight this again when all I want is to hide it from myself the way I've been so good at hiding it for so long.

When I get out of the shower, I throw on some pajama bottoms and a tank top before heading into the living room.

Jesse's working on a jigsaw puzzle on the coffee table. He's real good at those, finding the pieces, knowing where they fit. It reminds me of how well he knows me. The pieces are all there, and Jesse's the only one I've ever known who's able to find out how they go together.

He glances up, and I see that expression, like in the car, like he knows there's more to what I'm doing than I'm willing to admit.

God, I want to hide.

At the same time, this reminds me of how much I want him, to have him in a way that requires me to be honest with myself, requires a courage I haven't been able to discover before him.

I kneel on the other side of the coffee table and start picking up pieces. I want to talk to him about it, but the words...I can't find them right now. Everything seems so stupid, but not talking about it is almost as bad...if not worse.

"I'd heard before about that fungus that brainwashes the ants," Jesse says. "It's crazy to think of how fucked up nature can be."

He's trying to chat about the podcast, but I blurt out, "It's this exercise." I forced myself to say something—anything—that would give me the strength to reveal this thing that's weighing on me.

Jesse's gaze meets mine, and I wonder if he's thrown by how I randomly dropped it into conversation like that.

"What is the exercise?" he asks.

"It's this stupid thing. I'm supposed to write down my experience, the one I told you about that night—a detailed account. My therapist said that sometimes this first time can be without much detail, that it could read like a police report of the event, because it's hard to process the emotions. But he wants me to get it down, and I don't want to."

I feel as if I told him, *Because I'm a coward...because I'm weak...because I can't do this.*

"Eric," he says. I take a moment to appreciate my name on his lips once again. "That's totally understandable, and I'm so sorry you've been carrying this on your own all week. If I knew, I would have—"

"I didn't want you to know. It shouldn't be this fucking hard. It's a stupid thing that happened, and I should be able to sit down at my fucking desk and take the ten minutes to get it down, but I have a million reasons why not to, and I've kept putting it off. Today I was sitting in my office, thinking I could cancel my appointment tomorrow. I could reschedule it. I don't have to do any of this."

"Did you cancel it?"

I shake my head.

"Why?"

"I understand that's not the right thing to do. Regardless of all the reasons I have for not following through with this, it's a step in the right direction, but it's a step I'm not ready to take."

Jesse reaches across the table, setting his hand on mine. "But you don't have to take it on your own, Eric. I'm right here."

"I've tried since last week, so many times, but I'm sitting in my office on my own, thinking of all the things I could write, where to start, and it's too much."

His gaze wanders for a moment before he looks at me again. "What if I was in your office with you? Not so that I could see the page." He says that part quickly, as though he wants to be clear that he's not trying to invade my privacy. "Do you think it would help, or do you think it would make it harder? I don't want to do anything that makes it more difficult."

I could cry right now. Part of what makes it so difficult is —when I sit in that office, trying to write it down—I feel on my own all over again. I was oppressed by that feeling as I started to write the words, being transported back to this dark place where no one could hear my pain or my struggle or understand that cruel and twisted feeling of betrayal.

I couldn't do that again, and sometimes it's easy to forget that I'm not by myself this time. Jesse already knows my truth. I have an ally.

"Would you do that?" I ask. It's not that I think he wouldn't be there for me. It's just, I am willing to admit that I need help.

Jesse rises to his feet and holds his hand out. "Come on. Let's do this."

As I take his hand and he helps me to my feet, I feel my strength returning. We walk into my office, this place that the past few days, when I've been trying this exercise, has felt so oppressive to me.

Jesse leads the way. He rearranges my desk, putting up a folder to block his view of me writing. He pulls up a chair beside the desk, all this seemingly by instinct, by his awareness of what I could need in such a moment. Then he looks at me once again and asks, "Do you think this will help? So I can't see what you're writing, but be here."

"That will help a lot. Thank you."

"You don't think I'm doing anything wrong by being here for this, that I'm hindering your progress in any way?"

"No. Troy said it's likely I'll have to write out what happened that night a lot, as part of the healing process. Getting it down will help, and, Jesse, I'm not strong enough to do it tonight. Not on my own."

"Hey," he says. "Didn't someone tell me that no one gets to where they are without a little help?"

I remember him saying those same words to me that night when he held me in his arms and reassured me I wasn't alone, when he pulled this demon out of me, exorcized me of it for a moment. Even though the experience lingers with me, so does Jesse. That's something worth appreciating.

"That's right," I say, choking on the words. I hate how weak I feel right now. I hate that I'm still that sixteen-year-old kid—confused, scared, worried, nervous. All these emotions come back so quickly, a mix of emotional grief and physical numbness.

Jesse waits until I'm ready to sit down, and when I do, he

sits in the chair adjacent to mine, behind that folder barrier, which is more of a barrier than I want to have between us...ever.

"Are you okay with me putting my hand on you, or do you think that will be too much?" he asks.

"I would like it right now, but I don't know about once I get started. I might need you to take it off."

"It's fine, Eric. You have every right to push it away. I'm here, in whatever way you need me." He sets his hand on my leg, and it offers me an extra boost of confidence. Maybe what I needed. "You're strong enough to do this, Eric. You did it once, when you told me. You've talked about it with your therapists. You've got this."

Easier said than done. I grab the picture of me and Ty off the desk, open the drawer, and swap the picture with the notebook I've attempted to write this exercise in...again and again and again.

So many torn pages from my failed attempts at doing this.

I set the notebook down in front of me, and I feel bad that I'm making sure Jesse can't see it. Not that he would try, but this is such a vulnerable thing—too vulnerable—that I don't think I can handle him seeing my thoughts written out.

I pull a pen out of my case beside my laptop. Then I stare at the empty page.

It's so masochistic that I have to do this exercise to make myself better. The person causing me pain now isn't my uncle—it's me. I'm the one who has to put these words down, force myself to relive the horror, the terror of what happened. What kind of fucked-up universe do we live in where this is part of the healing process, where the only way to escape pain is to relive it again and again and again? Intellectually, I know it has to be this way, just based on what it felt like when I revealed the truth to Jesse.

That won't make it any easier, though.

I take a breath.

Like before, I don't know what to write or where to start, so I put the pen to page and go for it.

I don't return to that night, but to that day, when I was relaxing on their couch downstairs, laughing at some cartoons that were on. Sixteen and watching cartoons seems so childish now, but it gave me some relief after having ditched my asshole dad. I always felt like I had to be such an adult with my father hardly being attentive. It was nice to let go and laugh at some stupid characters doing ridiculous shit to each other.

As I write my way to that night, I stop, then dig my pen into the sheet of paper, driving it in. Anger wells up within me—so much fury and hate. What began as weakness and guilt and shame has transformed into unfettered rage, and I haven't fucking written anything about the assault yet.

I stop, lean back, take a breath. I can't bring myself to look at Jesse right now, but he can't know how much it helps knowing he's here.

I slide my hand onto his and grip. He grips back.

I can do this. I can do this with him here, I remind myself.

"You're not on your own," Jesse says. He's found the right words at the right time.

I take a shaky breath and pick up the pen again. I'm getting this down tonight if it fucking kills me. Filled with determination and a renewed sense of confidence, I press forward. I have so many false starts and tear a few pages out before tossing them aside.

I begin, finally, with the moment it happened.

I see my uncle coming into the room where I stayed when I visited my aunt. In my naivety, I assumed he was going to ask me to go see a movie with him, maybe invite me to go out to eat. As he sat down beside me on the bed, he wore an expression that even now, as I look back, doesn't seem malicious or angry or sinister. He looked like my friend.

As I describe that, I dig my pen into the paper once again. I find myself running it up and down, repeatedly driving into the paper, ripping it away, feeling like I'm right back where I started.

I don't realize until my rage settles that I'm crying...and my face is on fire.

I take a few more breaths.

Jesse must be tired of sitting here, but as I look at him, he's still right there, his expression as supportive as ever.

*You're not on your own.*

I start once again, getting a little further this time, and as I reach that instant, that first touch as my uncle slid his hand up my leg, an instinctual reaction, this crazed part of me that's so furious, forces me to push at Jesse's hand.

He said it was fine to push him away, so I start to, but why can't I let go of him?

Because I don't want to let go.

As the conflict rages in my brain, this painful knot tightens in my chest.

My desire to hold him outweighs my need to push him away, so I cling to it as I continue writing, forcing that same horror through my mind as I live it.

It all feels so real, but it's like I can only remember fractions of the incident. There are these vague recollections of the most painful parts, but the only thing that feels so real are the feelings—the pain my body experienced and the pain I felt inside as I thought, *But he's my friend.*

I couldn't have taken up more than half a page, but it feels as though I've been writing this for such a fucking long time. Before I know it, I've reached the end, and I turn to Jesse, feeling the tears dripping off my chin, still rushing down my face, as vulnerable as I've ever been.

I blurt out the words, "He was my friend."

I move toward Jesse, hooking my arms around him. I need to cling to something right now, someone, and as I feel his hold, I feel like I can breathe again. My thoughts are everywhere, dwelling on the pain, this crippling agony within me. I can hardly hear Jesse as he whispers softly, "I'm here, and I'm so sorry he did that. I'm so sorry he made you feel this way."

My body trembles feverishly. There's this tug-of-war within me. A part of me doesn't want any physical contact right now. Jesse's touch alarms something within me from everything I've worked up, yet there's a part of me that won't let him go, that can't let him go, because I need him so much. I need him more than I need to push him away.

"It's okay," Jesse says. "I love you. I love you, I love you."

After he spends some time soothing me, he asks, "Do you want to go lie down?"

"Please don't make me go anywhere. Please let's just stay here," I say.

"I'm not going to make you do anything, Eric."

It offers me an assurance I need right now, for some deep-seated fear that was awakened as I worked out that exercise.

After I calm down, I let Jesse guide me into the bedroom, and we lie together, gazing at one another, my hand on his face, my thumb sliding across his flesh, touching him the way I want to touch him right now.

"You did it, Eric. You got through it."

Even though I did, I know I couldn't have done any of it without him.

## 25

## JESSE

I appreciate Eric letting me be here for him tonight.

I'd considered that what was weighing on his mind had to do with meeting my parents, but I'd also considered, since his therapy appointment is tomorrow, it might have something to do with that. It wasn't until meeting my parents was out of the way and had gone so well, but his apprehension remained, that I decided to push...to see if he would open up to me about what he was really irritated with.

I'm so glad he did, especially after seeing him complete what was so clearly a very difficult process for him.

We lie in bed together until he finally passes out beside me. As much as I held him after he finished the exercise and broke down in my arms, I could tell he needed his space tonight...and I wanted to give it to him.

I would have preferred to have him in my arms. As I lie next to him now, I want to pull him into my chest...because even the inches that separate us are too much, every ripple in the sheet an affront to what we share.

On top of being pissed at the distance between us, I'm still rattled, shaken from watching him break down.

Not only because of that moment, but because it reminds me of another—when we were camping and he had that severe episode right before my eyes. Watching the man I love crumble—when he's normally so full of pride and strength—isn't something I revel in.

Not because I don't want to be here for him when he's vulnerable, but because I know how much he doesn't want me to see him like that...for anyone to see him like that.

But to see him there, fighting to face that demon that's been haunting him for so long...for that, I'm so goddamn proud of him...in a way I'm not sure he can ever really understand. That doesn't still the rage that swells within me, though, toward that motherfucker who did this to him.

How could his uncle be so cruel and selfish? What kind of monster would be so reckless, so thoughtless toward another person? Did his uncle have a clue he would have this effect on Eric...here, forty-three years old, dealing with the trauma of an event that happened to him when he was sixteen?

It's hard for me to remember so many things that happened to me at that age, and I'm only twenty-three. But I never had an experience like that. Nothing that could cripple me the way Eric is so obviously crippled.

I had shit, but nothing comparable, so I can't know what it's like for him.

I hate myself for that.

Because I want to help him.

But there's this feeling of helplessness in all this.

I can read all the crap I want, sit in on therapy sessions, try to help him through exercises, but at the end of the day,

I'm a kid again, at the mercy of forces outside myself. Back then it was being pushed from foster home to foster home, and now I'm at the mercy of this thing that terrorizes the man I'm in love with.

At one point in the night, Eric starts to stir, his face shifting about. He grunts as beads of sweat form on his forehead.

He's having a nightmare.

I've seen this happen a few times since we've been together, since I've slept in bed with him.

At first, when I would notice it, I thought it was just the sort of night terrors most people experience. Hell, even Whitney would stir and shake over some that she had, but these days, after the research I've done, I can't help but feel that these are linked to his trauma. I wonder what it's of... Is it that event...or something else?

I can't watch him struggle, not tonight, not when I fear he might be reliving that experience all over again in his dreams.

I gently nudge him, and his eyes pop open. He sits up, his arms coming up at either side as I move back quickly, giving him the space I'm sure he needs.

He breathes intensely as he glances around the room in a panic, like he's trying to orient himself.

As his breathing steadies and he seems to recognize me, I ask, "Are you okay?"

"I'm fine. Having a nightmare." He takes another breath, blinking deliberately, seemingly more at ease than before, and then lies back on his pillow.

So many questions I want to ask him, but I'm worried about pushing him too hard, and as his gaze meets mine, he says, "Quid pro quo." He forces a smirk, and I'm relieved that he's said that because I'm certain it's because he can sense my confusion right now.

"Ask away," I say.

He takes a moment, as though he's trying to be careful about his question. "Your biological parents...what do you think about them?"

That wasn't what I was expecting...at all, but I try for the best answer I can manage because I'd like the same from him when it's my turn. "I wish I could say I'm a big enough person to have gotten over it...that they made their decision and maybe they had very good reasons. I've told myself story after story of very valid reasons why they might not have wanted to know me. There's one where my mother couldn't afford to keep me...or her parents wouldn't let her. My father's dead in one scenario, a bastard in a couple hundred. There's one where my mom's a drug addict and realized it would be better for me not to know her. No matter what story I tell, it doesn't make me feel any better or any less upset."

"That's understandable, and I'm sorry you have to live with that. You know about my situation with my father. He hardly wanted to be that. I still wonder what I did. I, a kid, did something to piss him off that made him not give a shit, that I was so unworthy of his affection. I think some part of me always wondered if it was because I was gay. He could sense it, and that disappointed him in some way. Has to be a reason he never came looking for me after I ran."

It's a pain I share with him. This feeling of not being loved or wanted.

"I'm sorry, Eric."

"Regardless of why that was, it reminds me I could have been a lot better with Ty. I spent so much time regretting rather than appreciating what we had. I see that now that I feel as though he's not constantly trying to chase me out of his life. Now that, after I fucked up royally, he's listening and understanding. It's bizarre to think it took this to get me to a place where I actually believe my son wants me in his life." He takes a deep breath. "I'm not going to count that as my quid pro quo," he assures me. "That would be cheating since I was bouncing off what you said, and probably not anything you didn't know already."

"Not going to take advantage of the subject change?" I tease him, and I earn a smile, one I deeply appreciate.

He sits up and turns onto his side, propping himself up on his elbow.

"No, you deserve better than subject changes, Jesse. What do you really want to ask me right now? What was on your mind after you woke me up?"

"The nightmare you were having...I've seen you struggling in your sleep before. Was it about your uncle?"

He winces. "They've never been about that instance necessarily, but to say they aren't about him at all would be a lie."

He doesn't sound like he wants to share more than that, but I feel compelled to open up to him. This is quid pro quo, after all. "After the Morgans adopted me, I started having these nightmares. I still have them occasionally. I'm always younger, in high school, and for whatever reason...any number of reasons...Judy, that woman at the shelter, shows up and tells me that the Morgans don't want me anymore. In some of them, Stan and Charlotte actually tell me to my face. That they don't love me. They don't want me. Then I'm taken back to the shelter, and I'm on my own all over again."

He rests his hand on my arm. "Jesse, I'm so sorry."

I shrug. "I can't complain about it. They've never left me,

but it hasn't kept me from being afraid, on some level, of being abandoned...alone all over again."

"Oh, my Jesse. My beautiful Jesse."

"Even with how amazing they've been, some days I do feel like I could find out that they're the dream...all this is a dream, and I wake up...by myself." I can't believe I said that much. "Sorry, I didn't mean to make this a downer. I just... when I see you having a nightmare, I worry and think if it feels nearly as real as the ones I have, you shouldn't have to experience it."

"I really appreciate that," he says. "Mine have played a very similar role in my own life. It feels kind of the same, but different. I'm being chased by this creature. Something out of a horror movie...almost like that movie *Martyrs*. It's not exactly a monster, though. It's this faceless dark creature that's hunting me down. It can be through the woods, a dark alley, an office building...anywhere I can run. And I know, the way you sometimes know things in dreams, that when it reaches me, it's not going to kill me. No, much worse. It's going to torture me in the worst possible way, and it's going to make me watch as it forces me to endure this agony.

"I've had this dream—or some variation of it—so many times. Sometimes the creature takes on different forms, but it's always that feeling of overwhelming helplessness...like there's nothing I can do to stop it. In some of my dreams, I do turn around and kill it. Slay it like some kind of hero in a movie. But more often than not, I'm running, terrified, a fucking coward. And I despise myself for running. I've always hated the feeling that rises within me because it makes me feel weak...like a failure. And these dreams, which I've had since that experience with my uncle, they've been something that's always been playing on my thoughts through every career goal, every obstacle I faced. They've inspired me to find that control in my own life and make it the way I want it to be. To have success, to be someone worth something."

"You've always been someone worth something, Eric. And you've earned everything you've ever achieved." I'm trying to be honest with him, to reflect back what I see when I look at him.

He nods, but his expression doesn't suggest he believes my words. "Yes, but I realize, here I am, forty-three years old...and even I'm impressed with the stuff I have, but I'm still a sixteen-year-old kid, running from the darkness, the phantom. That's never the guy I wanted to be."

"You're not running anymore, Eric. You were. You had every reason to. But like with Ty, *this* isn't over yet. And there's still time to turn around and face this thing...like you did tonight."

His eyes widen, and he studies me before his expression twists up again. He reaches out and runs the back of his hand down my cheek. I don't really know why, but I lean into it, wanting him to know I'm here. "I'm not a big believer in reincarnation, Jesse, but you make me believe in karma... because whatever I did to deserve you, I sure as fuck didn't do it in this life."

I feel his tension's waned and he's more at ease than when he first woke up...and especially since we shared that moment in the office together, when he faced that demon despite all the pain it brought him. He allowed me to see what he doesn't allow most others to see—that vulnerable side of him, that side he'd rather not share, the side most of us would rather hide from the world.

He sets his hand on the back of my head and reels me in to him, not taking much effort since I go so willingly. He offers a firm kiss, rolling on top of me, and his weight feels so good against me. I want to be here for him. I want to give him the ease he seeks in this moment.

"I need...you...Eric," I whisper between kisses.

"I need you more," Eric replies as I feel his dick hardening against my hip.

## 26

## ERIC

Jesse and I sit on yoga mats in the living room.

We moved the coffee table back to give us space in front of my big-screen TV, which plays a video link our new mindful yoga instructor provided us with during our first session on Tuesday.

This is apparently how we'll be spending our Friday night.

I haven't been ecstatic about pursuing something that seems wooey...hokey, even. Hell, I've never been flexible, so yoga was never something I was all that great at. But when Troy brought it up again in a session Jesse sat in on, the way Jesse's eyes lit up, I knew he was excited about the idea of doing something outside of an office environment. Admittedly, so was I.

It's nice being able to do it together...because everything's better with Jesse.

My eyes are closed as Carolyn, our instructor, guides us through a meditation that encourages us to listen to different parts of our bodies. In our first session, she called this a body scan—listening to parts of my body being the goal.

She described her program as a combination of mindfulness and yoga. She'll work with Jesse and me as a couple, guiding us through meditation processes and yoga positions she claims will help me become less judgmental toward my body—to relax into the sensations within me when I focus on different parts of it. It's about adjusting to the sensations and thoughts that arise when I'm triggered by anything that comes up because of the encounter I had at sixteen.

Also, when discussing the specifics of my situation with Carolyn, she echoed Troy's encouragement about this approach potentially helping me reach my real goal—getting to the place where I can bottom for Jesse, give myself fully to him in the way I want to. Not only because he wants it, but because I want him that way.

I want to be totally open to him, vulnerable, to trust him in a way we haven't explored yet. Any tension or discord that stands between us is more than I care for, and if this mindful yoga bullshit will help me get there, I'm in. However, as I sit here, legs crossed in whatever the fuck they call this position, I have to admit I'm not all that receptive to Carolyn's directions, just as I wasn't all that keen about it in our session this week.

*"I invite you to pay attention to the sensation in your hips and torso...and to listen to your breaths in a way that is comfortable to you,"* she says in her high-pitched voice. It can be somewhat annoying, but there's something disarming about her gentle guidance. Still, I don't like the idea of relaxing at her encouragement, even if she is just a recording. I've never liked taking directions, and I enjoyed them even less when we worked on these initial poses that first day.

*"If you'd like to open your eyes now, I'll be walking you through a gentle movement,"* Carolyn says.

I open my eyes, seeing on the screen her bright maroon-dyed hair as she sits on her yoga mat in a neon-green shirt and black leggings.

I turn to Jesse, whose lips are pressed together tightly as he watches the video as though he's learning how to fix a clogged garbage disposal rather than how to navigate the next meditation.

He closes his eyes and takes deep, steady breaths. *"If you want, explore the sensations in your feet...your toes,"* she says, but all I can do is watch the way Jesse's chest pushes out and pulls back in. He's shirtless, in just gym shorts, which bulge with his thick cock.

God, he's so beautiful.

I love how vulnerable he is in this moment. How he's able to let go and appreciate a video like this. It reminds me of the way he is when we fuck—open and receptive. It's that carefree part of him that I envy...because it's so amazing.

That he's doing this with me makes this moment that much more special.

More than this, the way he's there for me, coming to therapy sessions and being present like he was three weeks ago when I needed him so badly for that CPT exercise, means more than he could ever possibly understand.

Jesse's my fucking hero.

He follows the instructions in the video, closing his eyes and resuming with the meditation. I want to give him shit for how seriously he's taking it, yet his own commitment makes me realize that I need to follow suit.

I awkwardly get into the position and take a breath, closing my eyes, focusing on the soft tune in the background of the video, especially as Carolyn stops directing us. I've never enjoyed sitting still with my thoughts like this. I prefer being busy, in the middle of something, especially trying to reach some goal, trying to become a better person.

*"If you can, listen to your movement,"* Carolyn prods. *"Try and really focus on what you're experiencing right now."*

Everything feels tense and knotted up, which Carolyn said would happen initially, but I don't like it, especially sitting here with it.

Of course I'm tense. I have so many things in my life to be stressed about. I run a fucking empire. That's not easy, especially when I'm so far away from San Diego, where I'm used to running my company from. Now I'm working remotely…but at least I have two of the best fucking reasons in the world—Jesse and my son.

*"It's okay. Your thoughts will drift, and when they do, pull back to focusing on your breathing as best you can,"* Carolyn says.

How the fuck can anyone do this shit without their thoughts drifting?

I continue sitting in silence…but different thoughts begin to crop up—thoughts I prefer to chase away. I open my eyes once again and sneak a peek at Jesse.

He seems unfazed as he's relaxed on his mat. I watch him like some kind of predator before he smirks.

"I can feel you watching me." One eye pops open, and he peers at me as that smirk expands into a grin. "I don't think the program is going to do us much good if you can't meditate for five minutes. We haven't even gotten to the hard part yet."

"I'm shit at all this."

"Eric, it's not about being good. As Carolyn said, it's about listening to your body and trying to be more attuned to it."

Yeah, I was there too. I heard her talk about what sounded like a bunch of New Age crap. But even when I was resisting, Carolyn soothed me by talking about her fifteen-year experience as a counseling psychologist, working specifically with patients dealing with sexual trauma.

And the more she discussed what mindful yoga was all about—becoming more aware of my body, in tune with it—the less resistant I became, especially considering part of my issue deals with how my body was treated...what I was forced to do.

"You're not even going to try it?" Jesse asks.

"I am trying it. This is me trying it."

He glares at me, knowing I'm bullshitting him right now.

I sigh as Carolyn begins the yoga portion of the video. I go with it, swaying my body side to side, hands over my head, imitating her in an overdramatic way.

Jesse moves more naturally, shaking his head. "You are totally going to throw out your hip that way."

"Are you saying that because I'm older than you?"

"I'm saying that because you're not taking it very seriously." He's being playful, but I can tell he's being sincere too. He doesn't appreciate that I'm not giving this my all.

I'm being an asshole about this because there's still a part of me that doesn't want to explore this.

I remind myself of why I'm really doing this: for Jesse.

Because I love him.

Because he wants this, and because if anything can possibly help me get to the point of sharing with him that intimacy I desire—*crave*—I'm willing to give it a chance.

I do my best to follow the video prompts and not goof off as we work our way through a few different positions. In one instance, I'm trying to position my legs the way Carolyn has them knotted up in the video, and I glance over at Jesse's mat and see that he's effortlessly twisted in the correct position.

Well, close enough.

With one leg tucked near his chin, it's as though he's displaying his ass for me.

I try to get my leg as close to my chin as Jesse has his, but I'm not nearly as flexible, and it frustrates me knowing he's better at this than me.

"What is this circus acrobatic act, and why have you been hiding this up until now?" I ask.

He laughs. "I didn't think I was this flexible until we were doing these, but I'm not too bad, am I?"

"I could have told you that you're pretty flexible, but this makes me feel like you've been hiding this Cirque du Soleil act from me. I think I'm going to have to be a little more demanding from now on."

"When haven't you been demanding?" As we switch positions so that he's sitting up again, he adds, "But you know I like the demands."

My gaze settles on his crotch once again, and I notice he's gotten a little hard. I growl softly.

"Focus, Eric."

I obey, working my way into the next position, more manageable, on my side. Then Carolyn asks us to reflect on our bodies once again in silence.

In this moment, though I find Carolyn's voice annoying, I miss the sound of it where she would give some sort of instruction.

I'm rarely silent. When I'm working in my office or even jogging, I'm usually listening to music. Seems like now I know why.

In the quiet, paying attention to my body, something unsettling rises up within me. It reminds me of the nightmares I have, this thing chasing me that in some ways I'm always running from, like if I sit still too long, it will somehow seize control, possess my mind, and before I know it, I will be this completely other person than the man I've come to know all these forty-three years of my life.

Such a silly exercise should be easy enough, but the silence becomes more and more agonizing as it stretches out.

When Carolyn directs us to sit back up, Jesse's gaze catches mine, and he asks, "Are you okay?"

Is it that transparent how bothered I am by this? Like I was that night before we worked on the exercise Troy gave me?

My concern about Jesse reading my discomfort is overshadowed by that compassionate expression on his face.

"It is a little difficult," I admit.

"She said it'll get easier, though."

"I know it will, Jesse. It's frustrating not being good at something."

"Well, how about once we're done with something you're not good at, we can do something you're really good at?"

He's trying to cheer me up, and considering how my cock is lengthening in my shorts, it's clearly working.

"I like the sound of that."

He crawls over to me.

"Do you mind if I kiss you?" he asks, his eyes lit up, his smile broad. "See? I'm already working on this stuff."

He's talking about the affirmative consent he discussed with Troy and Carolyn. It's all about Jesse asking for my permission before making physical contact, making sure I'm comfortable. They say it will help with our communication, and what I thought was stupid, because I love his touch so much, I realize makes such a difference because it makes me feel more at ease when he asks first. It reminds me that he cares about me—my feelings and my body. And just as amazing, he doesn't make me feel like I'm wrong or needy for appreciating it.

"If you don't fucking kiss me right now, I'm going to be pissed," I tell him.

"Does that mean you're going to hate-fuck me? Because then I might have to withhold it just for that."

"Kiss me," I tell him, and he pushes his lips up against mine. The anxiety, the tension that I've been feeling during this video, starts to dissipate.

I wrap my arms around him and guide him so that his back is on the mat. Spreading out on top of him, I force my lips from his and pull back, gazing down at him.

Carolyn's voice continues droning on and on in the background.

"I think we're going to have to take a break from this," I say as I feel his girth against my pelvis.

"Yeah, we can definitely get to it later." He grabs the back of my head, pulling me down to him so I can feel his own need, his own desperation for what I crave so badly right now.

## 27

## JESSE

"That was one hell of a spike," Ben says as he walks with me and Ty from the showers.

It's the first time Ty and I have gotten together to play since the epic fallout, and it's been about as awkward as I figured it would be. It's strange chatting up all our friends, having a good time, but none of them knowing about the tension that's been brewing between us these past few months.

Ty has hardly made eye contact with me despite the good times we shared on our camping trip, and the spike Ben's referring to...well, I can't help but feel like when Ty scored that point against my team, he was reveling in at least some catharsis of having evened the score a bit after everything that's transpired between us.

Not that it could ever be even. Not that we could ever find a way to make this fair and balanced, but it seemed Ty worked that hard out on the court because he felt like he could at least get some relief through volleyball.

When Ben heads off, Ty and I walk through the parking

lot together, the way we used to when we would usually finish catching up about our days or agree to head out to a restaurant or bar together, but it's not the same. It can't ever be the same again. I know that. I'm not an idiot about this, but it doesn't make this lingering discomfort easier to manage.

It's better than the alternative of not spending any time with him, but it leaves me wondering what our future will be...what it can really be, and if either of us can ever get to a place close to what we shared before.

I return home to Eric, and we eat dinner together. He doesn't waste time after—nails me twice, in the bedroom. I'm wondering if part of it is that he feels better now that he's taking steps toward his recovery. Whatever the reason, my body's all his. It has been since that first time he took me in PV...when he changed my whole fucking world.

The next day, I sit at my desk in my office, typing a report on my laptop, my earbuds in as I listen to the latest *Rocks and Hard Places* podcast. My phone buzzes on the desk, and I pick it up to see a text from Eric.

*Planning to skip lunch again today?* he asks.

He knows how busy I've been all week and that I've been doing my best to play catchup after we had an epic fail on a recent program test.

I reply: *All work and no play for Mr. Morgan.*

I wonder if he'll understand my *The Shining* reference before he responds with: *All work and no play makes Jesse a dull boy. ;)*

*I think I know what we'll be watching together next*, I send back to him.

Watching movies together, even ones I've seen before, is a treat because it's better getting to share those things with someone. Not just with anyone, but with Eric.

I've felt better about our time together since our camping outing with Ty a little over a month ago. Less guilty, maybe. That's not entirely gone, and I don't ever expect it to be, but just that seeing Ty easing up around us was nice. So fucking nice, and it's even better now that we're actually hanging again.

I set my phone back down because I need to be a "dull boy" to crank this work out and get back to the tasks I'm supposed to be dealing with today.

We have Eric's therapy visit tomorrow, and then we'll attend another mindful yoga session next week. I love being there for him like this, but I have to keep on top of my work to make sure no one complains about all this time I need during my weeks to be there for my boyfriend.

There's a knock at my door. Not going to get any of this done if I keep getting distracted.

"Yup?" I say before Sam enters and approaches my desk, a sneaky expression on his face, his ChapStick sparkling under the overhead fluorescent lights. "I can't imagine you're here because you have any good news."

He leans his hip against the side of my desk and folds his arms. I notice how tight the button-up he's wearing is and how he's left the collar undone...along with a couple of buttons. Considering how flirtatious he can be, I don't imagine this was by mistake.

"Maybe I just wanted to see you," he says, arching his blond brow.

I roll my eyes, and his expression twists up. "Okay, okay. I've got some not-so-great news about those results I sent you last week."

"You mean the ones I've been basing my report today on? The one I've spent hours trying to pull together?"

"Those are the ones," he whispers, cringing. "I got an

email from Carter, and apparently those results weren't the results I was supposed to send you. There were two tests performed on the same day. The one I sent you only includes a few of the issues we encountered, but there were more glitches in the second one that need to be resolved."

I sigh. "Yay," I say facetiously.

"I know. I only come visit when I have bad news. Don't shoot the messenger. But don't stress out too much. The ones that were on the other report came up again, so it's just adding to what you already have."

"Email away...and I'll see if I can get a report out that makes some sort of sense."

"On it. Sorry again."

He turns and heads out of the office, but then swings back around at the door. "And you know, Jesse, you still need to take your lunch break."

"Jesus, everyone's giving me shit about that right now. I'll take it today, okay?"

"You could always go with me," he says with a wink. "Or maybe dinner?"

*I'd have to take it up with my boyfriend.*

"Why don't you get back to work?" I say.

"Okay, but the offer is always on the table."

He heads out, and I roll my eyes once again.

I plant my head on my desk, in front of the keyboard. Great. All that work I was putting into this project has been for nothing. Maybe I do need to get some lunch, after all.

I pick up my phone, checking to see if Eric's texted.

I get back to work for a bit before there's another rap on my door, and if it's Sam again with more bad news, I'm gonna lose my goddamn mind.

"Come in," I groan.

The door opens, and a familiar face pops in—one that relieves me of all the stress I've been piling up since this day began.

"Eric Westright," I say, enjoying how those two simple words make me feel as I speak them. I narrow my eyes. "What are you doing here?"

I lean back in my swivel chair, folding my arms, sort of enjoying that he's stepping into my space. As he enters, letting the door close behind him, he glances around the office like he's impressed.

"Mr. Morgan," he says. "I should have visited your office sooner. I think I was a little undersold on how important your position at this company is."

"Oh, this old thing," I tease, because I know my corner office is fairly impressive. Fuck, I was impressed when they showed it to me. The position I have with this company isn't exactly entrance level, which was one of the reasons I wanted this job so much when we first started seeing each other.

He walks over to the window behind me, checking out the view. I follow his gaze, appreciating the skyscrapers and mid-rises it overlooks.

"This is better than the view from my condo," he says as though he's envious.

"Whatever," I say as I rise and hurry to greet him. "Get over here and give your man a kiss."

He obeys. My hand slides along his side, around to the small of his back as I taste his minty mouth.

"Mmm," escapes my lips. "I was hungry, but I didn't know what exactly for until you got here." Instinctively, my gaze sinks to his crotch.

"Mr. Morgan, you're awfully feisty this afternoon. You

don't have some assistant who can come in here and assist you with all your *needs*?"

"Who needs an assistant when I have a boyfriend who's willing to swing by and give me that?"

"Oh, really?" He glances around before retreating back toward the door. He turns the lock, and I make my way in front of my desk.

"Is anyone likely to interrupt us?" he asks.

I shake my head. "Nope."

"Any cameras?"

"Uh-uh."

He smirks. "Well, then. Mr. Morgan does need some lunch. And to relieve some stress, it seems. He's had a busy week."

I laugh.

"Take off your clothes," he commands, and my face flashes with heat.

The sex has always been hot, but since we've been practicing the mindful yoga techniques during the sessions and on our own at home, Eric's definitely upped his game. Maybe this work is already helping.

"Here in my office? You want to turn my respectable place of business into a porn shoot?"

"About as bad as I want to make you my bottom right now."

The way his eyebrow arches, I can't help but feel my dick twitch and appreciate that Eric has turned a stressful day into something a lot more exciting.

"Give me a little show, beautiful," he says, stepping into the middle of the room and folding his arms, putting me on the spot, reminding me of that night when he wanted me to do a little striptease for him.

It feels wrong doing this here, but then also so right.

And as always, I find him impossible to resist. I grab my tie and loosen it.

He bites his lip, which just means he wants me to continue even more.

After I remove my tie, I toss it onto the desk behind me and unbutton my shirt cuff links. Then I start at my shirt collar and make my way down the placket, undoing the buttons. When I've undone them all, I pull the shirt open very slowly...wanting to tease him...to torture him.

The way his gaze travels down my body, settling on my slight happy trail, I can feel his appreciation, his adoration. Eric gives everything away with the shift of his expression... that familiar hunger all over his face that's so easy to read.

The way Eric's jaw tenses and he squares off his shoulders, it's as though he's holding himself back, trying to keep from lunging at me, tearing my clothes off and forcing me onto the desk so he can take me, claim me. It's a savage side of him I enjoy so much.

But his clear attempt at stilling his desire, keeping himself back, only arouses me more—makes me feel like I have this power over him.

Eric notices the bulge in my pants, so I start removing my belt next, sliding it out of the loops in the waistband while kicking out of my shoes. I remove my socks because I feel like this will save us some trouble later.

"My stripping expert," Eric whispers, apparently noticing my attention to these details.

"Trying to put on a good show."

I pull down my pants, kick them off, and slide my thumbs under the waistband of my trunk boxers.

"Stop right there," Eric practically spits through his teeth.

I obey as he unfolds his arms and approaches me,

moving slowly, like he's still doing his best to keep from rushing me and ravaging my oh-so-fucking-willing body.

As he reaches me, he grabs either side of the collar of my shirt and pulls them back, moving the sleeves slowly down my arms, scanning me over, assessing my body like he approves of what he sees. When he gets down to my wrists, he releases the shirt, and gravity pulls it down to the floor behind me.

"Mr. Morgan," he says, "these Calvins look very good on you."

I chuckle, feeling silly and slightly embarrassed. But before I have a chance to think much about that, he moves forward quickly, his lips back on mine, his hands probing my body, feeling around in a frenzy, like all that tension he's been holding back, all that restraint is finally being unleashed on me.

"God, you're so gorgeous." He pulls away to say that before he kisses me again, pushing me back. My ass touches the desk, and I sit back on it. Eric slides me even farther across the desktop.

"My work," I say, turning to focus on my laptop. Eric reaches around and slides it out of our way.

I turn back, impressed and sort of intimidated by this energy he's coming at me with—his intensity. "I wasn't expecting all this," I say.

"Then you probably weren't expecting this either," he says, reaching into his pocket and retrieving a small bottle of lube.

"Thank fucking God. I need you in my ass." I'm so relieved because I was worried we'd be giving each other BJs or hand jobs, which wouldn't have been enough to satisfy me...not when I'm wanting to be totally possessed by him.

He sets the bottle on my desk and tugs at the waistband of my underwear. I press my palms behind me on the desk, lifting my ass in the air, helping him pull them down my legs, and as soon as he gets them off, he starts going down on me. I roll my head back, enjoying the sensation, completely losing myself.

"Fuck me, Eric. I need you to fuck me now."

He gasps as he pulls his mouth off my cock before he quickly begins removing his own clothes, dropping his pants and underwear, kicking off his shoes. He starts to remove his shirt but doesn't get very far before he gives up, growling as he takes the bottle of lube and wets his hand with some.

"I need you inside me, Eric."

He can't understand how much I want to feel his girth in me. We've fucked so much since we met, and goddammit, why isn't it ever enough?

He comes at me quickly, kissing my lips. I lift my legs as he pushes that stiff cock against my hole, and feel the pressure. It's so intense, reminding me of how big he is, but he doesn't rush.

We take our time so that he can work that cock into me, and as I'm about to call out, he clamps his hand down over my mouth, silencing me.

Thank God.

It takes some time and effort, but gradually we get to where he's buried inside me.

"That's it," I whisper when he removes his hand from my mouth. His cock is jamming into my prostate in that way that sends goose bumps prickling across my flesh and heat surging to my face.

I notice the wild, feral expression on his face as he takes me. He cups his hand behind my neck, locking me in place as he speeds up his pace, sensation rising within me, overwhelming me.

"You're so tight, Mr. Morgan," he whispers before his mouth clamps down against mine again.

He pushes me back down on the desk, fucking me harder, pushing deeper and deeper. I want to call out the way I call out when we fuck in one of our condos, but I know better. Instead, I dig my fingers into his back, appreciating what it's like to submit to him totally, to feel that girth within me, possessing me.

"I'm all yours," I mutter. "I'm all yours, Eric."

If only he could fathom how much.

He grunts and then groans softly.

"I'm about to come in you," he warns.

I grab my cock and jerk frantically. "Do it, Eric. I need it, Eric."

As soon as I speak his name, his face twists up, and he slams against my prostate in a series of powerful jerks, with such frenzy that it overwhelms my nerves. My load shoots out across me as I feel a familiar swell within me, and I gasp, appreciating this moment, the relief I've experienced from all the frustration my day began with.

I'm intoxicated…high…fucking addicted—addicted to Eric Westright. He's a drug I won't ever give up.

Soon we're panting, him lying on top of me, his sweat dripping from his bangs onto my face. I appreciate being trapped beneath his weight, our breaths syncing up as he clings to me, his cock still stuck within me.

No matter how many times we fuck, it's never enough, and I want to be closer. I want him to take me again and again.

He pulls away, looking down at me, a grin sweeping

across his face before he says, "Thank you for that, Mr. Morgan."

I laugh, and I can't help how loud it is. I'm sure someone outside the office could hear this part, but it's not a big deal, considering they didn't hear the rest.

"Now that I've fed your hole," he adds before leaning back and setting his hand on my abs, "why don't you let me fill your belly."

"Already needing a blowjob?" I tease, and he laughs.

"Food," he clarifies. "You know, the thing that keeps these muscles of yours so strong and firm."

"Oh, well, that would be okay too, I guess."

It's so funny how he managed to get me so worked up that my hunger for anything other than him wasn't on my mind, but he's probably right about me needing to get something other than cum inside me.

We clean up, my body shaking, reeling in pleasure, as we hurry back into our clothes.

"Where should I take my boyfriend out today?" Eric asks.

"And here I thought you were going to use me for my ass today."

"Nope," he says. "I'm going to treat my man right."

"But what about when I want you to treat me wrong?"

"I do that right too."

"Yes, you do," I admit with a chuckle as I finish buttoning my shirt.

As he tucks his shirt in his pants, he approaches me and offers another kiss, placing his hand behind my head and massaging gently, something so affectionate considering the intense fuck we just shared—something that reminds me that what we share is a lot more than the good fucks we enjoy together.

After we finish getting dressed, we head out of my office together. I notice my reflection in the glass across a framed print in the hall. My hair is tousled over my head...sex-hair, for sure. I run my hand through it to fix it a little so I don't look like the sort of trash Eric made of me minutes earlier.

As we're about to round the corner, I see Sam coming down the hall toward us.

Of course. Just my luck.

As soon as he spies me, his eyes light up. Then he sees Eric, and his expression shifts like he's equally intrigued by him.

"Oh, hi, Jesse." He glances between Eric and me. "You must be Jesse's dad." He reaches his hand out for a shake.

I blush, horrified by the misunderstanding.

"Um," Eric says, and I can tell by the expression on his face that he doesn't want to correct Sam.

"Sam, this is my boyfriend. His name is Eric."

I feel bad that it came out like this because I see Sam getting flustered and glancing between us like he's obviously embarrassed.

"Oh, well, it's very nice to meet you, Eric," he says politely. "Jesse is a great employee, and we love having him. Always professional and, yeah..."

This is the first time I've seen him at a loss for words.

"I'm glad to hear that," Eric says before Sam excuses himself and heads off.

Eric glances at me, his brows coming together. "Your dad, huh?"

"My incredibly hot daddy, more like it," I tease.

"As long as I get to fuck you, I don't give a damn how old anyone thinks I look."

I laugh. "Well, you're not going to have any issues there."

"I know. You're a pretty lucky guy."

I snicker before passing him. "You're so full of yourself today."

"You're full of me too," he reminds me as he slaps my ass, gripping on a little before releasing it.

I really am, and I'm so excited, I feel as though I could skip all the way out of the building.

## 28

## ERIC

I lie on the bed, my legs spread out over me as I assess my ass in a hand mirror. I feel like such an idiot. Here I am with a fucking hand mirror, following one of these crazy-ass exercises Carolyn recommended. It's part of her program, to help me get in touch with my body. Just look at it and try to relax into any sensations—particularly negative ones—I may experience during the process. Somehow this is supposed to help me get to what I want to share with Jesse.

Mindfulness techniques, huh? Such a load of bullshit.

I've only seen her twice since our intro session, aside from the videos Jesse and I watch together, but already, I'm over it. She's nice and understanding, but it doesn't change the fact that these exercises and bending into weird positions in sessions with her is weird as fuck. I don't see how this circus-acrobat crap is going to help us.

Obviously I can still please Jesse...something I've done plenty since even before we saw her or Troy. Although, I know a part of it is because all this work makes me feel broken or like less of a man...or that I can't give Jesse what he needs.

Like that office sex last week. That wasn't something I would have done normally. Not that I don't want to take Jesse's body wherever we are, but I was pushing myself, proving something to myself and to Jesse. I'm sure he didn't need me to prove anything, but I needed to, especially after all these goddamn exercises.

Between therapy and mindful yoga sessions, I feel as though I'm just submerging myself more and more in things that make me feel so vulnerable...and as undesirable as a person can feel.

We've hardly begun, but I've had to relive that painful experience over and over again, in more accounts for my therapist. He keeps wanting more description, more detail. He says it'll help, but it doesn't feel like it when it throws me right back to being a lost, confused kid all over again.

Even worse, going back and writing about that dark experience isn't enough for this asshole. There are all these talking points—I'm supposed to be questioning beliefs and thoughts around it and in my life that might have developed because of it.

What a crock of shit. He's almost as bad as Carolyn's nutjob yoga bullshit.

I'm supposed to change my thinking around something I've been doing for nearly thirty years now? It'd be laughable if it wasn't so goddamned pathetic.

What's the fucking point of any of this?

I set the mirror down beside me and look up at the ceiling, sighing.

How many other dumb exercises will I have to do before I can have what I want—Jesse the way I want?

How much good is any of this doing me anyway?

This isn't how I live my life, sitting here trying to push, and probe, and analyze. I'm a fighter. I push forward in the face of fear or worry. I disregard my insecurities…all the caution signs…and go after the things I want. I haven't acquired this wealth in my life by overthinking anything to the point of absurdity. All this dancing around what I want feels counterproductive.

I put the mirror away in the bathroom, feeling stupid. I'm way too rational for this.

Nice as the mindful yoga sessions have been, and as gung ho as Jesse has been about continuing with these ridiculous sessions, there has to be an easier way…a faster way.

I've sat here for so long, since sixteen, being this fucked up, and I'm tired of running. I've faced my fears with Jesse before…that night we confronted Ty and the night when he helped me with that exercise. If I can do this with anyone, I can do it with him.

As I look at myself in the mirror, I tense my jaw, making a decision.

I'm going to do this. I'm going to get through this the way I get through everything—by fighting.

I head into my office and throw myself into my work, trying to push that stupid mirror exercise out of my thoughts.

I've put the picture of Ty back up, and I take a moment to appreciate all that this fucked-up shit has brought into my life and how much Ty and I have chatted recently. Not much, but we've had some lunches and dinners again.

It's a start. I finally feel as if I'm on the right path.

I shower up before heading into the kitchen to make some dinner for Jesse and me tonight, selecting through what I have in my pantry before settling on a beef and broccoli stir fry.

As I cook, I'm working to mentally prepare myself for what I want to share with Jesse tonight. I'm not ready, but who needs to be fucking ready? When have I needed to be ready for anything else in my life? Yes, the anxiety's there, but that's to be expected. I might be uncomfortable or uneasy, but I don't believe I'll now have that experience I had when we went camping. Not now that Jesse understands my past.

When I hear the door open, I whirl around to see Jesse in a tank and basketball shorts, a little sweat on his brow. I approach him and he glances around me, at the dinner I'm fixing.

"Well, look who got all into wining and dining me tonight."

"How was the gym?" I ask him, but he hardly has a chance to respond before I take his lips. I don't care about the fact that he's all sweaty. Really, I welcome it as I take a whiff of his scent and pull him close to me so that our torsos are flush as our lips are sealed together.

This is what I want—him, just like this.

I take in his fragrance once again.

"I need...to shower," he says.

"You need to just keep kissing me. I think I've earned it after the meal I made you."

He doesn't fight me on that.

When I finally force myself to pull away, knowing he probably needs a chance to breathe, he looks at me with pleasant surprise.

"The best way to be greeted after a long day," he says.

"How's that issue you were dealing with...that report you had to fix?"

"Gave me a good excuse to pump a little harder than usual."

I want to make a joke about pumping harder than usual, but I'm struggling to do anything other than appreciate this man before me...the man I'm so enamored with.

I love him. I trust him.

He heads off to shower while I finish preparing dinner. After I set the table, he steps out of my bedroom dressed in shorts and a polo, clothes he had in his drawer.

His drawer. The drawer I set aside for him now that he's in my life.

As he approaches the table, his nostrils flare as he takes in the scent of my cooking the way I took in his scent when he walked into my place.

He smiles as he sits across from me. We catch up on each other's day.

I'm not going to force tonight, I'm not going to push so hard that it makes either of us uncomfortable. I'm going to wait until the moment arises naturally, and then face this demon that still haunts me to this day—a demon it's fucking time for me to exorcise.

We finish up dinner, then move on to a movie in bed. I'm having a difficult time watching it tonight, though, because all I can do is keep looking at my Jesse.

His beautiful face.

Those gorgeous dimples, and those eyes—those damn chestnut-brown eyes that get me every time.

"Why do you keep looking at me like that?" he finally asks, his lips curling into a smirk as though he already knows the answer.

"Can't I just appreciate how gorgeous my man is?"

"If you're going to appreciate him, he'd prefer you have your hands on him, at least."

He rolls onto me, crawling up my body before his lips slam down against mine. I submit to him, the way he's always so good at submitting to me, letting him guide this experience. I relax, gripping the back of his head.

I can do this…I can fucking do this. But the fact that I'm so goddamned determined reminds me of how much there is to overcome. And this determination reminds me of when we went camping and I pushed myself in a similar way. It's different now, though, because I can actually talk to him, because we can work through this together. I'm not on my own like I was then.

I tug at his shirt, pulling it off him. He does the same with mine before kissing his way down my chest and torso. When he gets to my boxers, he slides them off me before filling his mouth with my girth, going down on me.

Good as it feels, I know what I want tonight. I want him inside me.

Now. I want to face this.

I sit up, and he pulls his lips off my dick and kisses me. "Jesse…I need you tonight."

"I need you too."

"No, you don't understand my meaning. I need you inside me."

He pulls away, his expression unreadable for a moment, and then there's a sort of sadness to it.

"Eric," he mutters.

I set my hand against his face, running my thumb across his cheek. "It's fine."

"No," he says, sitting back quickly.

In an instant, I feel guarded, defensive…and embarrassed.

"It's too soon," Jesse says. "We just started seeing someone about this, and you know what they're saying.

There are steps we still have to take. Work we have to do. Come on, Eric. Let's give this stuff a try before pushing."

"Jesse, I don't live my life...any other aspect of it, at least, running from things, or taking fucking steps doing things the way other people do them."

"I just don't want things to end up like when we went camping."

I hate that he had to experience that. I despise myself for what I put him through, but I know better now.

"I know," I say. "But it was different then. I wasn't ready. I hadn't faced it yet. I couldn't talk to you about it, but I can now, and we can work on this together."

As much as I'm still trying to encourage him, I'm hurt by his skepticism...that he doesn't trust me to know what's best with this. And even after I tried to explain this to him, he looks confused, as though he doesn't understand what I'm saying.

"Eric, what's wrong with us waiting a little longer?"

"You don't think I can do this?" spits out of my mouth, and there's anger in my tone. It's been steadily building through this conversation, especially the more I've felt like he thinks he knows what's best for me, as though he doesn't believe I can do this.

"You don't believe in me?" I ask. "You don't think I'm qualified to know what I'm ready to do with my own fucking body?"

My words are harsh...because I feel so hurt.

"Eric, I believe in you, but it feels like you're trying to prove something to yourself, or to me."

"I'm not trying to prove anything, and if I was, don't I have a right to decide what I do with my own body?"

"Eric..."

I can tell he's trying to be gentle with me, which makes

me feel like he thinks what I'm sure Carolyn and Troy and Michelle think—that I'm weak.

I'm being severe right now, but I feel so fucking defensive. I don't know who I'm more angry with—him for not letting me try this, or me for not being able to do something that should be perfectly normal for me, that should be easy.

"Eric, come on." A warm smile spreads across his face as he seems to attempt to soothe his own concern as well as my own. That smile that could normally change my mood in an instant does little more than aggravate me.

"What does it matter if we first try some of these silly exercises or mindfulness stuff?" Jesse asks. "What does it matter if we do something tonight or when we've worked on this a little more? I'm still going to be here, and I'm still going to love you, Eric."

I can hear the sincerity in his words, but it doesn't change how I feel. "If you love me, then let me do this. Help me do this one thing tonight."

Tears well in his eyes as his gaze drifts from mine.

I feel abandoned.

"Please don't ask me to do that," he whispers, as though it's difficult for him to speak the words.

"Do you think I'm too weak to do this?" I ask through gritted teeth.

"Eric, that's not what it's about at all. I just don't want to do anything to keep you from making progress and—"

"Because you think I'm weak?"

"Because we're not ready."

Those boundaries Jesse is normally able to break through—all that time we've spent together that has led to me allowing them to shatter, to let him in—in a moment, it's as though a concrete wall has lifted from the ground, separated us.

I'm so hurt, so angry.

"Eric?"

"No, it's fine," I say curtly. "You obviously don't respect me…or think enough about my ability to gauge the situation, even though I have proven myself in every aspect of my life to be in control and able to handle myself. I don't need you or anybody else telling me what to do and when to do it."

"Eric, please, let's not fight."

"There's no fight, just an understanding that you don't get me. Not the way I thought you did." As I speak the words, I know they're not entirely true, but it doesn't keep me from feeling this pain…or wanting to push him away right now.

"Eric, I'm trying really hard to be here for you, to be what you need me to be."

"I don't need you to be anything other than my partner, my ally, which you clearly are not right now."

This conversation is over, and Jesse must know that by the way he studies my expression. "Are you mad?" he asks.

"I'm frustrated, Jesse."

"Sorry, we haven't really gotten into a fight, but do I need to go, or…"

I want him to leave. I don't want him to be near me when I feel so betrayed, but looking into his eyes, I see this worry, and his own pain, like he's wondering if I'm going to push him away. It makes me think of our conversation about his nightmares, about being abandoned by the Morgans.

Knowing that I could make him feel that way by pushing him away kills me. Angry as I am with him right now, I would never put him through that. I couldn't. But it doesn't keep me from resenting him.

"No, you don't need to go, Jesse. We're not children. No

one's storming out, making some big, dramatic gesture tonight. I think I sobered up about where we are in relation to each other in this relationship. I'm going to go get ready for bed."

As I slide out of the bed and head into the bathroom, I don't turn back to him.

Still, he must feel my rejection. Though I didn't storm off or ask him to leave, which a part of me desperately wants, I can't imagine he doesn't feel somewhat abandoned in this moment. In some ways we're even…because he abandoned me first, and now I'm wrecked, damaged.

I close the bathroom door and look at myself in the mirror. I recall what it feels like to stand before this mirror, feeling totally alone in the world. I know Jesse cares, that he wants to be here for me, but I can't shake this horrible feeling of betrayal. For not being here for me the way I needed him to be.

## 29

# JESSE

It's so fucking hard to concentrate on work when all I'm doing is stressing out about what happened between Eric and me last night.

As sure as I was about my response—that we needed to wait—I can't help but feel as though it would have been better to suck it up and follow through with his request.

It doesn't feel right, but after what went down, after how I hurt him, I realize I might have made a terrible mistake. He wanted to feel in control, and it's his body, as he said, but it reminded me of that night when we went camping and he totally lost it. He thought he could push, and he pushed too hard, too fast. I know he hurt that night, but so did I, watching this man I was falling head over heels for shaking, trembling, trapped in the horror of his terrifying memories.

Maybe it was selfish of me not to hear him out. Doesn't he have the right to decide how to handle all this?

God, I don't fucking know. There aren't manuals for how to handle something like this. Hell, I feel like everything I've read makes me more aware of certain things about what he's going through than what the hell is happening with me.

How the fuck am I supposed to handle a situation like the one that came up last night? That's not an easy Google search.

I keep pushing through my day, when my phone buzzes. I check, hoping it's Eric, who hasn't texted me all day...and who hardly spoke to me after our fight last night.

A fucking fight? This isn't us at all.

A combination of disappointment and excitement duke it out when I see Ty's name on my phone. I should be ecstatic that he's not texting, that he's fucking calling, but because of the mood I'm in, I don't want to answer. I have to, though. This isn't an opportunity I can pass up.

As Eric said last night, regardless of what's going on, it's not like we're going to have a big fight and storm out over it, but still, I fear it will change what we share—that I've pushed Eric, potentially in some way we won't be able to bounce back from.

"Hey, man, what's up?" I say, answering my phone. I'm trying to sound like everything's fine, but the harder I try, the more insincere my words sound.

"Hey." Ty sounds as unenthusiastic as I do, leaving me even more curious about why he's calling.

There's this delay, and I don't rush him.

"We're definitely getting together for volleyball next week. Just seeing if you can make it."

"Yeah, yeah. That'd be great."

My voice cracks slightly...because it feels like a fucking miracle that he's asking me for that. I'm so torn between excitement to be on the path toward getting my friend back and another of totally fucking up everything with Eric.

"Is everything okay, Jesse?"

As he speaks the words, this pain ripples through me, stinging in my chest. I want to tell him how not okay I am, yet I'm caught in this strange place. Ty and I haven't made up yet, and so much about what frustrates me has to do with things I hold in confidence with his father.

"I'll be fine." I should've said, "I'm fine," but lying to Ty right now seems like an even stupider move. "It's just...stuff. I'll be good."

The way I said *stuff*, I wonder if Ty can sense that I mean so much more than that.

"Okay, okay," he says. "If you're game, I'll text you next week, and we'll see if we can work it out."

Back in the day, I would have told him I was hurt and frustrated. We would have hung out. I would have been able to unload so much of my problems on him, and he would have complained about the shit in his own life.

But everything in my life in this moment is stuck in my throat.

I don't like this.

I want my friend back.

"All right. Cool, cool. Well, I'll talk to you later," he says quickly and then hangs up.

Probably for the best, because I could've ended up saying too much. Hell, I already did.

Tears stir in my eyes the way they did last night when I was talking to Eric, and I want to break down.

But I need to push forward. I have to at least keep the other aspects of my life together, if I'm going to royally fuck up all my relationships.

I press on with my work. It's hard to get anything done when I have all this hanging over my head, but I need to get this in before the weekend. However, fuck if I don't just want to call it quits and figure out this shit with Eric.

There's a knock on my door. I'm sure it's Sam, but there's a part of me that's hoping it's Eric, that he's rushed by today to talk to me, and actually talk to me, not blow it off like he did last night.

"Come in," I call out.

The door opens, but it's not Sam or Eric.

It's Ty, and that bastard is carrying a pizza, probably Meat Lover's. It reminds me of when he came and talked me through that shit with my granny.

And now I can't hold back the tears I've been fighting all day. They slide down my face...because god-fucking-dammit, how can he be so amazing when I've been such a shit to him?

He gets this whimsical little smile on his face. "I got this pizza," he says as he traipses into my office, "and it's not gonna eat itself."

It's like when he told me the same thing after I broke it off with Whitney.

He sets the box on my desk, beside my laptop, this knowing expression across his face, that awareness that I haven't shared the details about what's really upsetting me. It's as though he's pleading, "Please talk to me." If only he knew how much I could use a friend right now.

"Think you can take a break?" Ty asks.

I shrug. "I don't think I'm going to get much more done today anyway."

"Come on, then. Let's go crash at my place and talk shit about all our coworkers."

I'm laughing through my tears because he says it as though we're right back where we were before. I appreciate that he's even trying.

"You talked me into it," I say.

He takes the pizza with him, and we meet at his place. As we head to his unit, he's cracking jokes, talking to me about some of the guys we play volleyball with, catching me up on some gossip.

When we're in his condo, he sets the pizza box down on the coffee table, opens it, and grabs a slice before planting himself on the couch.

"Get us some beers?" he asks as he chews his pizza.

I do, and when I hand him one of the cans, I say, "I don't know that I deserve all this."

"Deserve what? Getting me a beer and hanging around so I can dump work shit on you? Then you can tell me why you sound like somebody shot your new puppy."

I sit on the cushion beside him on the couch, opening my beer, thinking about how incredible he's being, but also realizing I'm trapped. The things I need to talk to him about, I can't.

"I wish I could tell you," I say, "but I think I'm learning exactly how tricky this all is. The things we used to talk about if I had a fight with Whitney or something...now it's so complicated, isn't it?"

"Complicated? You had a fight with Eric? So what? That's what happens, and, Jesse, if we're going to find a way to make this weird-ass situation work, you can tell me when you're down. And I can be here to help."

"You can't know what this all means to me, but there are details to this that I can't really share...that aren't mine to share."

"Then share the parts you can." His words are so soft, such a contrast to when he was shouting at us that night in Eric's condo. It should help, but it can't.

"I'm trying to think of ways of saying what I need to that won't violate any trust he has in me," I say, "and I keep reaching a dead end. I mean, it wasn't a fight exactly, but it was more than we've had before, and I think I hurt him. I didn't mean to, but I'm not sure if I should have just done what he wanted because he asked me, or if what I was fighting for was worth it. God, see? That's the vaguest shit ever."

I wipe tears from my face with the backs of my hands.

"Find yourself hurting a lot of people without meaning to?" he asks, a sort of bitterness in his expression.

"Ty, I know no matter what I say, or do, you don't have a reason to ever forgive me."

"Whoa, whoa. That's not why I went to your office today. I went because, as fucked up as this situation is, I knew you were hurt. I've never liked to see you that way, even that first time we hung out together, when I brought over that pizza. And as for your issue with Eric, I definitely get that you can hurt someone without wanting to...because you hurt me." Now his eyes are turning red and watering up as though he's about to cry. "So much, Jesse. With Eric, it was one thing. I could have just written him off that day, really. There's always been this wall between us anyway. But with you, we've been through so much together, shared so much. I really didn't want to lose my best friend."

"I'm sorry."

"Those words don't really make it better, Jesse. You know that."

"I do."

"Although, as angry as I have been with you for what happened, I have to admit that I know you would never have done this to hurt me on purpose. And if you really are happy with Eric, if this really was as special as it must have been for you to talk to me about it, what kind of bastard would I be not to want that for you? I've always wanted you to be happy, Jesse. So in this moment, seeing you in pain hurts me, even though I am mad at you still. But I don't know how to get rid of that. I wish there was a way to erase the bad feeling, because intellectually, I can talk myself down. I keep thinking, if the shoe were on the other foot, I don't know that I would have handled it as well as you did. And if you were in my shoes, being Jesse Morgan, you would have been even more amazing to me after my being a dick than the other way around. I mean, I'm supposed to be the fuck-up, right?"

We chuckle at the same time, the way we would have at a joke we would have shared in the past, but I'm not sure if it's because he meant it to be funny or because there's so much truth to his words.

"But there's this feeling in me that I can't shake," he stresses. "It hurts, a lot, Jesse, and I'm not going to lie and pretend it doesn't. It's not only what you did behind my back, but like when we went camping and I had to watch you guys with your inside jokes, and then he was talking about how he flew to San Diego with you. Jesse, it's *my* goddamn father. And...I'm jealous that, in a few months, you've developed this special relationship with a man I've been trying to get to give a damn about me for most of my life."

And that's something I really fucking get.

He takes a shaky breath, as though he's trying to recover from the wound he exposed for me to see. He leans forward and interlocks his fingers. "But I can say that, regardless of how much all that hurts, this entire experience gave me something I never had before."

"What do you mean?"

He looks at his hands as he rubs his thumb over his other before saying, "Please don't tell Eric this. Although, I guess if you do, what does it matter at this point?"

"I won't say anything, Ty."

He eyes me uncertainly, as if he questions my allegiance now in a way he never would have before, but he presses on anyway. "That day when I ran into him here, he thought I was ignoring him. But I was out, and I came up the stairs, saw him. He was pleading for me to come to the door, and reflecting on back when we first met, and his hopes, his disappointment. He was crying, like really crying, Jesse, really hurt at the thought of me wanting to be out of his life. If you'd asked me a few days before if I thought he would have even cared if I wanted to be in his life or not, I would have said no.

"But I finally saw a man who cared about me, who loved me—the man I wanted to believe he was in the beginning, a man who I maybe stopped believing in too soon. And I thought, 'This is my dad, and he's here for me, and he's fighting for me.' Awful as I felt about everything else, and hurt...and betrayed, that outweighed the rest."

I'm so relieved to hear Ty say this, especially since that's what I see when I look at Eric. Ty deserves to know that Eric cares...that he wants that connection as much as Ty does.

"He doesn't know I saw that," Ty adds. "I snuck around the corner and pretended I was coming around it when he was done, but that's why I was willing to talk to him that day, because, Jesse, I do want my dad. Even just what we've all experienced, talking to each other again. No, it's not going to be great right away, but the person he is right now...I like him a hell of a lot more than the guy I've been spending years hanging out with—unable to communicate with, feeling like there was this invisible wall separating us."

He looks directly into my eyes, and even though he's looked at me while we've been talking, it feels as if it's the first time he's *really* looking at me. "But now I feel like there's a wall between me and my best bud since college, and that sucks, because I could really use a hug right now."

"I could use a hug too," I confess with a sort of bitter chuckle.

Ty scoots across the couch and puts his arms around me, pulling me in close for a hug, very familiar, similar to so many times we've shared before, just holding me.

It's a hug like we shared after my granny passed, and I cry because I can't help myself.

"I don't deserve this," I say, my voice cracking as I speak the words.

"Maybe you don't, but I do," he says, and I surrender, giving him the hug he deserves, for the pain he's experienced and for the hope he's found that maybe, just maybe, he can have the father he's always wanted.

We cry together, shamelessly, each for our own reasons, as I find everything I dealt with last night with Eric creeping up on me and colliding with the pain I've put Ty through.

When Ty finally pulls away, he wipes his hands under his nose.

"Well, there we go, being all ridiculous and sappy," he says, "and we still have to get to why you're a mess right now."

"Thank you. I'm glad you talked to me about it."

"I am too. I don't know the details of what you're working out with my...Eric..." I can tell he stopped himself from saying dad or father—something I more than understand. "...but if we've learned anything through this whole mess, it's that talking is important. Christ, if I can be sitting here talking to you, certainly there's nothing you could have fucked up so much that Eric won't be willing to hear you run your chatty mouth." He winks, but then his expression turns serious once again. "Jesse, I may not know Eric as much as I've always wished I could, but what I do know is that he gets guarded. He shuts down, but there's something else under there. I can't say I've really figured out what, but...I think I'm realizing it's more than just about me."

He's right about that. If only he knew how right.

I have to believe—despite how he got last night, how he clammed up with me—that I can remind him that I am here for him, and I do care, even though it may not have looked like that to him.

"I believe in you guys," Ty says. "You've put too much on the line to throw in the towel now, right? So get your fucked-up shit worked out."

He can't know what those words mean to me...what this afternoon has meant to me.

He smirks, and I burst into laughter, a laughter I've needed after everything that's happened.

"Now one more hug, and then I'm evicting you from my place," he teases.

I laugh again as we exchange another hug, this time less sad, just appreciating that, even though it's not great, or perfect...it's better.

# 30

## ERIC

I force my fingers against the keyboard, struggling to push through an email to Vanessa about setting up a meeting between me and this CEO who's been making some pretty fucking terrible business decisions for what was a major investment for me. The company is based in Portland, and I wouldn't mind meeting the CEO there next week.

Now's a good time to get away, I figure. Maybe I've been in Atlanta too long.

Despite my justifications, deep down, I realize what I'm doing. Running again from the demon as it hounds me through some dark forest. I need to get away from it all, I keep telling myself, especially after what happened with Jesse last night.

As much as I know he's been my ally through all this, I feel so fucking betrayed. He's supposed to be on my side.

Jesse's a good guy, I remind myself, but I've learned how pointless those sorts of assurances are since our fight. Despite what I know about Jesse, and how supportive he's been, in his response to my request, I feel totally alone.

But knowing he cares, knowing how much he has understood me...more than most...makes his betrayal cut like a fucking knife.

I care about him so much. It aches when I think about leaving him for any amount of time—a knot twisting in my chest—stinging, burning.

How can I live with this painful feeling?

This isn't about leaving him, I tell myself. I need time and space. My feelings about what happened will pass, but even though I know that's true, what I fear is that all those defenses I worked to pull down for Jesse, those will return...and I will push him away, the way I push everyone away.

I don't want to do this, but this is who I am.

I'm about to hit Send on the email, but I stop myself. I don't want to do this to him...to us. But that I even got as far as writing that email terrifies me about where we're at right now.

There's a knock on my office door. I hadn't even realized he'd gotten home. I must have been too distracted to hear him come in.

"Come in," I say. "It's unlocked."

Jesse must know that. Although, I don't figure he was knocking because he thought it was locked, but because he felt like he needed my permission.

Amazing how that incident last night could leave us both feeling as though we're walking on eggshells around one another. There's this rift between us.

As I turn around in my swivel chair, I see this sad expression on his face that I want to kiss right off. I imagine that kid who had all those nightmares about being abandoned, and I'm already glad I couldn't force myself to send that email.

I'm not leaving him. Still, he must sense that I've already abandoned him emotionally.

I rise to my feet. I'm trying to avoid looking at him because I don't know that I can stand that expression he's making.

"I think we should talk about last night," he mutters.

That's so him. He doesn't play games or beat around the bush, just goes right for it. It's that maturity that I've always seen in him, and in many ways, he has something I've lacked—the ability to face a difficult situation. In most areas of my life, that's not an issue, but with this particular subject, I'm still running from this phantom, scared and afraid.

"We don't have to discuss it, Jesse. We're not going to agree on this. You made it very clear that you don't want to help me and—"

"Not help you?" Jesse asks, interrupting me. "Eric, I'm here because I'm trying to help you. I'm going to therapy sessions and yoga. I've been trying to figure this out."

I hear the hurt in his voice, the pain that I saw in his expression last night when I shut down...because he knows me better than most people, who wouldn't pick up on those subtle cues, who would just think something else about it.

Not my Jesse, though.

"That's not what I meant, and you know it," I snap. "I'm very appreciative of you being there for all that." Despite my curtness, I'm sincere in that much, and I would never want him to think otherwise. "I see everything you do, Jesse, and I appreciate it. That's why I didn't make a scene about last night, because I know you think you're doing what's right. But it hurts that you didn't trust me on this."

"Is that what this is about to you?" he asks. "Trust?"

"Of course that's what this is about."

"Eric, that night when we were camping, I thought we were going to share something magical and special. You were so excited, and I thought, 'Now is the time.' And what happened? There I was, thinking I was going to make you feel amazing, and suddenly I put you into the worst panic attack I've ever seen anyone have. Do you have any idea what that did to me?"

His words tear through my defenses as I imagine his pain that night—the horror of watching someone going through that. "Jesse, I am so sorry—"

"I'm not asking for an apology. You didn't do anything wrong, but it's still there in my head. I still see this image of you, struggling, fighting something within you. Do you know how difficult it is for me to watch? It's not even just that night. Every day, I see a little bit of it still there, and I'm terrified that I'm going to do something to be the cause of that pain again.

"So last night, when you said you wanted to try, it scared the shit out of me because, not only did I have that image playing in the back of my mind, but you were asking me to do that...and to me, you might as well have been asking me to stab you in the gut with a knife...because you wanted me to."

As guarded as I've been, maybe even unreasonable about not seeing this through his eyes, I start to see beyond my own selfish desire to push past this insecurity within me. How this isn't just about me.

"I'm so sorry," I say.

"I'm sorry too." Jesse approaches cautiously. This isn't what I want. I like that Jesse pushes my buttons and gets me riled up. I've enjoyed how he pushes through my boundaries, not this trepid man who's treating me the way I fear so much.

"I'm not weak, Jesse," I blurt out. "You don't have to walk on eggshells around me. You don't have to put on rubber gloves."

"Eric, I've never seen you as a weak man. I know you're hurt, and I've seen the strength you've built from that. But it's okay to be vulnerable. It's okay to not have every single thing in your goddamned life figured out or put together."

As he reaches me, I take his hands, and he rubs his thumbs softly into my palms.

"I'm on your side, Eric."

I feel the truth of his words, which disperse all that pain I've been feeling in my chest.

As I look up to face him, I realize he's doing the same until our gazes meet.

This quiet between us is so familiar.

For the first time since our fight, I see the boy and the man before me—the one I fell in love with, who captivated me from the very start. I see his sympathy, his understanding.

"I love going to your sessions with you and working on these exercises," he continues. "And I'm trying to Google and read up on all this, figure out what you need from me. But fuck, last night wasn't in anything I've read, and I didn't know the right answer. I didn't want to fuck everything up, and I'm terrified of being the one who makes things worse for you. But really, as much as it would horrify me to see that happen to you again, if you need this, then I'll do it, Eric. I'll do whatever the fuck you need me to do. I don't care what the therapists say is right or wrong for you because I don't ever want you to feel like I'm not on your side. I don't ever want you to feel as though you can't count on me in this fucked-up mess we're in."

As he speaks those words, in the way tears fill his eyes

and his face trembles, I can see how scared he is of following through with his offer to—as he put it—stab me with a knife if that's what I really want. After hearing his side, I feel like such a cruel bastard for asking that of him.

Despite everything I've been telling myself, trying to use as a reason to keep a distance between us, I realize he's on my side and that he has been this entire time.

Steadily, that wall I put up last night collapses, and though it shouldn't surprise me that the man who was able to tear it down once before could wreck it once again, it does. Because Jesse never ceases to amaze me.

"You've always had a talent for this," I tell him.

"For what?"

"Leaving me without reasons to fight...making me not want to fight. To just be with you."

I cup my hand behind his head and stroke my thumb behind his ear as a tear releases from his eye. "I've been very selfish about this. I made last night about me, about your loyalty. That's what this has been about for me all day. I'm realizing how wrong that was. It was wrong of me to ask you to do that, and it would be wrong of me to ask you tonight."

His face trembles and he gasps, like he's relieved to hear my words, reminding me of what a piece of shit I was to ask him to do that, not considering his own pain in all this. I hook my arms around him, pulling him close. "I'm so sorry, Jesse. I'm so sorry."

"What did I tell you about saying I'm sorry?" he tries to joke, but the way his voice cracks, I can tell it's a struggle for him.

I pull back because I want to look him in the eyes as I say, "But I am sorry. This isn't about just me anymore. This is about *us*, and as much as I felt let down last night, I let you down. I didn't want to abandon you, but I did...in my heart. I put up my defenses and pushed you away. Before you knocked on the door, I was trying to find an excuse to run…from you."

His eyes widen, as though the thought rouses that fear I know is within him.

"I couldn't do it, Jesse. I couldn't do that to you. I never want to be the reason you feel abandoned any more than you want to be the reason I'm suffering. And I know I did that to you last night with how I reacted. This is a lot for me because I've never had to deal with anything like this before."

"Yeah, you just started therapy and—"

"I'm not talking about the therapy, Jesse. I'm talking about being in love with you. I'm talking about finding myself opening up to another person, finding a way to build that bridge when I have spent my entire life trying to be good at being on my own. Even when I was with Casey, what I liked about that relationship was that it was superficial. He never pressed in the areas that mattered because he enjoyed not knowing the real me. It's not easy for me to trust since my bastard uncle, but you're the first person who's given me a reason to open my heart again, and I'm scared. When I got defensive last night, I felt like I was so stupid for opening myself up to get hurt. But that's part of what this is. We get hurt, even when the other person doesn't mean anything by it, just like I didn't mean to hurt you that night when I had that episode."

"Eric, I wasn't trying to make you feel bad about that night."

"I know you weren't, but it doesn't change the wound that it put inside you, the wound I opened."

He sniffles. "I'm pretty resilient. I'll be fine."

"I know you will be, Jesse. We'll both be fine. And even if

it kills me to wait through this stupid therapy and yoga antics...and maybe some stupid tango classes like Carolyn mentioned in that last session, I'll suck it up. Like you said, what difference does it make if we do this tonight or six months from now or a year from now? The only thing I need right now in my life is *you*."

"I need you too, Eric."

I move toward him quickly. Before I know it, my lips are against his as I push him back against the doorframe. My hands have minds of their own as I pull off his shirt. He submits so easily.

As I kiss his face, I feel another tear slide out of his eye before I realize there's one falling out of mine as well.

All I want is to show him how sorry I am for pushing him away.

I want to show him how close we can truly be tonight.

I tug at his waist, pulling his torso flush against my own, and I force my lips away from his. He takes a shaky breath as I look into his eyes.

My little lost boy.

I take his hand. "Come on," I tell him.

He doesn't fight me or resist as I get him into my bedroom, and soon we're on the bed, naked, kissing. I'm lost in him again, appreciating his mouth, his tongue, his flesh, the feel of his fingers and hands against my back.

As I push deep within him, the sounds of his moans are...everything. I revel in his pleasure, those sounds reminding me that I'm making him feel good, that he wants this, that he wants me.

And I feel like the luckiest motherfucker who ever lived for getting to share this delicious experience with the only man who's ever been worthy of my trust.

With his arms over his head as I thrust into him, he calls out my name. "Eric...I love you, Eric."

"I love you too, Jesse," I say before taking his mouth again, feeling that spark between us, one that sets fire the way it always has, feeling the intensity of the inferno that has transformed into a supernova as I decide to spend the rest of the night loving my gorgeous man the way he deserves to be loved.

## 31

## JESSE

When Ty and I finish playing volleyball with the guys at the park, I grab my backpack from the picnic table where we always put our stuff.

"Hey, man, mind giving me a lift back to my place?" Ty asks as he comes up beside me.

It's not the first time I've given him a ride after we've played volleyball, but it's the first time he's asked since our fallout. I can tell by the sympathetic expression on his face that this is one of many peace offerings he's extended since all this shit went to hell.

It's been a few weeks since he came into my office with that pizza and helped me sort through my thoughts about the fight Eric and I had, and while things still aren't the best between Ty and me, I don't expect that. They're better than before, though, and that's all that matters. It gives me hope.

I agree to take him back to his condo, and as we walk to my car, we chat about the game and the gang before Ty says, "Did Eric tell you he's talking to my mom tomorrow...about you-know-what?"

"He may have had a mini-breakdown about it," I say. "He's not exactly thrilled."

"Really? Because I'm ecstatic. I want to hear how this all plays out... Eric telling my mom that he's fucking around with my best friend. I'm sure she'll be stoked about having you over for dinner parties."

I'm blushing at the thought. "God, that's gonna be awkward."

"Hey, it's only fair, considering I'm not exactly eager to see your parents since all this went down, which by the way, I do feel like I deserve your dad's lasagna at some point, so if you could make that happen..."

We reach my car, and I walk around to the driver's side while he waits at the passenger's side.

"Yeah, I think I can make that happen, Ty."

He smiles before we get in, and I head to his place.

I turn the music up. I don't want this to get any more awkward than it is, since there's plenty of opportunities for that on the ten-minute ride to his building.

He's quiet for a bit before he says, "We could swing by that pizza place we used to go to, maybe grab a bite to eat...if you don't have plans with Eric, that is."

"We were going to make dinner, but—"

"Oh, well, then don't..."

"Ty, I really want to get pizza, so I'll just text him. It's not a big deal."

Eric wouldn't want me to miss out on this chance to reconnect with Ty any more than I do. Besides, considering how much time Eric and I have spent together these past few weeks, attending therapy and yoga sessions... And on top of those, we've started taking tango lessons at Carolyn's recommendation. She said she thought it would benefit Eric to learn how to follow instead of trying to lead all the time...

giving up some control to me in a less triggering environment. Can't say either of us is particularly good, but it's fun learning something new with Eric. Hell, everything is better when Eric's involved.

Ty and I head to the local pizzeria we used to frequent and get our usual Meat Lover's.

We sit across from each other in a booth, and as he devours a slice, I think about how lucky I am to have him in my life still—this guy who gets me so much that he fucking gets me a pizza and forces me to open about shit, even when that's the most difficult thing for me in the world.

Ty talks through chewing, telling me about some work shit.

It's nice doing this again. I wish I could pretend everything's all better between us and that we're fine, but I can't shake the feelings I carry about what I did...about how I hurt him...or how amazing he's been to me in spite of all that.

As he's being open about his life, I can feel this lingering discomfort between us—a wall that reminds me of the walls I am still tearing down with Eric. The difference is that these walls weren't there when Ty and I first met.

But now, because of what Eric and I did, we have to fight this battle. I'm lucky he's willing to fight with me.

We get to talking about some of the shit I've been hearing on *Rocks and Hard Places* and *Damn Interesting* when the waitress places the check on the table.

I reach for it, but Ty's too quick for me as he nabs the bill, a sneaky expression across his face. "Uh-uh. You've been guilt-paying one too many times, and even though I'm enjoying taking advantage of you and stealing all the mad monies you're making at your bougie-ass job, I can at least pay while I'm still getting a good salary."

"What do you mean?"

He hesitates for a moment, his expression twisting up... like he's considering telling me something. "Don't tell Eric this because I want to be the one. Already talked to my boss about getting my certification. They're going to find a way to work with me a bit so that I can cycle out and train another guy to take my position. That way I can go back to school in the fall and be a student all over again."

"Are you serious, Ty?"

"I know, right? Who woulda thought I'd be the one going back to school?"

"I'm really impressed. Jesus, I remember you making fun of grad students because you couldn't imagine going back once you broke out of the joint."

He laughs. "I'm surprised I wanted this too, but I think if I've learned anything these past few months, it's that sometimes you got to take a risk, even if it fucks up everything." As he speaks the words, he looks directly into my eyes. It's not approval, not exactly. That would be too much. But it's still a lot coming from him.

More than what he said, the fact that he's even trying to soothe this uneasy tension that remains between us...he can't know what that means to me.

We chat a little more about his plans before we leave and drive to his place.

I park in the lower parking deck with the entrance to the building. He fishes his duffel bag out of the back seat, closes the door, and heads to the passenger's side, ducking down as he rests his hands on the window sill.

"Remember when you used to park here and we'd go up and watch a movie in my condo...or we would have gone out to a bar and gotten drunk?"

"Yeah," I say, wondering where he's going with this.

Ty's lips curl into a wry smirk. "I miss those times."

"I miss them too, Ty."

"Not saying we can do those things, or that I want to do them with you right now, but you know, maybe one day, five years from now, when I don't hate your guts."

I laugh. God, he's the best. "Guess we'll take it one day at a time."

"That's right, man," he says. "One day at a time. Later."

Waving, he offers a goofy expression—narrowed eyes, his tongue hanging out. Then he whirls around and heads toward the door into his building.

*One day at a time...*

With Ty. With everything.

## 32

# ERIC

"You ready?" Ty asks as he sits at the table across from me. We agreed to meet for lunch before I head over to Tricia's to do the deed. To face the music.

"I guess as ready as I can be for this," I tell him before taking a deep breath.

"I do have some news. I decided I'm going to be getting my CPA certification."

"What? Really? That's incredible news, Ty. I'm so proud of you." I make sure to stress that, since he was so dumbfounded the last time I used that word with him.

"Thank you. That means a lot."

"Ty, I've always been proud of you, even when I've had a hard time communicating that. I'm sorry I let you down. Not just with all this...but throughout your life."

He nods, and I can see the sorrow written all over his face. "We were both in over our heads back then," he says. "I don't think either of us realized how much until after we met. And I've been doing a lot of thinking recently...had to do a lot of thinking, really. But I think I might have given up on you sooner than I should have. The kid who wanted to meet you didn't realize his dad would wind up being this super-successful control-freak with every aspect of his life nailed down. You were so cool and tough as fucking nails. I was this fuck-up kid, making mistakes and without any real ambitions."

"I never saw you like that."

"But it didn't change that I felt like you were...disappointed with the son you had. It was a lot of pressure to suddenly be in the shadow of a great man. Someone I thought of as a god back then. And at some point, I started holding back, never trying to be the best I could, because I was so afraid...what if my amazing dad didn't like the best version of me?"

"Ty, I've never expected you to be anything other than yourself."

"How can I look at your life, everything you've accomplished, and compare myself to that without feeling like you have to look at what I do and think that it's just...nothing."

"You've never been nothing to me, Ty. That's not how I've ever seen you."

His chin quivers. "I'm starting to realize that, and it's time for me to grow up and face the fact that, even if that best version isn't good enough for you, maybe it has to be enough for me."

"I never realized you cared that much about what I thought, Ty. And really, after everything that's happened, I can't imagine why you'd give a damn what I think now."

"Because we're human beings, and we're all messed up in the head, I guess," he says with a laugh.

I see before me, my son, this incredible person who has

allowed me back into his life despite that shit I pulled... being honest and open and fighting for the things he wants. He can't know the pride it fills me with knowing that such an incredible human could be my own son.

And now I really get why Jesse and Ty are friends...how two such impressive, compassionate, strong individuals would have found one another.

Like me and my own friends.

"Well, I'm very proud of the man sitting across from me right now," I say. "I'm very proud of you, Ty."

His eyes water before he says, "No, I'm not doing this again. I've done this too much recently. Nope. Not today. I'd better go. And I think you have a date with Mom, which I want to hear all about when you're done."

"Ty..." I want to tell him so much more.

"We're done with that conversation," he says. "For now. We can reminisce on that shit another day."

"Fair enough." I remind myself that this isn't the last time I'm ever going to see him, or my last chance to let him know how amazing he is. And for that, I'm so fucking grateful.

He drinks some of his unsweetened tea before setting his glass down. "So go get it done, and then we'll try to get together for dinner soon. Not with Mom, but you, me, and Jesse. Cool?"

"Very cool," I say, filled with appreciation for this second chance I have with my son...but fearing my discussion with Tricia.

~

I STAND outside the door to Tricia's house. I'm more reluctant to knock now than when I was standing outside Ty's condo that day when I went to see him.

So many emotions are wrapped up in her. Not just the time we shared in our youth, but the pain of leaving her when I acknowledged who I really was—a gay man—combined with the pain of her not telling me about my son. As much as she fucked up back then, I know it's my turn now.

Once again, I have to out what Jesse and I have been doing, and aside from Ty, Tricia is the last person in the world I want to confront about this, but it's important. If we're ever going to have any chance of moving forward, I have to deal with this.

I take a breath before I knock.

When the door opens, Tricia stands there, dressed in flats, jeans, and a white button-up. Her blonde hair is shorter than it was when she was younger, falling to her shoulders. There's concern in her expression because surely she must know I wouldn't be here with good news.

"Well, this is unexpected, Eric," she says, sighing as though she's tired. "Come on in."

She sounds resigned, accepting of whatever it is I'm about to dump on her, as though she's been beaten down by life one too many times and is just tired of it.

As soon as I enter the kitchen, she opens the refrigerator. "You want a glass of chardonnay?"

"Not particularly."

"Too bad. I have a feeling I'm gonna need one, and I'm not drinking alone for this."

She fetches a bottle from the fridge, then heads to the cabinet and retrieves two glasses.

"I feel like," she says as she pours our drinks, "I should be pretending I'm oblivious right now. That I think you stopped by to say hi, or you have some incredible news you'd like to share with me, but I'm tired of pretending. What about you, Eric?"

She approaches with the two glasses, handing me one.

I start to pull it to my lips when she says, "No, wait. Let's at least toast before you tell me whatever it is. I said I don't want to pretend, but it's not a race to the truth, is it?"

She smiles, but it's bittersweet.

"What do you want to toast to?" I ask, playing along.

I see in her expression the sadness, the worry, and that resigned sense that whatever it is I'm about to share, she'd rather get it over with.

"To our son," she says. "Because as fucked up as all this is, he's the one thing I can look at every day that reminds me there is some good in this world."

She clinks her glass against mine.

I can't help but feel as though somehow she psychically picked up on what I have to share with her. I know that can't be the case. After all, what she's saying is likely true, but it's still bizarre the way she said it, considering what I'm about to tell her.

She relaxes in the chair adjacent to me at the kitchen table, taking a sip of her drink before setting it on the table and saying, "Okay, now I think I'm ready."

"I'm not sure you are," I warn her.

I don't delay. I get right to the point, telling her about what I've been doing with Jesse—the most incredible man I've ever met in my life, the man I got in over my head with, the man I can't envision my life without.

I confess my sin. My crime against our son.

A crime I feel so guilty for, yet that brought me more joy than I believed I was capable of feeling ever again.

A crime I am really not sure I could truly live without having committed.

She's quiet through the reveal, her expression stoic, as though she's waiting for me to say this is all some disturbing joke or that she has been fooled for some candid-camera show. Not that those are nearly as popular as they have been in the past.

"You motherfucker," she finally says. Her face twists up as tears fill her eyes, reminding me of a similar confession a long time ago...when I came out to her. "You fucking bastard. You fucking, selfish bastard."

I deserve it. So fucking much.

"Do you know how many years I spent feeling guilty for not telling you about Ty? How much time I spent thinking what I was doing was so shitty?"

"It certainly wasn't right, what you did," I remind her.

"Oh, are you gonna tell me what's right? You, the guy who's screwing around with your son's best friend?"

"No, I'm not saying what I did was right, or that I deserve Ty's forgiveness. Ty knows about all this."

She freezes, as though she can't believe that part. She takes a moment to process it before saying, "I knew you liked guys, but I didn't realize you liked them so young...as young as your son." Clearly, she says it to hurt me. "Does it make you feel young and sexy again screwing around with a kid?"

"It's more than that, Tricia."

She assesses my expression before her face twists up. "As if Ty hasn't been fucked up enough. Between not knowing his dad and then having his dad come into his life and be anything but what he needed."

"Tricia, I understand why you're angry. You think I didn't

know how this script was gonna play out when I came over here?"

"Script?" she asks. "Is it a script to you? Some movie of the week where our lives are some senseless drama? I hurt, Eric, so fucking much. I'm in pain right now, and it's not just because of this fucked-up thing you did, but because of every mistake I've made in my life. The hurt, the drama, the mistakes, and the judgment I've had for those mistakes."

I know she's referring to my reaction to hearing about my son so late, but even though I'm in the wrong now, I refuse to let her off the hook for that.

"Do I play a part in this script?" she adds. "Background noise in your life? That thing you feel burned by because of what I did? I'm just the horrible bitch who never let you know you had a son. I don't have feelings. I wasn't crying every day after you left because I was a stupid, naive girl who believed you loved me, who you were so good to."

While her accusatory response has left me feeling the need to defend myself, I've held back, reminding myself I deserve her judgment. But in a moment, her rage shifts to something else. "You listened, you wanted me, I thought you desired me. And then I find out that was all a lie, that you never loved me, that you *couldn't* love me. You might have been able to walk away all those years ago, but I couldn't."

"I tried to contact you."

"No, Eric, you don't understand. I *couldn't* be around you because I couldn't walk away from how I felt. I never would have gotten over you. I was a kid and I was in love. In love, Eric. And I do know what that means, especially with all the assholes I've met over the years. So there I was, a young woman in love, and when I found out I had a child on the way, the thought of raising him with you...having to live my life pining right next to the man I was in love with, watching him care for our child...do you know what that would have done to me, Eric? You can't, and you can't know how depressed I was leading up to giving birth...or after. Not a day went by where I didn't think I needed to track you down and tell you. Everything in me told me it was the wrong decision...every day I was haunted by that mistake, and the longer I carried it, the worse it became...till eventually Ty was constantly reminding me of what I was depriving him of, what I was depriving both of you of. But I don't like this part you've cast me in. Because while I'm this two-dimensional monster, you get to make a mistake that feels pretty damn cruel to me and then judge me all these years for what I did?"

"Yes, I am," I say, "because in the same way that I think Ty has every right to feel hurt and betrayed by what I did, I have the same right with this. It wasn't fair what you did... the choice you never gave me. I can hear your excuses all day, but it can't take my pain away, just as I can't take away your pain about what I've done to our son, so don't ask that of me. No amount of 'I'm sorry' can take away Ty's pain in this, and I've been lucky that our son is a good, compassionate person who sees beyond all this."

"Well, what about his father?" Tricia asks. "Where has my compassion been?"

Her words aren't lost on me, and even though intellectually I'd already had this conversation in my mind before we reached this point, it really hits home in the moment. "I haven't been cruel to you about this or brought it up incessantly to cause you any grief," I say.

"You've never needed to, Eric. You think I can't see it in your eyes? I may have missed some pretty important things about you when we were younger, but I still *know* you." She shakes her head. "God, the world's so fucked up. It isn't easy, is it? It seems we can't get through it without hurting ourselves, and hurting each other." She takes a breath and a sip of her wine. "Oh, Eric, when we were in school, sneaking off into the woods to laugh and tell stories, sharing so much, could you have ever imagined this is what our lives would become?"

"I sure didn't."

She sighs as though releasing so much pent-up emotion, much of which we've unearthed in this conversation. "Jesse...do you love him?" she asks.

"I do."

Tears flow freely from her eyes. She doesn't try to wipe them away. "It seems almost unfair that you get to find happiness all these years later, and here I am trapped in this goddamn house, trying with this guy who's a waste of my fucking time and I know it, but still trying anyway."

"There are good people. I couldn't have said that before, but I do believe it now."

I'm referring to Jesse...this dream of a man...a man I wouldn't have believed existed until I was lucky enough to meet him.

"I'm sorry for hurting you, and I'm sorry for hurting our son," I add.

She nods. "I know that, Eric, and I never reveled in bringing pain into your life."

"I know, Trish. Oh, what are we gonna do?"

"In fairness," she says, "family dinners were already awkward for us."

I chuckle, and she smirks as though she's pleased at how she was able to lighten the mood.

"And here I am back to hating you," she says, "because you flashed that smile, and I'm in love all over again."

She reaches over and takes my hand. "You did a shit

thing. We all do shit things sometimes, and they have consequences. I could kick your ass for hurting our kid...but...I'm glad you have a reason to smile, Eric."

I appreciate her honesty and, once again, the ease of letting the truth just be out there. So many truths I've had to face, and so many truths I'm only facing because of Jesse.

## 33

## JESSE

Eric steps on my toe again.

"Fuck," he says, frustrated—angry even—as he looks down at our feet.

"It's okay," I tell him. "Relax. Deep breath."

"This isn't the easiest thing in the world for me."

We've only had two tango lessons so far, and we definitely have a lot to work on, so we've taken a break tonight, pushed the coffee table against the couch to make space for a dance floor as a tango song plays in a loop for us to practice.

I'm kind of glad Carolyn encouraged us to try this. As much as I know this has a greater benefit for Eric, I'm enjoying getting to share this with him.

We start once again and make it maybe three steps before he trips up and stops. "Can you lead more with your chest, like Raul said?"

"Remember, the whole idea is for you to let go of that need for control," I remind him.

He sighs, seeming as frustrated as ever with this whole thing. Like he's angry with himself for not being able to do this right away.

"Hey, hey, hey, Eric, it's okay. Everything's fine. We're both learning this together, and I'm fucking up plenty, but you have to accept that we're going to make a mess of it a little bit in the beginning."

He chuckles for the first time since we started practicing a little over fifteen minutes ago. I can tell because of how many times the song has started over.

"Knowing that I need to do this to help with the other stuff," Eric says, "adds pressure, you know?"

"Then let's pretend for a moment that it's not related to anything, okay? We're two idiots trying to learn to tango for tango's sake."

"Easier said than done."

I start singing the words to "Hounds of Love" by Kate Bush, sort of to the music that's playing, but mainly creating my own annoying song in my shit-voice.

He cringes, then says, "Those aren't the words."

"Shut up and keep moving."

He follows, and I can already feel that he isn't as tense as before. Once again, I've broken through yet another barrier he's put up. My favorite game.

"You're an awful singer, Jesse."

"I'm *your* awful singer, and with a face like this, do I really need to be good at singing?"

He laughs heartily before saying, "Not when you're that gorgeous...and cocky."

"Well, you know I love anything involving cock." I wink as we continue in our circle around the room.

Again, he stumbles. "Shit."

"It's all good," I assure him, and I continue with the Kate Bush song. "Do you know what I really need? Do you know what I really need? I need la-la-la-la-yay-yo-yay-yo-your love."

His gaze meets mine, and I see that desire in his eyes, like when we first met. Although, it's different now.

Back then, it was just this inexplicable chemistry between us, but now I see much more in his gaze, as though he can see so much more of me—the way I see more of him since that first electric handshake that made me hungry for Eric in a way I've never been hungry for anyone in my entire life.

He woke something within me that I don't know if I'll ever entirely understand.

But I don't need to understand it—all I *need* is Eric.

It's not perfect, no. We're just starting on our journey, and we've hardly made a dent with therapy, but we're taking those first steps. It's a process, but like with tango, it's a journey—one I'm eager to take since it's with him. And each time we get through a counseling session, or with yoga, or a tango lesson, I feel like I get to know him better. I get to know the man who is so much more than the front he shows the world, the front he puts up because of how he was injured so long ago.

"I don't think I want to keep dancing right now," he says, squatting down, hooking his arm around me, and throwing me over his shoulder. "Definitely time for me to take the lead."

"Okay," I say as he carries me to the bedroom, "but we are getting back to tango later."

"Yeah, yeah," he says, tossing me onto the bed. "All in good time."

We work together, pulling off each other's clothes. There's an added intensity to it...as though he wants to take some of his tango frustration out on me—something that's more than fine with me.

He grabs the lube from the nightstand, and I notice the condoms we still have in there, which we haven't used in months.

Reminds me of how far we've come.

He slathers lube across his cock before moving close and pushing steadily within me. I adjust and relax, appreciating that determined and excited expression across his face.

"How does it feel?" he asks, a question that means so much more to me now that I know more about him, now that I know why he's always cared so much about my own pleasure, especially with how little his was considered on that horrifying day.

"It feels so goddamn good." I moan immediately after as he pushes farther in.

He sets his hand behind my neck while wrapping another under my arm as he begins thrusting, his thick girth reaching farther and farther.

I roll my head back, enjoying the sensation, loving that I'm able to share this with him, loving how close we are.

I'm lost in my own pleasure when I look up at him and realize he's gazing down at me, not offering the usual kisses, just watching my own arousal.

He glances down at my dick, which is leaking precum.

"Do you like watching what you do to me?" I ask him.

"I love seeing you get so worked up. How you get totally lost in it. Let go entirely. I love being the reason you're so happy, and excited, and on edge...feeling so good. I want to keep being the reason you're like this."

"I want to be the reason you feel good too. Do you mind if I kiss you?"

He chuckles. "You're good at this affirmative-consent thing."

"I'm good at a lot of things," I tease.

"Yes, I would love if you kissed me, Jesse Morgan." He's not joking, though, so I lean up and take his lips.

He licks and nips, his hot breath pushing against my face as he feels his fingers across my body and offers another powerful thrust.

Like on so many other nights, he rocks my world. His passion, his intensity, his frustration, his appreciation, all reveal themselves as we continue fucking.

When he's got me on my knees, facing the headboard, gripping it with both hands as he takes me from behind, he jerks me off while inside me. He leans down close, and I turn to see his face.

"You're about to come," he tells me.

He knows my body that well now. He can tell by every movement I make, the same way I can tell that he's about to come.

Almost as if he was demanding I shoot my load, I erupt. He twists and jerks before doing the same within me. We pant together before our lips meet once again. We come down from the experience together, not in any rush, not racing to clean up.

We lie together so that soon I'm in his arms, him gazing down at me with a familiar look of satisfaction across his face. I imagine mine is equally easy to read.

"What is it?" I ask as I notice his expression shift to something more serious.

"I don't like how easy it is for you to read me. Most people aren't that good at it."

"Well, most people aren't as amazing as me."

He smiles. "No, they aren't. I was thinking that one day, I

hope you're able to give me what I clearly am able to give you in moments like this. That I'll be able to bottom for you."

"We'll get there, Eric. It might take us a little longer than it does for most people, and we might be a little more fucked up, but I think we're on the right path now. Don't you?"

"For sure, mostly about the fucked-up part," he teases.

"Whatever. You have to admit you have kind of an incredible boyfriend." I cock a brow.

His eyes narrow. "Look at that conceited expression...like you know what you've claimed."

"What have I claimed?"

"My heart."

"It's only fair, Eric, since you've already claimed mine."

And as he kisses me once again, I appreciate the moment, this satisfaction that we're here for each other. Yes, there's work to be done. No, we're not perfect, and we probably never will be, but I'm fine with this journey we're on, as long as I'm on it with Eric.

One day at a time...one step at a time...

THE END

## ABOUT THE AUTHOR

A good ole Southern boy, Devon McCormack grew up in the Georgia suburbs with his two younger brothers and an older sister. At a very young age, he spun tales the old fashioned way, lying to anyone and everyone he encountered. He claimed he was an orphan. He claimed to be a king from another planet. He claimed to have supernatural powers. He has since harnessed this penchant for tall tales by crafting worlds and characters that allow him to live out whatever fantasy he chooses. Devon is an out and proud gay man living with his partner in Atlanta, Georgia.

Lightning Source UK Ltd.
Milton Keynes UK
UKHW020643251022
411061UK00015B/1114

9 781642 046694